The Magical City of Al-Qamar

The Magical City of Al-Qamar

Published by AD Publishing

Texas,USA

ISBN: 979-8-218-47015-9

Dedication

To the reader, your imagination brings these characters to life, and for that, they are eternally grateful.

CHAPTER 1: THE WINDS OF CHANCE

The sails of Tariq's ship, once billowing with pride and purpose, now lay tattered and weary, victims of a tempest that had raged with the fury of the gods. The vast ocean, indifferent to the struggles of man, had cast him adrift, a solitary figure at the mercy of its whims. Yet, in its capricious nature, the sea had also guided him, delivering him to the shores of an unknown land with the gentleness of a whispered promise. As dawn's first light kissed the horizon, Tariq found himself gazing upon a port of ethereal beauty, shrouded in a mist that seemed to dance with the morning breeze. The port, a haven for souls weary of their journeys, beckoned with an allure that spoke of mystery and promise. Its docks, lined with ships from distant realms, told tales of adventures both grand and harrowing.

Tariq's ship glided into the harbor with the grace of a dream, its arrival unnoticed save for the curious seagulls that circled overhead. As he disembarked, the land greeted him with the scent of salt and spices, a symphony of aromas that told of trade and exploration. The cobblestones beneath his feet were worn smooth by the passage of countless travelers, each one leaving an indelible mark on this place of convergence.

His heart, a compass guided by fate, urged him forward. He wandered through the bustling market, where merchants hawked their wares with voices as varied as the goods they sold. Silks from the East, jewels from the South, and the heady aroma of exotic fruits created a tapestry of sensory delights that filled Tariq with both wonder and nostalgia. Amidst the cacophony, an elderly merchant caught Tariq's eye. The man's face, etched with lines of wisdom and experience, bore a kind smile that spoke of stories untold. Tariq approached, his curiosity piqued and his spirit seeking solace. "Kind sir," Tariq began, his voice carrying the weight of his journey, "what is this place that the winds of chance have brought me to?" The merchant's eyes twinkled with a knowing light. "You stand in the port of Al-Madina, a place where paths converge and destinies intertwine. It is said that those who arrive here are brought by fate, guided by the unseen hand of destiny." Tariq's heart quickened. "Al-Madina... a name as beautiful as the place itself.

What stories does this port hold?" The merchant chuckled softly, a sound like the rustle of ancient scrolls. "Stories of love and loss, of adventure and discovery. Each soul that steps upon these shores adds their chapter to the endless book of Al-Madina. Tell me, young sailor, what chapter do you seek to write?"

Tariq pondered the question, his mind drifting back to the storm that had brought him here. He thought of the sea, its vastness a mirror to his own soul, and of the adventures that awaited him in this new land. The winds of chance had carried him far, but it was his own heart that would guide him forward. "I seek to discover, to understand," Tariq replied, his voice filled with a quiet resolve. "The sea has been my guide, but now it is time to find my path upon the land."

The merchant nodded, his smile widening. "Then welcome, Tariq, to Al-Madina. May your journey be filled with the wonders you seek and the answers you desire."

With those words, Tariq felt a newfound sense of purpose. The port of Al-Madina was not just a place of arrival, but a gateway to destiny. As he ventured further into the city, he knew that the winds of chance had brought him here for a reason. His story was just beginning, and the pages of Al-Madina awaited the touch of his journey.

CHAPTER 2: DISCOVERIES AT AL-MADINA PORT

Tariq wandered deeper into the port of Al-Madina, his eyes wide with wonder as he took in the vibrant tapestry of life around him. Each step he took revealed a new marvel, a new piece of this enchanting place that seemed to blend the mundane with the magical. The market was a kaleidoscope of colors and sounds, a bustling hub where merchants from distant lands showcased their exotic wares. Tariq paused before a stall draped in rich silks, the fabrics shimmering like liquid jewels in the morning sun. He ran his fingers over a length of emerald-green silk, marveling at its softness. "A silk from the lands of the East," the merchant explained, his voice tinged with pride. "Spun by the finest weavers, it is said to be as light as a whisper and as strong as a promise."

Tariq nodded, lost in thought. "Such beauty, woven from threads so fine. It speaks of craftsmanship and dedication, of a desire to create something lasting and exquisite."

Next, Tariq's attention was captured by the heady aroma of spices. He followed his nose to a stall overflowing with baskets of brightly colored powders—saffron, turmeric, paprika, and more. The air was thick with their rich scents, each one telling a story of distant lands and culinary traditions. A merchant, his hands stained with the hues of his trade, offered Tariq a sample. "Taste, my friend. This is cardamom, a spice as ancient as the sands of time." Tariq tasted a small pinch, the flavor bursting on his tongue. "It's as if the essence of the land it comes from has been captured in this tiny seed. A reminder that even the smallest things can hold great power."

Further along, Tariq found a stall filled with artifacts and curiosities—items that seemed to whisper of magic and mystery. There were intricately carved amulets, ancient scrolls with indecipherable scripts, and vials of shimmering liquids. One item in particular caught his eye—a small, ornate box made of ebony and inlaid with silver. The merchant noticed his interest and leaned in. "This is a puzzle box, crafted by a master artisan. It is said to hold a secret within, a treasure that only the cleverest can uncover." Tariq picked up the box, feeling its weight in his hands. "A treasure hidden within a puzzle. It is a metaphor for life itself, where the greatest rewards come not from the obvious, but from the effort and ingenuity we put into uncovering them."

As he moved through the market, Tariq came upon a circle of people gathered around a troupe of street performers. Jugglers tossed flaming torches into the air, acrobats tumbled with effortless grace, and musicians played melodies that seemed to dance on the breeze. A young girl, her face painted with bright colors, performed a delicate dance, her movements fluid and enchanting. Tariq watched, captivated by the elegance and joy she brought to her performance.

"This dance," he mused, "is a celebration of life. It is a reminder that even in the midst of chaos, there is beauty and grace to be found. We must cherish these moments of wonder, for they give us hope and remind us of the goodness that exists in the world."

As Tariq continued to explore, he realized that Al-Madina was more than just a port—it was a microcosm of the world, a place where cultures converged and shared their treasures. Each item, each scent, each performance was a testament to the richness of human experience and the endless pursuit of beauty and meaning. With every discovery, Tariq felt his purpose solidify. The winds of chance had brought him here for a reason, and it was up to him to uncover the secrets of Al-Madina and weave his own story into its tapestry. He was no longer just a sailor adrift; he was a seeker of knowledge, a guardian of balance, and a bearer of hope.

As the sun began to set, casting a golden glow over the port, Tariq felt a sense of calm and determination. The journey ahead was still unknown, but he was ready to face it with an open heart and a curious mind.

CHAPTER 3: WISDOM OF THE BEGGAR

As the sun dipped below the horizon, casting long shadows across the bustling port of Al-Madina, Tariq continued his exploration. The vibrant market began to quiet, its once-bustling energy transforming into a serene hum as merchants closed their stalls and the day's activities wound down. Tariq's mind was alive with the myriad wonders he had encountered, each one adding a new layer to the tapestry of his journey. Near the edge of the market, Tariq noticed a figure huddled against the wall of a narrow alley. The man's clothes were tattered, his face weathered by time and hardship. Yet, there was a spark in his eyes, a glimmer of something beyond the physical. Intrigued, Tariq approached the beggar, his heart moved by the man's plight. "Good evening," Tariq said softly, kneeling down to meet the beggar's gaze. "Can I offer you something to ease your burden?" The beggar looked up, his eyes reflecting gratitude and surprise. "I ask for nothing, kind stranger, but if you have something to spare, it would be a gift from the heavens." Tariq reached into his satchel and pulled out a small pouch filled with coins, a modest fortune by his standards but a generous gift for one in need. He handed it to the beggar, who accepted it with trembling hands. "Thank you, noble soul," the beggar whispered, his voice choked with emotion. "Your kindness is rare in these times. Allow me to repay you with knowledge, for gold and silver are fleeting, but wisdom endures."

Tariq sat beside the beggar, eager to hear what wisdom he had to share. The beggar began, his voice soft but filled with a profound resonance. "This land, Al-Madina, is a place where magic and illusion intertwine, creating a reality that is both wondrous and deceptive. To understand this place, one must first understand the nature of magic itself."

"Magic," he continued, "is the art of manipulating the unseen forces that bind the world. It can be used to create beauty and wonder, but also to deceive and control. Here in Al-Madina, magic is woven into the very fabric of the city. The port, the market, the people—they are all touched by its influence." Tariq listened intently, the beggar's words resonating with the lessons he had learned during his travels. "How does one discern what is real and what is an illusion?" he asked.

The beggar smiled, a wise and knowing expression. "Perception is the key, wanderer. Magic thrives on the power of perception. It can make the ordinary appear extraordinary, and the extraordinary seem mundane. To see through the illusion, one must look beyond the surface, to the heart of things. Trust your instincts and the wisdom you have gained, for they will guide you through the veils of deception." He paused, his eyes distant as if recalling a long-forgotten memory. "I was once a man of means, a merchant who dealt in rare and precious artifacts. But I became entranced by the illusions of power and wealth, losing sight of what truly mattered. It was only when I was stripped of my material possessions that I began to see the world as it truly is."

Tariq pondered the beggar's words, reflecting on his own journey and the lessons he had learned. "Magic and illusion," he mused. "They can shape our reality, but they can also blind us to the truth. It is up to us to seek balance, to use our knowledge and instincts to navigate the world." The beggar nodded, his eyes shining with approval. "You have a wise heart, Tariq. Remember, the true magic lies not in the manipulation of the world, but in understanding it. Use your knowledge to guide others, to bring light where there is darkness, and to find the balance that sustains life."

With a deep sense of gratitude, Tariq thanked the beggar and rose to his feet. The sun had set, and the port of Al-Madina was now bathed in the soft glow of lantern light. He felt a renewed sense of purpose, his path illuminated by the wisdom he had gained. As he continued his journey through the port, Tariq carried with him the lessons of magic and illusion, knowing that the true power lay in understanding and balance. The winds of chance had brought him to Al-Madina, and it was here that he would find the answers he sought, not just for himself, but for the world he had come to cherish.

CHAPTER 4: REFLECTIONS ON FATE

As the port of Al-Madina settled into the tranquility of night, Tariq found a quiet spot near the harbor to sit and reflect. The water gently lapped against the docks, its rhythmic motion a soothing counterpoint to the day's chaotic events. The conversation with the beggar had stirred something deep within him, prompting questions about his journey and the mysterious forces that had brought him here.

Tariq gazed out over the moonlit waters, his mind turning inward. "What is it that brought me here?" he wondered. "Was it merely chance, the whims of the sea? Or is there a greater force at play, guiding my path through these uncharted waters?" The idea of fate, a concept both elusive and profound, had always fascinated him. As a sailor, he had learned to trust the winds and the stars, believing that they held the secrets of his destiny. Yet, here in Al-Madina, a place where magic and reality intertwined, the notion of fate took on a new dimension.

"Why me?" Tariq asked himself, his thoughts drifting back to the storm that had diverted his ship. "Why was I chosen to witness the wonders and perils of this land? Is there a purpose to my journey, a reason behind every encounter and challenge?" The wisdom of the beggar echoed in his mind: "The true magic lies not in the manipulation of the world, but in understanding it." Tariq pondered these words, realizing that his quest was not just about discovering new lands or acquiring knowledge, but about finding meaning in the journey itself.

Tariq considered the people he had met since arriving in Al-Madina—the merchant who spoke of the port's history, the performers who celebrated life through their art, and the beggar who revealed the nature of magic and illusion. Each encounter seemed to weave a thread into the tapestry of his fate, connecting him to the fabric of this land in ways he was only beginning to understand. "Perhaps fate is not a predetermined path," Tariq mused, "but a series of choices and connections, each one leading us closer to our true purpose. The winds of chance may have brought me here, but it is up to me to navigate the journey with wisdom and courage."

As the night deepened, Tariq felt a renewed sense of determination. He had been given a gift—the opportunity to explore a land rich with history, magic, and potential. It was his responsibility to uncover its secrets, not just for his own sake, but for the benefit of all who called this place home. "I will embrace this journey," Tariq vowed, "and seek to understand the forces that shape our lives. In doing so, I will find my place in the world and fulfill the destiny that the winds of fate have set before me."

With this newfound clarity, Tariq rose to his feet, his spirit buoyed by the promise of discovery. The port of Al-Madina, with its many mysteries and wonders, awaited him. Each step he took would be guided by the lessons he had learned and the wisdom he had gained.

As he walked back towards the heart of the city, the moonlight casting a silvery path before him, Tariq felt a profound sense of peace. The journey ahead was uncertain, but he was ready to face it with an open heart and a curious mind, trusting that the winds of fate would guide him to where he needed to be.

CHAPTER 5: TALES OF THE DESERT

The streets of Al-Madina were quiet as Tariq made his way to a tavern nestled at the edge of the bustling market. The warm glow of lanterns spilled out from the windows, casting inviting pools of light on the cobblestone streets. He stepped inside, greeted by the murmur of conversations and the comforting aroma of spiced ale and roasted meats.

The tavern was a cozy, welcoming place, filled with travelers and locals alike. Wooden beams overhead supported a ceiling adorned with dried herbs and lanterns, casting a warm, golden light. The walls were decorated with tapestries depicting scenes of sea voyages and desert landscapes, each one telling a story of adventure and exploration. Tariq found a seat at a corner table, ordering a simple meal and a tankard of ale. As he settled in, he couldn't help but overhear a group of travelers at a nearby table. Their animated discussion piqued his curiosity, and he listened intently to their conversation.

The travelers were an eclectic mix—a weathered caravan leader, a young scholar with a satchel of scrolls, and a mysterious figure cloaked in shadows. They spoke in hushed tones, their voices filled with wonder and excitement. "You speak of the desert as if it is alive," the young scholar said, his eyes wide with fascination. The caravan leader nodded, his face illuminated by the flickering light of the lantern. "It is, in a way. The desert holds many secrets, some as old as time itself. There are places where the sands shift like water, and the air shimmers with magic." The cloaked figure leaned forward, their voice a soft whisper. "Have you heard of the City of Mirages? It is said to appear only under certain circumstances, when the stars align and the moon is full."

Tariq's interest was piqued. He had heard tales of such places before, cities that existed on the edge of reality, appearing and disappearing like dreams. He leaned closer, eager to hear more. "The City of Mirages," the caravan leader continued, "is a place of great beauty and mystery. Its streets are paved with gold, and its towers reach towards the heavens. But it is also a place of great danger. Those who enter the city must prove their worth, for it is guarded by ancient spirits who protect its secrets." The young scholar nodded eagerly. "I have read about this city in ancient texts. It is said that only those with a pure heart and a clear mind can find it. The city reveals itself to those who are truly worthy, offering wisdom and treasures beyond imagination."

As Tariq listened, he felt a stirring in his heart. The idea of a magical city hidden within the desert resonated with him, echoing his own journey of discovery and self-realization. The tales of the City of Mirages spoke of a quest for knowledge and truth, a path that aligned with his own desires. "Fate has brought me to this place," he thought. "Perhaps it is also guiding me towards this city, a place where I can find the answers I seek and fulfill my purpose."

The conversation at the neighboring table continued, but Tariq's mind was already racing with possibilities. He finished his meal and drained his tankard, feeling a sense of resolve wash over him. He knew that his journey was far from over and that the desert held new challenges and wonders waiting to be discovered. As he left the tavern, the moon hung low in the sky, casting a silver glow over Al-Madina. Tariq's heart was light, filled with the promise of new adventures. The winds of fate had brought him here, and now they were guiding him towards the desert and the enigmatic City of Mirages.

With renewed determination, Tariq set his sights on the horizon. He would seek out the City of Mirages, uncover its secrets, and continue his quest for knowledge and balance. The path ahead was uncertain, but he was ready to face whatever challenges lay in his way. The desert called to him, a vast expanse of mystery and magic. Tariq answered its call, stepping into the night with a heart full of hope and a spirit ready for the journey ahead.

CHAPTER 6: BARGAINING FOR PASSAGE

With the tales of the City of Mirages fresh in his mind, Tariq set out to find transportation into the desert. The bustling market of Al-Madina was now cloaked in twilight, lanterns casting warm, flickering light on the faces of traders and travelers. Determined to begin his journey, Tariq knew that he would need to barter for passage into the vast and mysterious sands.

Tariq made his way to the edge of the market, where caravans and traders gathered to prepare for their journeys. The air was filled with the scent of spices and the sounds of animals readying for the trek ahead. He approached a group of seasoned travelers, their faces weathered by countless journeys under the scorching desert sun. "Excuse me," Tariq began, addressing a caravan leader who appeared to be in charge. "I seek passage into the desert. Can you help me find a way to reach the heart of the sands?" The caravan leader, a tall man with a thick beard and piercing eyes, looked Tariq up and down. "You wish to enter the desert?" he asked, his voice tinged with curiosity. "It is not a journey to be taken lightly. The desert is unforgiving to those who are unprepared."

Tariq nodded, understanding the gravity of the situation. "I am prepared to offer what I can in exchange for your guidance and transportation. I have coins, but perhaps there is something more valuable I can provide." The caravan leader stroked his beard thoughtfully. "Coins are useful, but in the desert, knowledge and resources are far more valuable. What skills do you possess, traveler?" Tariq considered his answer carefully. "I am a sailor by trade. I have navigated treacherous waters and survived many storms. I am also knowledgeable in the ways of the stars and can help guide us through the desert by night." The caravan leader's eyes lit up with interest. "A navigator, you say? That could indeed be useful. The desert stars can be as tricky to read as the ocean's waves. Very well, I will accept your offer. You will join our caravan as a navigator, and in return, we will take you as far into the desert as we dare."

Tariq thanked the caravan leader and set about preparing for the journey. He gathered his belongings, ensuring he had enough provisions for the trek. The caravan leader introduced him to the rest of the group—a mix of traders, scholars, and guards, each with their own purpose for venturing into the desert. As they loaded their camels and secured their supplies, Tariq felt a sense of anticipation and excitement. The tales of the City of Mirages had ignited a fire within him, and he was eager to see if the legends were true.

With the preparations complete, the caravan set out under the cover of darkness, the stars overhead guiding their way. Tariq rode alongside the caravan leader, his eyes scanning the horizon for any signs of danger or opportunity.

As they traveled deeper into the desert, the sands seemed to come alive, shifting and shimmering in the moonlight. Tariq used his skills as a navigator to keep them on course, reading the stars and interpreting the subtle changes in the landscape.

That first night, as they made camp beneath the vast desert sky, Tariq sat by the fire, his thoughts drifting to the tales of the City of Mirages. The other travelers shared stories of their own, recounting legends and myths passed down through generations. One of the scholars, a woman with keen eyes and a gentle demeanor, approached Tariq. "You seek the City of Mirages, do you not?" she asked softly. Tariq nodded. "I do. I have heard it is a place of great beauty and wisdom, a city that appears only to those who are truly worthy." The scholar smiled. "Many have sought it, but few have found it. The desert tests those who enter it, revealing their true selves. Perhaps you will be among the fortunate ones. Keep your heart pure and your mind clear, and the desert may reveal its secrets to you."

As the fire crackled and the desert winds whispered through the night, Tariq felt a renewed sense of purpose. The journey ahead would be challenging, but he was ready to face whatever trials the desert had in store. The City of Mirages awaited, and with each step, he drew closer to uncovering its mysteries and fulfilling his destiny. The next leg of Tariq's journey had begun, and the sands of the desert held the promise of new adventures and discoveries.

CHAPTER 7: NIGHTMARES
IN THE DESERT

The desert night was a canvas of stars, their light piercing the vast expanse of darkness. The caravan had settled into a quiet stillness, the only sounds the soft murmurs of the camels and the occasional rustle of the wind through the dunes. Tariq lay on his mat, the warmth of the campfire slowly fading as he drifted into a restless sleep.

In his dreams, Tariq found himself in a place both familiar and alien. The sands of the desert had turned dark, almost black, and the sky above was roiling with storm clouds. A chilling wind swept through, carrying whispers of fear and despair. Before him, a great battle unfolded—warriors clad in shimmering armor clashed with shadowy figures, their weapons glowing with an eerie light. He saw flashes of magic, bursts of energy that crackled and seared the air. The ground trembled with the force of their conflict, and the cries of the combatants echoed in his ears. Amidst the chaos, Tariq felt a dark presence, a malevolent force that seemed to draw strength from the destruction.

As the battle raged, Tariq's eyes were drawn to a figure cloaked in shadow, standing at the heart of the maelstrom. This figure wielded dark magic, its power radiating out in waves of corruption. Every touch, every spell cast, seemed to sap the light from the world around it, leaving behind only darkness and despair. Tariq felt a profound sense of dread as the figure turned its gaze upon him. Its eyes glowed with an unholy fire, and in that gaze, he saw visions of ruin and suffering. The dark figure raised its hand, and a torrent of black energy surged towards Tariq, enveloping him in its cold embrace.

With a gasp, Tariq awoke, his body drenched in sweat and his heart pounding in his chest. The desert night was still around him, the stars above serene and indifferent to his terror. He sat up, drawing deep breaths to calm himself, the echoes of the dream still vivid in his mind. The campfire had burned down to embers, casting a faint glow that barely pierced the darkness. Tariq glanced around, ensuring that the camp was undisturbed. The other members of the caravan slept soundly, unaware of the nightmare that had shaken him to his core.

Tariq knew that dreams could be powerful omens, messages from the subconscious or even the supernatural. This dream, with its vivid imagery and intense emotions, felt like more than just a figment of his imagination. It was a warning, a glimpse of a potential future shaped by dark forces. He thought back to the stories he had heard about the desert and the City of Mirages. The scholar's words echoed in his mind: "The desert tests those who enter it, revealing their true selves." Perhaps this dream was part of that test, a challenge he needed to face to prove his worth.

Determined to understand the meaning of his dream, Tariq decided to seek guidance from the scholars and the elders of the caravan. As dawn approached, he prepared himself to share his vision and learn what he could about the dark magic and the battle he had witnessed. The desert was a place of mystery and power, and Tariq knew that he had to be vigilant. The dream had revealed a new layer of the challenges he would face, and he needed to be prepared for whatever lay ahead.

As the first light of dawn crept over the horizon, Tariq felt a renewed sense of purpose. The journey through the desert was fraught with danger, both seen and unseen, but he was determined to uncover the truth and protect the land from the darkness he had seen in his dreams.

With the rising sun casting its golden light over the sands, Tariq rose to his feet, ready to face the day. The path ahead was uncertain, but he knew that he could not turn back. The winds of fate had brought him here, and it was up to him to navigate the challenges and uncover the secrets of the desert.

CHAPTER 8: REFLECTIONS ON PROPHECY AND ILLUSION

As the dawn light bathed the desert in a warm glow, Tariq sat at the edge of the caravan camp, reflecting on the haunting dream that had shaken him the night before. The images of the great battle, the dark magic, and the shadowy figure still lingered in his mind, filling him with a sense of urgency and foreboding. Tariq pondered the idea of prophecy, a concept that had fascinated and perplexed him in equal measure. Throughout his journeys, he had encountered tales of seers and oracles, individuals gifted with the ability to glimpse into the future. These prophecies often came in the form of dreams or visions, cryptic messages that required careful interpretation. "Was my dream a prophecy?" he wondered. "A warning of what is to come, or merely a reflection of my deepest fears?" Tariq knew that prophecies could be double-edged swords, offering glimpses of potential futures while also shaping the actions of those who received them. The knowledge of a possible future could be both a guide and a burden. He remembered the words of an old seer he had met during his travels. "The future is not set in stone," she had said. "It is a tapestry woven from countless threads, each one representing a choice or a possibility. A prophecy is but a glimpse of one such thread, a potential outcome that can be altered by the actions of the present."

Tariq's thoughts then turned to the concept of illusion, a theme that had been a recurring element in his journey through Al-Madina. The beggar's words echoed in his mind: "Magic thrives on the power of perception. It can make the ordinary appear extraordinary, and the extraordinary seem mundane."

In the desert, where the lines between reality and illusion were often blurred, Tariq understood that perception played a crucial role in shaping one's experience. The dream he had experienced could have been an illusion, a manifestation of his subconscious fears amplified by the magical nature of the land. "Illusions can deceive the senses and cloud the mind," Tariq mused. "They can create false realities, leading us astray if we are not vigilant. Yet, they also hold the potential to reveal deeper truths, forcing us to confront our innermost thoughts and desires."

33

Tariq realized that his journey through the desert would require a delicate balance between understanding prophecy and navigating illusion. He needed to remain open to the possibilities of the future while grounding himself in the reality of the present. The dream had given him a glimpse of a potential future shaped by dark magic, but it was his actions that would determine its outcome. "Prophecies and illusions," he thought, "are like the shifting sands of the desert—ever-changing and unpredictable. To navigate them, I must trust in my instincts and the wisdom I have gained. I must seek clarity and balance, using my knowledge to guide my path."

With these reflections, Tariq felt a renewed sense of determination. He rose to his feet, the morning sun casting his shadow long across the sand. The desert stretched out before him, a vast expanse of mystery and potential. The City of Mirages awaited, a beacon of hope and wisdom that he was determined to find. As the caravan began to stir and prepare for the day's journey, Tariq joined them, ready to face whatever challenges lay ahead. The dream had given him a warning, but it had also strengthened his resolve. He would uncover the secrets of the desert, confront the dark forces that threatened the land, and fulfill the destiny that the winds of fate had set before him.

With each step, Tariq moved closer to the heart of the desert and the answers he sought. The path was uncertain, but he was guided by the wisdom of prophecy and the understanding of illusion. The journey ahead would test him in ways he could not yet imagine, but he was ready to face it with courage and clarity. The desert called to him, and Tariq answered, his heart filled with hope and determination. The winds of fate carried him forward, into the unknown, where the true magic of his journey awaited.

CHAPTER 9: THE PRINCESS'S DREAM

High in her castle tower, Princess Layla gazed out over the vast expanse of her kingdom. The golden sands of the desert stretched endlessly towards the horizon, their undulating waves shimmering in the heat of the midday sun. Al-Madina, with its bustling market and lively streets, lay at the heart of this majestic landscape. Yet, despite the beauty that surrounded her, Layla felt a profound sense of yearning. For several nights now, Layla had been visited by dreams of a wanderer—a mysterious figure who had arrived in her land under the most unusual circumstances. The dreams were vivid and filled with a sense of destiny that she could not ignore. In her dreams, the wanderer moved with purpose and determination, his eyes filled with a deep understanding of the world. She wondered who this wanderer was and what had brought him to Al-Madina. Her heart told her that his arrival was significant, a pivotal moment in the unfolding story of her kingdom. She could feel an invisible thread connecting their fates, pulling her towards him with an irresistible force.

From her vantage point, Layla could see the port where the wanderer had arrived, his ship battered by a storm and guided to her shores by the whims of fate. She imagined him now, navigating the streets of Al-Madina, seeking answers and forging new paths. There was a sense of adventure about him, a quality that stirred something deep within her. Layla's life in the castle was one of privilege and responsibility. As a princess, she was expected to uphold the traditions and duties of her position, guiding her people with wisdom and grace. Yet, she often felt confined by the walls of the castle, yearning for the freedom to explore the world beyond.

In her dreams, Laila saw the wanderer facing great challenges—battles against dark forces, encounters with magical beings, and journeys through treacherous landscapes. She saw him standing at the edge of a great desert, the same desert that stretched out before her now, his eyes filled with determination and hope. She felt a deep connection to this wanderer, as if their destinies were intertwined. There was a sense of urgency in her dreams, a feeling that their meeting was crucial to the future of Al-Madina. The wanderer seemed to carry with him a light, a beacon of hope that could guide the kingdom through the darkness that threatened to engulf it.

Layla knew that she could not ignore these dreams. They were more than mere figments of her imagination; they were a call to action, a reminder that her role as a princess was not just to govern, but to protect and nurture her people. The wanderer represented a new beginning, a chance to bring balance and harmony to a land that had seen too much strife. She resolved to learn more about the wanderer, to seek him out and understand the purpose of his journey. Perhaps, together, they could uncover the secrets of the desert. Layla felt a renewed sense of purpose, a fire ignited within her heart by the dreams that had shown her the path forward.

With this resolve, Princess Layla turned away from the window and descended the winding staircase of her tower. She would seek counsel from the elders and scholars, learn all she could about the wanderer. Her journey was just beginning, and she was determined to see it through. As she stepped into the grand hall of the castle, her thoughts were filled with the image of the wanderer, his eyes bright with purpose and his heart steadfast in the face of adversity. She knew that their paths would cross, and when they did, it would mark the start of a new chapter for Al-Madina—a chapter written by the hands of fate and guided by the dreams of a princess.

CHAPTER 10: REFLECTIONS ON LOVE AND FATE

As Princess Layla descended from her tower, her mind was a whirlwind of thoughts and emotions. The dreams of the wanderer had stirred something deep within her, not just a sense of purpose, but a contemplation of love and fate—two forces that had always seemed intertwined in the stories she had grown up with.

Love, Layla mused, was a force as ancient and enduring as the desert itself. It was a bond that could bring people together across great distances and through immense trials. She had seen love in many forms: the tender affection of her parents, the loyalty of her closest friends, and the unspoken bonds that held her people together. But the love she felt stirring within her for the wanderer was different. It was born of dreams and whispers, a connection that seemed to transcend the physical world. "Is it possible," she wondered, "to love someone you have never met? To feel a bond so strong that it defies logic and reason?" Layla had always believed in the power of love to heal and transform. She had witnessed it in the way her parents ruled their kingdom with compassion and justice, and in the sacrifices her people made for one another. Love was a guiding force, a beacon of light in the darkest of times.

Fate, on the other hand, was a more enigmatic force. It was the thread that wove the tapestry of life, guiding individuals along paths they could not foresee. Layla often pondered the role of fate in her own life. She had been born into royalty, her path seemingly predetermined by her birthright. Yet, she felt that her destiny was not solely defined by her lineage, but by the choices she made and the actions she took.

The dreams of the wanderer had given her a glimpse of a different fate—one that was intertwined with his journey. She wondered if it was fate that had brought him to Al-Madina, and if it was fate that had guided her dreams to connect with his. "Are our lives truly governed by fate," she mused, "or do we have the power to shape our own destinies through our choices and actions?"

Layla realized that love and fate were not mutually exclusive. They were two sides of the same coin, each influencing the other in profound ways.

Love could guide one's choices, steering them towards their true path, while fate could bring people together, creating opportunities for love to flourish.

She thought of the wanderer, his presence in her dreams a testament to the mysterious ways in which love and fate operated. "Perhaps," she thought, "fate has brought him to this land not just to fulfill a prophecy, but to find love and connection. And perhaps my role is to help him realize that destiny."

With this understanding, Layla felt a sense of peace. Her dreams of the wanderer were not just visions of a distant future, but a call to action in the present. She would seek him out, learn from him.

Love and fate had guided her to this moment, and she was ready to embrace whatever challenges and joys lay ahead. The wanderer's journey was her journey too, a shared path that would lead them both to greater understanding and fulfillment.

As Layla stepped into the grand hall, her heart filled with resolve, she knew that her destiny was unfolding before her. She would follow the threads of love and fate, trusting in their guidance as she sought out the wanderer and the answers they both needed. The castle, once a symbol of confinement, now felt like a place of possibility. The desert beyond its walls beckoned, a land of mystery and magic that held the key to their future. Layla was ready to face it, with love and fate as her guides.

CHAPTER 11: REFLECTIONS ON AL-MADINA

Princess Laila stood on the balcony of the Sultan's palace, her gaze sweeping over the magnificent city of Al-Madina. The city was a jewel in the desert, a vibrant blend of culture, architecture, and history that reflected the soul of its people. As she took in the sights, she felt a profound sense of pride and wonder for the place she called home.

Al-Madina was a masterpiece of architecture, its skyline punctuated by minarets and domes that reached towards the heavens. The buildings, constructed from sandstone and adorned with intricate mosaics, glowed with a warm, golden hue in the light of the setting sun. The narrow streets and alleys, lined with bustling markets and vibrant bazaars, were a maze of activity and life. From her vantage point, Layla could see the grand temple at the heart of the city, its elegant arches and towering minarets standing as a testament to the city's spiritual heritage. Rhythmic chants echoed through the air, a melodic reminder of the faith that united the people of Al-Madina.

The souks of Al-Madina were renowned throughout the land, drawing traders and travelers from distant realms. Each market stall was a treasure trove of exotic goods: silks from the East, spices from the South, and handcrafted jewelry that sparkled like stars. The air was filled with the scents of saffron and incense, mingling with the sounds of haggling merchants and laughing children. Layla marveled at the diversity of the marketplace, where cultures and traditions blended seamlessly. It was a place where stories were exchanged along with goods, and where the pulse of the city could be felt most strongly.

Scattered throughout Al-Madina were lush gardens and tranquil courtyards, oases of greenery in the midst of the desert. These spaces offered respite from the bustling streets, their fountains and shaded pavilions inviting moments of reflection and peace. The palace gardens, in particular, were a marvel of landscape design, with flowering plants and fruit trees that thrived under the care of skilled gardeners. Layla often found solace in these gardens, their beauty a reminder of the delicate balance between nature and human endeavor. She admired the way the people of Al-Madina had harnessed the desert's resources to create such verdant spaces, a testament to their ingenuity and perseverance.

Beyond the city walls lay the port, where ships from all over the world docked to trade and resupply. The waters of the port sparkled in the sunlight, reflecting the vibrant sails of the merchant vessels. The docks were a hive of activity, with sailors unloading their cargo and exchanging tales of their voyages. The port was a gateway to the world, and Layla loved the sense of connection it provided. It was here that new ideas and innovations flowed into the city, enriching its culture and inspiring its people.

As she looked out over Al-Madina, Layla felt a deep sense of responsibility. The city was more than just her home; it was a living entity, a place where history and progress coexisted. She thought of the wanderer from her dreams, wondering how he would perceive this vibrant tapestry of life and what role he might play in its future. "Al-Madina is a city of contrasts," she mused. "A place where the ancient and the modern meet, where tradition and innovation walk hand in hand. It is a city shaped by its people, by their dreams and their struggles. And it is a city that holds the promise of so much more." With a renewed sense of purpose, Layla turned away from the balcony and made her way back into the palace. The wanderer's journey had become entwined with her own, and she was determined to see where it would lead. The city of Al-Madina, with all its wonders and mysteries, awaited their next chapter.

The princess knew that the path forward would be challenging, but she was ready to face it with courage and wisdom. The winds of chance had brought the wanderer to her city, and together perhaps they would uncover a new destiny for Al-Madina and its people.

CHAPTER 12: THE SULTAN'S COUNSEL

At the heart of the palace, in a grand chamber adorned with opulent tapestries and ornate furnishings, sat the Sultan. He was a figure of immense power and stoicism, his presence commanding respect and reverence. His beard, meticulously groomed, framed a face etched with lines of wisdom and concern. His eyes, sharp and discerning, constantly scanned the horizon of his thoughts, always contemplating the future of his beloved city, Al-Madina.

The Sultan's mind was a fortress of strategic thoughts and careful planning. He had led Al-Madina through times of prosperity and peril, always with the well-being of his people at the forefront. He was a guardian of the city's legacy and a steward of its future. Every decision he made was weighed with the gravity of its potential impact, ensuring that the city and its people thrived. This day, as he sat upon his ornate throne, the Sultan pondered the recent whispers of strange occurrences in the desert, the arrival of the wanderer, and the ever-present challenge of maintaining balance in a land where magic and reality intertwined. His thoughts were interrupted by a gentle knock on the door.

"Enter," the Sultan called, his voice resonant and authoritative. Princess Layla stepped into the chamber, her presence a breath of fresh air in the solemn room. She approached the Sultan with a graceful bow, her eyes reflecting the respect and love she held for him. "Sultan," she began, her voice soft yet steady, "I seek your counsel. There are matters of the city and its subjects that weigh heavily on my heart." The Sultan gestured for her to sit beside him. "Speak. Your insights are always valued." Layla took a seat, gathering her thoughts. "I have been thinking about Al-Madina, about its people and the future that lies ahead. The city is a beacon of culture and progress, yet it is also a place of deep mystery and magic. I have dreams, Sultan, dreams of a wanderer who has come to our land. I believe his arrival is significant, that it is tied to the fate of Al-Madina." The Sultan listened intently, his expression thoughtful. "This wanderer," he said, "is he the one who arrived at the port recently? I have heard whispers of his presence and the unusual circumstances that brought him here." Layla nodded.

"Yes, Sultan. His name is Tariq. I feel that his journey is intertwined with the destiny of our city. The dreams I have suggest that he is a bearer of change, one that could either bring great fortune or unforeseen challenges."

The Sultan leaned back in his chair, his eyes narrowing as he considered the words of the princess. "The future of Al-Madina has always been my greatest concern. We stand at a crossroads, where the decisions we make now will shape the lives of our people for generations. Magic is a double-edged sword, capable of both creation and destruction. We must tread carefully." Layla could see the weight of responsibility in the Sultan's eyes. "What do you propose we do? How can we ensure that the path we choose is the right one?" The Sultan stood, his gaze fixed on the city beyond the palace walls. "We must learn more about this wanderer, about his purpose and the nature of the magic that surrounds him. Knowledge is our greatest ally. We will seek counsel from our scholars and sages, and we will watch him closely. If he is to be a part of our city's future, we must understand his role in it."

Layla felt a sense of relief at the Sultans wisdom and decisiveness. "I will aid in this endeavor. I believe that understanding the wanderer and his journey is crucial to our future." The Sultan turned to the princess, his expression softening. "Your heart is as wise as it is kind, Layla. Together, we will navigate these uncertain times. Al-Madina is strong because of its people, and with their support, we will ensure its prosperity."

The princess and the Sultan stood together, looking out over the city they both cherished. The journey ahead was fraught with challenges, but they were united in their resolve to protect and guide Al-Madina. The winds of chance had brought Tariq to their land, and with him, the promise of change. It was up to them to ensure that this change was for the better.

As the sun set over the golden sands, casting long shadows across the city, the Sultan and Princess Layla knew that their path was clear. They would face the future with wisdom and courage, guided by the love they had for their people and the city that was their home.

CHAPTER 13: THE SULTAN'S SECOND

As the Sultan and Princess Layla stood in silent contemplation, a knock echoed through the grand chamber. A tall, imposing figure entered, his presence commanding attention. Malik, the Sultan's trusted counsel, moved with the grace and confidence of a man who knew the corridors of power intimately. His dark eyes flickered with intelligence and ambition, and his robes, adorned with intricate patterns, flowed like liquid night.

The Sultan turned to greet him. "Malik, thank you for joining us. There are matters we must discuss concerning the future of Al-Madina." Malik bowed deeply, his voice smooth and measured. "Of course, Your Majesty. I am always at your service." Princess Layla watched him closely. There was something about Malik that unsettled her, though she couldn't pinpoint why. He had always been respectful and courteous, yet she sensed an undercurrent of something darker, a shadow that lurked behind his polished exterior.

"Malik," the Sultan began, "we have been discussing the recent arrival of a wanderer named Tariq. His presence in Al-Madina is intriguing, and we believe it may be tied to the fate of our city. What do you know of him?" Malik's eyes narrowed slightly, a flicker of interest crossing his face. "I have heard whispers, Your Majesty. The man arrived under unusual circumstances, and there are rumors of strange dreams and prophecies surrounding him. It would be wise to learn more about his intentions." The Sultan nodded. "Precisely. I intend to keep a close watch on him. Layla has offered to assist in this endeavor. She believes that understanding Tariq's journey is crucial to our future."

Layla felt Malik's gaze shift towards her, his expression unreadable. "Princess, your insights are always valuable. It is commendable that you take such an active interest in the well-being of Al-Madina." "Thank you, Malik," Layla replied, her tone polite but guarded. "I believe that Tariq's presence here is not a mere coincidence. There is something more at play, something we must understand." Malik inclined his head. "Indeed. The desert holds many secrets, and those who come from it often carry stories and knowledge that can shape our destiny."

After their discussion, the Sultan requested a private word with Malik. Layla excused herself, her thoughts still preoccupied with the enigmatic counsel. She wandered through the palace gardens, seeking the solace of nature to clear her mind. The flowers and fountains, usually a source of peace, did little to dispel her unease.

Inside the grand chamber, the Sultan and Malik spoke in hushed tones. "What is your assessment of this Tariq?" the Sultan asked, his eyes piercing. Malik's voice was calm and measured. "He is an unknown variable, Your Majesty. While he may bring new opportunities, he also poses a potential threat. It is essential to understand his true purpose." The Sultan nodded, his expression thoughtful. "Keep a close eye on him, Malik. Use whatever means necessary to uncover his intentions. Al-Madina's future depends on our vigilance."

As night fell, Layla returned to her chambers, her mind racing with questions. She trusted the Sultans judgment, but her instincts told her to be wary of Malik. There was something about him that felt wrong, something she needed to uncover. She resolved to keep a close watch on Malik, determined to protect her city and her family. Layla knew that the journey ahead would be fraught with challenges and uncertainties. The winds of chance had brought Tariq to Al-Madina, and with him, the promise of change. It was up to her, the Sultan, and even Malik to navigate these turbulent times. The city of Al-Madina, with its rich history and vibrant culture, deserved nothing less than their unwavering dedication.

As the stars illuminated the desert night, Layla felt a renewed sense of purpose. The future of Al-Madina lay in their hands, and she was ready to face whatever came their way, guided by love, wisdom, and the enduring spirit of her people.

CHAPTER 14: THE COUNSEL OF AMBITION

Malik left the Sultan's grand chamber, his thoughts swirling with plans and possibilities. As he walked through the dimly lit corridors of the palace, he reflected on the nature of ambition and the forces that drove him and others to seek power and influence. Ambition, Malik mused, was a double-edged sword. It was the driving force behind great achievements and monumental progress, yet it could also lead to downfall and destruction. For him, ambition was a necessity, a guiding light that had shaped his path from a young age. He remembered his childhood, growing up in a modest home, dreaming of a life far removed from the struggles he had known. "Ambition is the fire that burns within," Malik thought. "It is the desire to rise above one's circumstances, to carve out a place of significance in the world. Without it, we are mere shadows, existing but not truly living." As Malik ascended the ranks within the Sultan's court, he had come to understand that power was not simply handed to those who desired it. It was earned through cunning, intelligence, and a willingness to make difficult decisions. He had observed many who sought to rise to greatness, their paths littered with the remnants of failed attempts and broken alliances. "To become a person of great importance," Malik reflected, "one must be willing to take risks, to navigate the treacherous waters of politics and intrigue. It requires not just ambition, but the ability to see several steps ahead, to anticipate and outmaneuver those who would stand in your way."

Malik's thoughts turned to those who, like him, had sought to rise to positions of influence. He considered the various motivations that drove people to seek power—some were driven by a desire to make a difference, to leave a lasting legacy; others were motivated by a thirst for control and dominance. "For me," Malik pondered, "it is a combination of both. I seek to guide Al-Madina towards a future of prosperity and strength, but I also desire the control and recognition that come with my position. It is a delicate balance, one that requires constant vigilance and adaptation."

Malik thought of Princess Layla and her wariness towards him. He respected her intuition and intelligence, recognizing her potential to be a formidable ally or adversary. Her dreams and connection to the wanderer Tariq intrigued him, and he wondered how their paths would intertwine with his own. "Layla is perceptive," Malik acknowledged. "She senses the undercurrents of my ambition, but she does not yet understand the full extent of my plans. I must tread carefully, for her support could be invaluable, but her opposition could prove detrimental."

As Malik reached his private chambers, he felt a renewed sense of determination. The arrival of Tariq and the dreams of the princess signaled a time of change and opportunity. His ambition would drive him to navigate this new landscape, to seize the chances that arose and to shape the future of Al-Madina to his vision.

"Ambition is the path to greatness," Malik concluded. "It is the force that compels us to strive for more, to reach beyond our grasp and to transform the world around us. It is not without its dangers, but for those who master it, the rewards are boundless." With these thoughts, Malik prepared for the days ahead. The journey of Al-Madina was intertwined with his own, and he was ready to face the challenges and opportunities that lay in wait. The winds of chance were shifting, and Malik intended to harness their power to achieve his ultimate goals.

As the first light of dawn began to filter through the palace windows, Malik felt the fire of ambition burn brighter within him. The path to greatness was fraught with peril, but he was ready to embrace it, to rise to the heights he had always dreamed of and to leave an indelible mark on the world.

CHAPTER 15: THE NOBLE SOLDIER

As Malik prepared for the days ahead, he knew he would need the support and loyalty of those closest to him. Among them was his brother, Khalid—a noble soldier whose strength and courage were matched only by his internal conflict over duty and devotion. Khalid had always been Malik's steadfast ally, though their paths and motivations often diverged.

Malik summoned Khalid to his chambers. As his brother entered, Malik couldn't help but admire Khalid's imposing figure. Tall and broad-shouldered, Khalid carried himself with the discipline and grace of a seasoned warrior. His armor, though worn from countless battles, gleamed with the pride of his station. "Khalid," Malik greeted, his voice warm yet authoritative. "Thank you for coming. We have much to discuss." Khalid bowed respectfully. "Brother, it is always an honor to serve. What is it that you require of me?"

Malik motioned for Khalid to sit, his gaze intense. "The arrival of the wanderer, Tariq, has brought new challenges and opportunities to Al-Madina. The Sultan has tasked us with understanding his purpose and ensuring the stability of our city. Your strength and loyalty are crucial in these uncertain times." Khalid nodded, his expression thoughtful. "I have heard of this Tariq. There are whispers of prophecies and dreams surrounding him. It is said he carries a great destiny, one that could shape the future of our land." Malik's eyes narrowed. "Precisely. And it is our duty to ensure that his presence does not disrupt the balance of power. We must be vigilant and prepared for any eventuality."

Khalid sighed, his internal conflict evident. "Malik, you know I am devoted to our city and our people. My duty as a soldier is clear—to protect and serve. But sometimes, I wonder if there is more to our purpose than just maintaining power and control. What of the people's needs? What of justice and honor?" Malik's gaze softened, recognizing the depth of Khalid's struggle. "Brother, our roles are not without their burdens. The path of power is fraught with difficult choices. We must be strong and resolute, for the sake of Al-Madina. Your sense of duty is admirable, but we cannot afford to let sentiment cloud our judgment."

The brothers sat in silence for a moment, reflecting on their shared history. They had grown up together, faced countless challenges, and risen through the ranks side by side. Yet, their motivations often diverged—Malik driven by ambition and the desire for control, while Khalid was guided by a sense of honor and a deep commitment to justice. "Khalid," Malik said finally, his tone sincere, "I need you by my side. Your strength and integrity are invaluable. Together, we can ensure the future of Al-Madina. But you must trust me and understand that our actions, though sometimes harsh, are necessary for the greater good." Khalid met his brother's gaze, the conflict in his eyes slowly giving way to resolve. "I will stand with you, Malik. But I ask that we remember the principles that make us who we are. Let us strive for a future where power and justice coexist, where our people can thrive in peace."

Malik nodded, a sense of relief washing over him. "Agreed, brother. We will face the challenges ahead together, as we always have. The path will not be easy, but with your strength and my guidance, we will prevail." As the brothers stood, ready to face the uncertainties of the future, Malik felt a renewed sense of purpose. Khalid's unwavering loyalty and sense of honor would be crucial in the days to come. Together, they would navigate the complexities of duty and devotion, ensuring the stability and prosperity of Al-Madina.

With the dawn breaking over the horizon, Malik and Khalid stepped into the light of a new day.

The challenges ahead were many, but united in their resolve, they were ready to face whatever fate had in store. The winds of chance were blowing, and the brothers were determined to steer the course of Al-Madina towards a future where power and justice could coexist.

CHAPTER 16: A FASCINATION WITH MAGIC

As the dawn light filtered through the palace windows, casting a golden glow across the chamber, Malik and Khalid prepared to face the challenges of the day. The brothers had always shared a deep bond, but their recent conversation had brought them closer, aligning their goals and strengthening their resolve. However, there was still one topic that Khalid had yet to broach with Malik, a subject that had fascinated and perplexed him for years—magic. As they walked through the grand halls of the palace, Khalid turned to his brother, a thoughtful expression on his face. "Malik, there is something I have been meaning to discuss with you. It is about magic and its place in our world." Malik glanced at Khalid, intrigued. "Magic? What specifically about it?" Khalid hesitated for a moment, then continued. "I have always been fascinated by magic, by its power and its potential. In our land, it is both revered and feared, a force that can create wonders and cause devastation. I want to understand it better, to learn how it works and how it can be used for the benefit of Al-Madina."

Malik nodded, his expression thoughtful. "Magic is indeed a powerful force. It has the potential to shape our world in profound ways. However, it is also dangerous, unpredictable. Those who wield it must do so with great caution and responsibility." Khalid's eyes lit up with curiosity. "That is what intrigues me. How can we harness such a force without falling into the traps of greed and corruption? How can we use magic to enhance our city's prosperity without losing sight of our principles?" Malik considered his brother's words carefully. "Magic, like any other form of power, requires balance. It is not enough to simply possess it; one must also have the wisdom to use it wisely. In our history, there have been those who sought to control magic for their own gain, leading to great suffering. But there have also been those who used it to heal, to protect, and to inspire." He paused, his gaze intense. "The key, Khalid, is to approach magic with respect and humility. It is a tool, one that can amplify our strengths and magnify our flaws. If we are to incorporate magic into our governance, we must do so with a clear understanding of its risks and rewards."

Khalid nodded, absorbing his brother's wisdom. "I believe that with the right approach, we can use magic to benefit our people. We can create innovations that improve their lives, protect them from harm, and help our city flourish. But we must also be vigilant, ensuring that magic does not corrupt our intentions or our actions." Malik smiled, a rare expression of genuine warmth. "I trust your judgment, Khalid. Your fascination with magic is not just idle curiosity; it is a desire to understand and to improve. Together, we can explore this path, always mindful of the balance we must maintain." As they continued their walk through the palace, the brothers felt a renewed sense of purpose. The challenges ahead were many, but with their combined strengths and shared vision, they were ready to face them. Magic, with all its complexities and potential, would be a part of their journey, a tool to be wielded with care and wisdom.

The future of Al-Madina lay in their hands, and they were determined to guide it towards a new era of prosperity and innovation. Magic would play a crucial role in this future, but it would be tempered by the principles of justice and honor that Khalid held dear. As the day began in earnest, Malik and Khalid prepared to meet with the Sultan and the other advisors, ready to discuss their plans and strategies. The winds of fate were shifting, and the brothers were determined to steer their city towards a brighter, more magical future.

CHAPTER 17: KHALID'S REFLECTION ON POWER AND CHARACTER

As Khalid walked through the palace gardens, his mind lingered on the conversation he had just had with Malik. The potential of magic was undeniable, but so were its risks. He found a quiet spot beneath a towering palm tree and allowed his thoughts to wander, contemplating the nature of power and its impact on the character of those who wielded it.

Khalid had seen firsthand how power could change a person. As a soldier, he had watched comrades rise through the ranks, some growing more honorable and others succumbing to arrogance and corruption. Power, he knew, was a potent force that could amplify both virtues and vices. "Does power inherently corrupt?" he wondered. "Or does it merely reveal the true nature of a person?" He thought about the various leaders and figures of authority he had encountered. Those who had remained steadfast in their principles, even as their influence grew, had earned his deepest respect. Conversely, those who had allowed power to erode their integrity had served as cautionary tales.

Khalid considered his own character and values. He prided himself on his sense of duty and honor, qualities that had guided him throughout his life. But he could not ignore the nagging doubt that power, especially the mystical kind, might alter even the most steadfast of hearts. "Can a strong character truly prevent corruption?" he asked himself. "Or is there a point at which the allure of power becomes too great to resist?" His thoughts turned to the wanderer, Tariq. From what he had heard, Tariq seemed driven by a noble quest, one that resonated with Khalid's own sense of purpose. But the stories of dreams and prophecies hinted at the potential for great power. Would Tariq remain true to his values if he harnessed such power, or would he be changed by it?

Khalid realized that the key to preventing corruption lay in maintaining a balance. Power should be tempered with wisdom, and ambition should be guided by a commitment to the greater good. This balance was delicate, requiring constant vigilance and self-reflection. He thought about Malik and their differing approaches to power. Malik's ambition was undeniable, but Khalid believed that his brother's heart was in the right place. They both wanted what was best for Al-Madina, even if their methods sometimes diverged.

Khalid resolved to stay true to his principles, even as they explored the potential of magic. He would strive to ensure that any power they harnessed was used for the benefit of their people, not for personal gain or dominance. His sense of duty would be his anchor, preventing him from losing sight of what truly mattered. As the sun began to set, casting long shadows across the garden, Khalid felt a renewed sense of clarity. Power, whether mundane or magical, was a tool that could be used for both good and ill. The character of the person wielding it was the determining factor. He rose to his feet, ready to face the challenges ahead with a steadfast heart and a clear mind. The path they were on was fraught with uncertainty, but he was determined to navigate it with honor and integrity.

Khalid made his way back to the palace, ready to rejoin Malik and continue their discussion. They would need to work together, balancing their strengths and ensuring that their ambitions did not overshadow their responsibilities. As he walked, Khalid thought about the future of Al-Madina and the role he would play in shaping it. With Malik by his side and his own unwavering commitment to duty, he felt confident that they could harness the power of magic for the greater good, preserving the integrity of their city and its people.

CHAPTER 18: TARIQ'S CONVERSATIONS IN THE DESERT

Tariq continued his journey through the vast and mysterious desert, the sands stretching endlessly around him. As he ventured deeper into the heart of the desert, he found solace in the company of the desert's inhabitants—its animals. These creatures, with their unique perspectives, offered Tariq a wealth of wisdom about human nature and the world he sought to understand. One evening, as the sun dipped below the horizon and the cool desert night began to unfold, Tariq encountered a wise old owl perched on a gnarled acacia tree. The owl's eyes glowed with an ancient knowledge, and Tariq felt compelled to speak with it. "Owl, what can you tell me about the nature of humans?" Tariq asked, his voice soft in the twilight. The owl blinked slowly, considering the question. "Humans are complex creatures," it began. "They possess great intelligence and curiosity, but they are also driven by desires and fears. They have the capacity for profound wisdom and kindness, yet they often fall prey to their own ambitions and insecurities. It is this duality that defines them."

Further along his journey, Tariq came across a gazelle, its slender form standing gracefully against the backdrop of the desert dunes. The gazelle's eyes were gentle, reflecting a deep understanding of the natural world. "Gazelle, what do you think of human nature?" Tariq inquired. The gazelle paused, its ears twitching thoughtfully. "Humans are restless," it replied. "They are always searching for something— be it knowledge, power, or fulfillment. This endless pursuit drives them to create and to destroy. They have the potential for great harmony with nature, but too often they allow their desires to lead them astray."

As night fell and the stars illuminated the desert sky, Tariq encountered a serpent slithering silently across the sands. The serpent, often feared and misunderstood, had its own perspective on humanity. "Serpent, what insights can you share about human nature?" Tariq asked, his curiosity piqued. The serpent's eyes glinted in the starlight. "Humans are creatures of passion and instinct," it hissed. "They are capable of immense love and loyalty, but also of great deceit and betrayal. Their nature is neither entirely good nor evil; it is shaped by their choices and experiences. They are always balancing on the edge of light and darkness." One night, Tariq rested beside a caravan of camels. The lead camel, with its weathered face and patient demeanor, seemed to have a story to tell. Tariq approached it, seeking its wisdom. "Camel, what do you think of human nature?" he asked. The camel regarded Tariq with a calm, knowing gaze. "Humans are resilient and resourceful," it said. "They adapt to their circumstances and persevere through hardships. Yet, they are also prone to forgetfulness, often losing sight of what truly matters. They have the strength to endure, but they must learn to remember their origins and their interconnectedness with all life."

As Tariq continued his conversations with the desert's inhabitants, he realized that each creature offered a unique perspective, reflecting different facets of human nature. The wisdom he gained from these encounters deepened his understanding of the complexities and contradictions within himself and his fellow humans.

With each interaction, Tariq felt a growing sense of clarity. The desert, with its harsh beauty and timeless wisdom, was teaching him valuable lessons. He understood that the journey he was on was not just about discovering a magical city, but also about understanding the deeper truths of existence. As he prepared to continue his journey, Tariq felt a renewed sense of purpose. The wisdom of the animals had given him a new perspective on human nature, one that he would carry with him as he navigated the challenges ahead. The desert was a place of mystery and magic, and it had much to teach those who were willing to listen.

CHAPTER 19: AN OASIS ENCOUNTER

As Tariq continued his journey through the desert, the midday sun blazed overhead, casting long shadows across the sand dunes. His steps were heavy, but his resolve was unwavering. In the distance, he spotted a verdant patch of green—a welcome sight amidst the barren landscape. An oasis. The sight filled him with a renewed sense of hope and anticipation. The oasis was a paradise of lush greenery and sparkling water, a stark contrast to the harsh desert that surrounded it. Palm trees swayed gently in the breeze, their leaves whispering secrets of the ancient land. Tariq approached the cool waters, bending down to quench his thirst. As he drank, he heard a soft, melodic voice behind him. "Isn't it beautiful?" the voice said. Tariq turned to see a woman standing a few paces away, her features delicate and her eyes filled with warmth and curiosity. She wore flowing garments that fluttered in the breeze, and a small smile played on her lips. Tariq felt an immediate connection, a sense that this encounter was destined. "Indeed, it is," Tariq replied, his voice filled with wonder. "I am Tariq, a wanderer in these lands. And you?" The woman stepped closer, her smile widening. "I am Layla, of Al-Madina. It seems fate has brought us together in this tranquil place." Tariq's eyes widened in recognition. "I have heard tales of your wisdom and beauty. It is an honor to meet you." Layla laughed softly, a sound like the tinkling of bells. "You flatter me. But tell me, what brings you to our desert?"

They sat by the water's edge, the oasis providing a serene backdrop to their conversation. As they talked, their words flowed easily, filled with curiosity and playful banter. "Life is such a curious thing," Layla mused, her fingers trailing in the cool water. "We are like the sands of the desert, constantly shifting and changing, yet always connected to something greater." Tariq nodded, thoughtful. "And love? What of love in this ever-changing landscape?" Layla's eyes sparkled with mischief. "Love is the oasis in the desert of life. It is a place of refuge and renewal, where one can find peace and joy amidst the trials and tribulations." Tariq smiled, captivated by her words. "You speak wisely. Love is indeed a powerful force, one that can guide us through the darkest of times."

As the afternoon turned to evening, their conversation deepened, exploring dreams and desires. They spoke of their hopes for the future, the challenges they faced, and the strength they found in each other's company. "I often dream of a world where people understand and respect each other," Tariq said, his voice earnest. "A place where love and compassion guide our actions." Layla looked at him, her gaze soft and understanding. "That is a beautiful dream and I believe it is possible. But it requires courage and faith, qualities that I see in you."

As the sun began to set, casting a golden glow over the oasis, Tariq and Layla stood and embraced. It was a moment of connection, a promise of support and understanding. "Thank you, Layla", Tariq whispered. "For this moment, and for your wisdom. I feel as though I have found a kindred spirit in you." Layla smiled, her eyes reflecting the colors of the sunset. "And I in you, wanderer. May our paths continue to cross, and may we find strength in each other's presence." They stood together, watching as the sun dipped below the horizon, painting the sky with hues of pink and orange. The oasis, with its tranquil beauty, became a symbol of the bond they had formed—a bond that would guide them through the challenges ahead. As night fell, the stars began to twinkle in the vast desert sky, and Tariq felt a profound sense of peace.

CHAPTER 20: THE NATURE OF REALITY

As the first rays of dawn broke over the horizon, Tariq stirred from his slumber. He found himself lying on the soft sands near the oasis, the memories of the previous evening swirling in his mind. The serene encounter, their heartfelt conversation, and the embrace at sunset all seemed so vivid. Yet, as he fully awoke, a sense of confusion washed over him. The Blurred Line Between Dream and Reality Tariq sat up, rubbing his eyes and gazing around the oasis. The tranquility of the scene was unchanged, but he couldn't shake the feeling of uncertainty. "Was it all a dream?" he wondered aloud. "Or was it an illusion conjured by the magic of this land?" He stood and walked to the edge of the water, staring at his reflection. The rippling surface seemed to mock his confusion, distorting his image as if to remind him of the elusive nature of reality in this magical place.

Tariq began to pace along the water's edge, speaking his thoughts aloud in an attempt to make sense of his experiences. "What is real?" he asked himself. "Is reality defined by our senses, by what we see, hear, and feel? Or is it shaped by our beliefs and perceptions?" He thought of the desert animals he had spoken with, their wisdom and perspectives on human nature. They had taught him that reality was often subjective, influenced by one's experiences and interpretations. Yet, the encounter with Layla felt different—it had a depth and clarity that seemed beyond mere illusion.

Tariq paused and took a deep breath, trying to center himself. "If what I experienced was a dream, then it was a dream that spoke to my deepest desires and fears. If it was an illusion, then it was an illusion that revealed truths about myself and this land."

He recalled the conversations he had with Layla, the insights they shared about life and love. Those moments felt undeniably real, filled with genuine connection and understanding. "Perhaps," he mused, "the distinction between reality and illusion is not as clear-cut as I once believed. Maybe both can coexist, each offering their own truths."

Tariq knelt by the water and cupped his hands, taking a long drink. The cool liquid refreshed him, grounding him in the present moment. He realized that whether dream or illusion, the experience with Layla had left a lasting impact on him. It had deepened his understanding of himself and his journey, giving him new insights into the nature of reality. "Reality is what we make of it," Tariq concluded. "It is shaped by our experiences, our beliefs, and our interactions with the world. What matters is not whether something is real or illusory, but the meaning and truth we derive from it." With this newfound clarity, Tariq stood and looked towards the distant castle. His journey was far from over, and he knew that many more challenges and revelations awaited him. The encounter with Layla, whether a product of his mind or the magic of the oasis, had strengthened his resolve and given him a deeper sense of purpose. Tariq felt a renewed sense of determination. The desert, with all its mysteries and illusions, had taught him valuable lessons. He was ready to face whatever lay ahead, guided by the truths he had discovered and the strength he had gained.

The path before him was uncertain, but Tariq was prepared to navigate it with wisdom and courage. The journey to the castle, and the answers it held, awaited him. And with each step, he carried the memories of the oasis and the connection he had felt with Layla, grounding him in his quest for truth and understanding.

CHAPTER 21: A CASTLE IN THE DISTANCE

As the first light of dawn began to illuminate the desert landscape, Tariq stood atop a sand dune, gazing at the distant silhouette of a castle. Its towers and spires rose majestically against the horizon, a beacon of civilization amidst the vast expanse of sand. Determined to uncover the mysteries of this land, Tariq decided to venture towards the castle. As he walked, Tariq reflected on the journey that had brought him here. The winds of chance had carried him far from his home, to a land where the desert met the sky and magic intertwined with reality. The people he had encountered were as varied and complex as the landscape itself, each with their own customs, beliefs, and secrets. "This land is so different from home," Tariq mused. "The desert is both harsh and beautiful, a place of great trials and hidden wonders. The people here live with a closeness to magic that I have never seen before. Their ways are foreign to me, yet there is a wisdom in their traditions that I am beginning to understand."

The castle seemed to grow larger as Tariq approached, its details becoming clearer with each step. The walls were made of sandstone, intricately carved with patterns and symbols that spoke of a rich history. The castle of Al-Madina stood proudly against the azure sky, its sandstone walls gleaming in the sunlight. The architecture was a blend of intricate designs and robust fortifications, showcasing the skill and artistry of those who had built it. Towers and spires reached towards the heavens, adorned with ornate carvings and colorful mosaics that depicted the rich history of the land. As Tariq neared the entrance, he was greeted by a grand gateway flanked by statues of legendary warriors and mythical creatures. The massive wooden doors, reinforced with iron and decorated with intricate patterns, opened slowly, revealing a bustling courtyard within. The guards, dressed in resplendent uniforms, stood tall and vigilant, their presence a testament to the strength and security of the castle. Tariq paused for a moment, gathering his thoughts. "I do not fully understand these people or their ways," he thought, "but I must try to learn. There is much at stake, and my journey is far from over."

With a deep breath, Tariq approached the gates. The guards eyed him warily, but he sensed no immediate hostility. He introduced himself, explaining his journey and his desire to speak with the leaders of the castle. The guards exchanged glances, then nodded and opened the gates, allowing him to enter. As he stepped inside, Tariq was struck by the contrast between the harsh desert outside and the cool, serene beauty within the castle walls. The air was filled with the scent of jasmine and citrus, and the sound of water flowing from a nearby fountain provided a soothing backdrop.

The courtyard was a hive of activity, filled with people from all walks of life. Traders displayed their wares, colorful fabrics and exotic goods from distant lands. Musicians played enchanting melodies, their tunes mingling with the laughter and chatter of the crowd. Fountains adorned with sculpted figures sprayed cool, refreshing water, providing a welcome respite from the desert heat.

Beyond the courtyard, Tariq discovered the castle gardens, a lush oasis of greenery and tranquility. The air was filled with the sweet scent of blooming flowers, and the sound of birds singing added to the serene atmosphere. Pathways lined with vibrant plants led to secluded groves and peaceful ponds, each area meticulously designed to offer a moment of calm and reflection.

Tariq was led to the grand hall, the heart of the castle where important matters were discussed, and decisions made. The hall was a marvel of architecture, with high ceilings adorned with intricate frescoes depicting scenes of heroism and legend. Golden chandeliers hung from above, casting a warm, inviting glow. The walls were lined with tapestries and banners, each telling a story of the castle's past.

As he walked through the castle, Tariq pondered the nature of understanding. He had come to this land with little knowledge of its customs or people, yet he had learned much through observation and conversation. The animals of the desert had taught him valuable lessons about human nature, and now he sought to understand the people who lived here. "Understanding is a journey," Tariq thought. "It requires patience and an open heart. I may not fully grasp the ways of this land, but I am willing to learn. Each step I take brings me closer to the truth, and closer to my own destiny."

Tariq's thoughts were interrupted by the arrival of a servant, who led him to a grand hall. There, he would meet the rulers of the castle and seek the answers he so desperately needed. As he walked, he felt a renewed sense of determination. The journey ahead would be challenging, but he was ready to face it with courage and wisdom. The castle, with its ancient walls and hidden secrets, awaited him. Tariq knew that his path was just beginning, and that the lessons he had learned in the desert would guide him as he navigated the complexities of this new world.

CHAPTER 22: THE CASTLE OF AL-MADINA

At the far end of the grand hall, Tariq entered the throne room, a space of unparalleled beauty and majesty. The throne, crafted from gold and inlaid with precious gems, stood on a raised platform. Behind it, a large window offered a breathtaking view of the city of Al-Madina and the desert beyond. Sunlight streamed through, casting an ethereal glow over the room.

As Tariq took in the splendor of the castle, he felt a deep sense of awe and wonder. Every corner of the castle seemed to tell a story, each detail a testament to the rich culture and history of Al-Madina. He marveled at the craftsmanship and artistry, the blend of beauty and strength that defined the castle. "This place is truly a wonder," Tariq thought to himself. "It is a testament to the ingenuity and spirit of its people. I can see why it has stood the test of time and why it remains a beacon of hope and prosperity."

As Tariq stood in the throne room, he knew that his journey had brought him to a place of great significance. The castle of Al-Madina was not just a physical structure; it was a symbol of the resilience and unity of its people. His arrival marked the beginning of a new chapter, one filled with promise and potential. With a heart full of hope and determination, Tariq prepared to meet the leaders of the castle and to learn more about the destiny that awaited him. The splendor of the castle had inspired him, and he was ready to face whatever challenges lay ahead, guided by the wisdom and strength he had found within its walls.

CHAPTER 23: THE MARKET OF AL-MADINA

After marveling at the grandeur of the castle, Tariq decided to explore the city of Al-Madina further. The vibrant life and bustling energy of the market called to him, promising a glimpse into the heart of the city and its people. He walked through the castle gates and into the streets, eager to experience the sights and sounds of the market.

The market of Al-Madina was a sprawling expanse of stalls and shops, filled with a dazzling array of goods from all corners of the world. The air was thick with the scents of exotic spices, freshly baked bread, and fragrant oils. Merchants called out to passersby, extolling the virtues of their wares, while shoppers haggled over prices with practiced skill.

As Tariq wandered through the market, he struck up conversations with the various inhabitants, eager to learn about their lives and their perspectives on the city and the land. Tariq stopped at a spice stall, captivated by the vibrant colors and intoxicating aromas. The merchant, a jovial man with a twinkle in his eye, greeted him warmly. "Welcome, traveler! What brings you to our beautiful market?" the merchant asked. Tariq smiled. "I am a wanderer, exploring the wonders of Al-Madina. Tell me, what do you think makes this city so special?" The merchant chuckled. "Ah, Al-Madina is a place of magic and mystery, my friend. Our city thrives on diversity and the exchange of ideas. People come here from all over, bringing with them their traditions and knowledge. It is this blend that makes our city so unique."

Further along, Tariq encountered a weaver, her hands deftly working at a loom, creating intricate patterns in vibrant fabrics. He paused to admire her work. "These are beautiful," he said. "You must take great pride in your craft." The weaver looked up and smiled. "Thank you. Our textiles are known throughout the land for their quality and beauty. We draw inspiration from our surroundings—the desert, the stars, the history of our people. Each piece tells a story." "What story does this city tell?" Tariq asked. The weaver's expression grew thoughtful. "Al-Madina is a story of resilience and transformation. We have faced many challenges, but each time, we rise stronger. The city is a testament to the strength and spirit of its people. We honor our past while embracing the future."

At a stall filled with ancient scrolls and books, Tariq met a scholar, an elderly man with a long, white beard and eyes that seemed to hold the wisdom of the ages. "Knowledge is the greatest treasure one can possess," the scholar said as Tariq browsed the collection. "What brings you to these pages, young man?" "I seek to understand this land and its people," Tariq replied. "What can you tell me about Al-Madina?" The scholar nodded. "Al-Madina is a place where history and innovation coexist. Our libraries hold the wisdom of centuries, and our scholars are always seeking new truths. This city is a beacon of learning and enlightenment. But it is also a place of great magic, where the lines between reality and illusion often blur."

Through his conversations, Tariq gained a deeper understanding of Al-Madina and its people. He learned that the city was a melting pot of cultures, a place where history, tradition, and innovation came together to create something truly unique. The inhabitants spoke with pride about their resilience, their love for knowledge, and their appreciation for the magic that permeated their lives.

As the sun began to set, casting a golden glow over the market, Tariq felt a profound sense of connection to Al-Madina. The city, with its rich tapestry of stories and perspectives, had welcomed him with open arms. He knew that his journey was far from over, but he felt more prepared to face the challenges ahead with the knowledge and wisdom he had gained. With a renewed sense of purpose, Tariq started to make his way back to the castle, ready to continue his quest. The voices of the market inhabitants echoed in his mind, their stories and insights guiding him as he navigated the complexities of his journey. Al-Madina had become more than just a stop on his path; it had become a part of his story, a place where he had found wisdom, inspiration, and a deeper understanding of himself and the world around him.

CHAPTER 24: AN UNEXPECTED ENCOUNTER

As Tariq wandered through the bustling market of Al-Madina, taking in the vibrant sights and sounds, his attention was suddenly drawn to a commotion near a stall selling exotic fruits. People were shouting, and he saw a figure darting through the crowd, clutching something tightly to his chest. It was the beggar from the port city—the same man Tariq had generously given to upon his arrival.

The beggar's eyes were wide with fear as he weaved through the throng of market-goers, trying to evade the angry shouts of the fruit vendor and a couple of city guards who had joined the pursuit. Tariq's heart went out to the man. Without thinking, he moved to intercept the guards. "Stop!" Tariq called out, stepping into their path. The guards skidded to a halt, glaring at him. "Out of the way, traveler!" one of the guards barked. "That man is a thief!"

Tariq raised his hands in a calming gesture. "Please, let me speak with him first. There may be a misunderstanding." The guards hesitated but allowed Tariq to approach the beggar, who had taken refuge in a narrow alleyway. The man was trembling, clutching a few pieces of fruit to his chest. His eyes met Tariq's, filled with a mixture of fear and desperation. "Why did you steal?" Tariq asked gently, stepping closer. "You know this will only bring trouble." The beggar's voice was a mere whisper. "I had no choice. I was starving, and no one would help me."

Tariq turned back to the guards and the angry vendor, who had followed them into the alley. "This man stole because he was hungry," Tariq explained. "I will pay for the fruit and ensure he receives help."

The fruit vendor crossed his arms, his expression stern. "He cannot simply steal and get away with it, no matter the reason." Tariq nodded. "I understand. But sometimes, mercy can achieve more than punishment. Let me make amends for him." Reluctantly, the vendor agreed. Tariq handed him a few coins, more than enough to cover the stolen fruit. The vendor's expression softened slightly as he pocketed the money.

Tariq turned to the beggar. "You should not have stolen, but I understand your desperation. Come with me. We will find you food and shelter." The beggar looked at Tariq with gratitude. "Thank you. I did not expect such kindness." As they walked away from the alley, Tariq spoke quietly to the beggar. "You taught me about the nature of magic and illusion. Now, let me teach you about the power of compassion and community. Al-Madina is a city of opportunities. If you are willing to work, I will help you find a way to improve your circumstances."

Tariq led the beggar to a small inn, where he arranged for food and a place to stay. He spoke with the innkeeper, ensuring that the beggar would have an opportunity to work in exchange for his keep. "This is your chance to start anew," Tariq told the beggar. "Do not squander it. Al-Madina is a place where people can rise above their past, where they can find hope and redemption." The beggar nodded, tears in his eyes. "I will not forget your kindness, Tariq. You have given me a second chance, and I will do my best to make the most of it."

As Tariq prepared to leave the inn, he reflected on the events of the day. The encounter with the beggar had reinforced his belief in the importance of compassion and understanding. The market, with its vibrant life and diverse people, had shown him the many faces of humanity—its struggles, its hopes, and its capacity for change. "Human nature is complex," Tariq thought. "But it is in our moments of compassion and kindness that we find our true strength. In helping others, we help ourselves, and we create a world where everyone can thrive."

CHAPTER 25: THE BEGGAR'S EXPLANATION

Tariq couldn't shake the feeling that there was more to the beggar's story. Finding, the beggar seated at a table, slowly eating the meal that had been provided, Tariq approached and sat down across from him; sensing that the man had something more to say.

The beggar looked up, his eyes filled with a mixture of gratitude and sorrow. "Tariq, there is something I must confess. When you gave me that generous gift in the port city, I tried to use it to better my situation. But things did not go as planned." Tariq leaned forward, listening intently. "What happened?"

The beggar sighed. "I took the coins you gave me—as beautiful and unique as they were, —to the market, hoping to trade them to start anew. But when I showed it to a merchant, he accused me of stealing it. He claimed that such valuable items could not possibly belong to someone like me." Tariq's heart sank as he listened. "So, you were branded a thief not because of your actions, but because of your appearance and circumstances." The beggar nodded. "Yes. The merchant alerted the guards, and I was chased through the market. In my desperation, I grabbed some fruit to sustain myself, which only made matters worse. That is why I was running when you saw me."

Tariq felt a deep sense of injustice on behalf of the beggar. "I am truly sorry that my gift brought you such trouble. It was meant to help you, not cause you more pain." The beggar shook his head. "Do not blame yourself, Tariq. Your kindness was genuine, and it gave me hope. It is the prejudice and mistrust of others that turned a gesture of goodwill into a source of strife."

Determined to rectify the situation, Tariq devised a plan. "I will speak with the merchant and the guards. They need to understand the truth of your situation. And together, we will find a way to help you start anew without the burden of these accusations." The beggar's eyes filled with tears of gratitude. "Thank you, Tariq. Your belief in me means more than you know."

Tariq and the beggar returned to the market, seeking out the merchant who had accused him. The man was busy at his stall, but Tariq approached with a calm yet firm demeanor. "Merchant," Tariq began, "we need to speak about the incident involving this man. He is no thief. The item he tried to sell was a gift from me, given out of kindness." The merchant looked skeptical. "And how am I to believe that?" Tariq reached into his bag and produced similar coins, one that matched the description of the item the beggar had tried to sell. "These are items from my homeland, symbols of goodwill. I gave one to him to help him improve his life. Your accusation was based on prejudice, not fact."

Seeing the matching coins and hearing Tariq's sincere explanation, the merchant's expression softened. "I see now that I was wrong. My apologies. It is easy to jump to conclusions when one sees only what they expect." Tariq nodded. "We all make mistakes. What matters is that we correct them. Let us work together to help this man find a path to a better life."

With the merchant's support and the guards' understanding, the beggar was given a second chance. Tariq ensured that he had a place to stay and an opportunity to work at the inn, helping him to rebuild his life with dignity and respect. As they walked back to the inn, the beggar turned to Tariq, his eyes shining with hope. "You have given me more than just a second chance, Tariq. You have shown me that there is goodness in the world, even when it is hard to see."

Tariq smiled. "We all deserve a chance to prove ourselves. Use this opportunity wisely, and you will find your place in Al-Madina." With a heart full of gratitude and a renewed sense of purpose, the beggar began his new life, knowing that kindness and compassion had made all the difference.

CHAPTER 26: THE SHADOWS OF AMBITION

As Tariq and the beggar walked back to the inn, Khalid, who had been nearby, overheard their conversation with the merchant. His mind raced as he processed the information he had just learned. The wanderer had access to treasures—items of significant value from distant lands. This was an opportunity that could not be ignored, especially considering the Sultan's interest in rare and valuable artifacts.

Khalid's sense of duty and his loyalty to his brother Malik, as well as to the Sultan, guided his actions. He knew that presenting this man and his potential treasures to the Sultan could earn him favor and strengthen his position within the court. Without wasting any time, Khalid decided to intervene. Khalid approached Tariq and the beggar with an air of authority. "Wanderer, a word, if you please," he called out, his tone firm but not unkind. Tariq turned. "What do you need of us?" Khalid's gaze shifted to the beggar, who looked nervous under his scrutiny. "I overheard your conversation with the merchant. You have access to valuable items, treasures that could be of great interest to the Sultan. It is my duty to bring you before the court to explain yourself." Tariq frowned, sensing the tension. "If that is what you wish, but I pose no threat." Khalid nodded. "I understand, but the Sultan has a right to know about these treasures. If they are indeed as valuable as they seem, they could be of great benefit to Al-Madina. We must ensure that they are handled appropriately."

Reluctantly, Tariq agreed to accompany Khalid and the beggar to the Sultan's palace. The beggar, though frightened, trusted Tariq's presence to protect him from unjust treatment. They walked through the bustling streets of Al-Madina, the grandeur of the palace growing larger as they approached.

In the grand hall of the Sultan's palace, Khalid presented Tariq to the court. The Sultan, a figure of immense authority and presence, sat on his throne, his keen eyes assessing the situation. "Sultan," Khalid began, bowing respectfully, "this man, who was initially mistaken for a wanderer, possesses items of great value from distant lands. We believe these treasures could be of significant interest to you." The Sultan leaned forward, curiosity piqued. "Show me these items." The beggar, trembling slightly, produced the coins that Tariq had given him. The Sultan examined it closely, his eyes widening with appreciation.

"This is indeed a fine piece," the Sultan said, looking at the beggar. "Tell me, how did you come by this?" The beggar swallowed nervously. "It was a gift, Your Majesty, from this kind man, Tariq. He gave it to me out of generosity when we met in the port city." The Sultan turned his gaze to Tariq. "You have a good heart, Tariq. But I must ensure that such items are not misused or undervalued. This man will be under the protection of the court, and I will see to it that he is given a fair chance to improve his situation." Tariq felt a mixture of relief and apprehension. "Thank you, Your Majesty. I only wish for him to be treated justly."

The Sultan nodded. "He will be. And perhaps, Tariq, you can assist us in understanding more about these items. Your knowledge and integrity could be invaluable." Khalid watched the exchange, satisfied that he had made the right decision. The Sultan's interest in the treasures could lead to new opportunities and strengthen Al-Madina's position. As they left the throne room, Khalid turned to Tariq. "You did well, Tariq. The Sultan's interest could bring great benefits to our city." Tariq nodded, still processing the turn of events. "I hope so, Khalid. I only wish for everyone to be treated fairly and with respect." Khalid clapped a hand on his shoulder. "Together, we will ensure that happens."

CHAPTER 27: A FATEFUL ENCOUNTER

After the audience with the Sultan, Tariq wandered through the palace grounds, his mind still reeling from the events of the day. As he walked, he found himself drawn to the gardens, a place of tranquility amidst the grandeur of the palace. The scent of jasmine filled the air, and the gentle sound of water from a nearby fountain provided a soothing backdrop.

As Tariq turned a corner, he stopped abruptly, his heart skipping a beat. Standing by the fountain was, the woman he had met at the oasis. She looked up, and their eyes met. For a moment, time seemed to stand still. "Life is such a curious thing," Tariq whispered, stepping forward. "We are like the sands of the desert, constantly shifting and changing, yet always connected to something greater." Layla's eyes widened in recognition, and a smile spread across her face. "It's you. I had hoped our paths would cross again." They moved towards each other, and without thinking, they embraced. It was a moment of pure connection, a reunion that felt both unexpected and destined.

As they pulled back, Tariq looked at Layla with a mixture of wonder and confusion. "You are the princess," he said softly. "Why did you not tell me at the oasis?" Layla's smile faded slightly. "I wanted to be just Layla for a while, to speak freely and enjoy your company without the weight of my title. The oasis is a place where I can be myself, away from the responsibilities and expectations of the palace." Tariq nodded, understanding. "I am glad we met there. It was a moment I will treasure always."

Unbeknownst to them, Khalid had been watching from a distance. He saw the embrace and the familiarity between Tariq and the princess, and a sense of unease settled over him. He knew that such a close relationship between a wanderer and the princess could complicate matters, especially with the delicate political situation in Al-Madina. Determined to protect the interests of the city and the Sultan, Khalid decided to inform Malik of what he had seen. He made his way to his brother's quarters, his mind racing with thoughts of what this new development could mean.

Malik was deep in thought when Khalid entered his chamber. He looked up, sensing the urgency in his brother's demeanor. "Khalid, what is it?" Malik asked. Khalid closed the door behind him and spoke in a low, serious tone. "I have just seen Tariq with the princess. They were in the gardens, and it was clear that they have a close relationship. They embraced, Malik." Malik's eyes narrowed. "The wanderer and the princess? This could complicate things. The Sultan must not be pleased to hear that the princess is so familiar with a wanderer." Khalid nodded. "Exactly. We must tread carefully. Tariq has proven himself to be honorable, but his relationship with the princess could jeopardize our plans and the stability of Al-Madina."

Malik thought for a moment, then nodded. "We must ensure that this relationship does not interfere with our goals. I will speak with the Sultan and make him aware of the situation. In the meantime, keep a close watch on Tariq. We need to understand his intentions and ensure that he does not overstep his bounds." Khalid agreed, his mind already working on how to discreetly observe Tariq without raising suspicion. "I will handle it, brother. We cannot afford to let emotions and personal relationships disrupt the delicate balance of power."

As Khalid left Malik's chambers, he felt the weight of his responsibilities pressing down on him. He knew that the coming days would be crucial in determining the future of Al-Madina and the roles that Tariq and Princess Layla would play in it.

Tariq, meanwhile, continued to enjoy the brief, precious moments with Layla in the garden, unaware of the storm brewing around them. The connection they shared was genuine and deep, but it was also fraught with challenges and uncertainties. With each passing moment, the delicate balance of Al-Madina's political landscape shifted, and Tariq's journey became even more complex and intertwined with the fate of the city and its people.

CHAPTER 28: MALIK'S CONCERNS

As Malik sat in his chambers, his mind was consumed with thoughts of Tariq and the princess. The implications of their relationship were far-reaching, and he knew that the situation required careful handling. The potential dangers posed by Tariq, should the princess truly love him, weighed heavily on his mind.

Malik paced the room, his thoughts racing. "If the princess loves Tariq," he mused, "it could destabilize the delicate balance of power in Al-Madina. The Sultan's authority could be undermined, and the loyalty of the court could be divided." He knew that love could be a powerful and unpredictable force. It had the potential to inspire great deeds and noble sacrifices, but it could also lead to impulsive actions and dangerous alliances. The idea of the princess being swayed by her feelings for Tariq was troubling.

Malik's mind turned to the Sultan. "The Sultan must be made aware of this situation," he thought. "If Tariq has the princess's heart, he could wield significant influence over her. This could pose a direct threat to the Sultan's control and to the stability of the kingdom." Malik considered the possibility of Tariq using his relationship with the princess to further his own ambitions. While Tariq had shown himself to be honorable, Malik could not afford to be complacent. The stakes were too high.

"The court will not look kindly on a wanderer aspiring to be with the princess," Malik continued his internal dialogue. "There could be unrest, and other nobles might see this as an opportunity to challenge the Sultan's rule. It could lead to a power struggle, weakening our defenses against external threats."

Malik knew that the Sultan's strength lay in the unity and loyalty of his subjects. Anything that threatened to disrupt that unity had to be addressed swiftly and decisively. As he pondered the situation, Malik realized that he needed to gather more information about Tariq's intentions. Was he truly driven by noble ideals, or did he have ambitions that could pose a risk to the throne? Malik needed to understand Tariq's character and motivations more deeply. "I must observe him closely," Malik decided. "I need to see how he interacts with others, how he handles challenges, and what his true goals are. Only then can I determine the best course of action."

With a sense of purpose, Malik formulated a plan. He would subtly increase surveillance on Tariq, ensuring that his every move was monitored. He would also seek to gain the princess's trust, hoping to influence her decisions and protect her from making choices that could endanger the kingdom. Malik knew that he had to tread carefully. The bonds of love and loyalty were delicate, and a heavy-handed approach could backfire. He needed to be strategic, using his influence and insight to guide the situation towards a resolution that would safeguard Al-Madina's future.

As the evening wore on, Malik felt the weight of his responsibilities pressing down on him. The future of the kingdom rested in his hands, and the decisions he made in the coming days would have far-reaching consequences. With a determined heart, Malik prepared to face the challenges ahead. He knew that he must protect the kingdom and its people, even if it meant making difficult and painful choices. The path before him was fraught with danger, but he was resolved to navigate it with wisdom and strength.

CHAPTER 29: MALIK'S SCHEME

As Malik sat in his chambers, contemplating the potential threat that Tariq and the princess's relationship posed, he devised a plan. He would subtly manipulate the princess's curiosity about the magical items in the castle, knowing that these artifacts held dark secrets and potential dangers.

Malik knew that the princess was intelligent and inquisitive. By piquing her interest in the magical items stored within the castle, he could lead her into a situation that would discredit her or at least distance her from Tariq. He decided to start with a seemingly innocent conversation, planting the seeds of curiosity that would grow into an insatiable desire for knowledge.

The next day, Malik arranged to meet the princess in the castle gardens, where they often strolled together. As they walked, Malik steered the conversation towards the history and mysteries of Al-Madina. "Princess Layla," Malik began, his tone light and conversational, "have you ever wondered about the origins of some of the artifacts in the castle? Many of them have fascinating histories and, I dare say, more than a few secrets." Layla looked intrigued. "I have heard stories, Malik, but I've never delved deeply into them. What do you know?"

Malik smiled, knowing he had captured her interest. "There are countless tales, each more intriguing than the last. For instance, the Mirror of Shadows, said to reveal not only one's true self but also the darkest fears that lie within. Or the Pendant of Dreams, which is rumored to grant visions of the future, though at a great personal cost." Layla's eyes widened with curiosity. "These sound like the stuff of legends. Are they truly here, within our castle?"

Malik nodded. "Indeed they are. And there are many more. Each artifact holds its own mystery, its own power. Some say that understanding them could unlock secrets that have been lost to time." As Malik continued to weave his tales, he could see Layla's curiosity growing. She was fascinated by the idea of exploring these magical items, of uncovering the truths hidden within the castle's walls. "Perhaps I could see them for myself," Layla mused aloud. "It would be an adventure, and there is much I could learn." Malik hid his satisfaction. "If you wish, I could arrange for you to explore these items. But be cautious, princess. Magic is a powerful force, and not all that glitters is gold. There are dangers, as well as wonders, within those artifacts."

Over the next few days, Malik made subtle arrangements, ensuring that the princess would have access to the magical items. He instructed the castle staff to allow her entry into the vaults where the artifacts were kept, but to maintain a discreet distance. Malik wanted Layla to feel free to explore, but also to be unwittingly monitored.

Princess Layla's explorations began innocently enough. She marveled at the beauty and craftsmanship of the artifacts, each piece more enchanting than the last. But as she delved deeper, she began to encounter items with darker auras, objects that seemed to whisper warnings and secrets. One evening, she found herself standing before an amulet. Its surface was smooth and dark, reflecting not just her image but a deeper, more unsettling version of herself. As she gazed into it, she felt a strange pull, as if the amulet were drawing out her fears and doubts.

Malik watched from the shadows, his plan unfolding perfectly. He knew that the more Layla explored, the more she would be ensnared by the amulet's dark magic. It would only be a matter of time before something went wrong, and when it did, he would be there to control the fallout.

As Layla continued her explorations, she began to feel the effects of the dark magic. Nightmares plagued her sleep, and she felt a growing sense of unease. She tried to shake it off, attributing it to her overactive imagination, but the feeling persisted. Tariq, noticing her distress, grew concerned. "Layla, are you alright? You seem troubled."

Layla forced a smile. "I'm fine, Tariq. Just a little tired. There is so much to discover here, and it can be overwhelming."

Despite her reassurances, Layla knew that something was amiss. The magical items were affecting her in ways she hadn't anticipated, and she began to fear that she had ventured too far into the unknown. As Malik watched her struggle, he felt a pang of guilt. But he reminded himself of the greater good—protecting the Sultan's rule and ensuring the stability of Al-Madina. His plan was in motion, and he would see it through to the end.

CHAPTER 30: THE LEGEND OF AL-QAMAR

As the days passed and Princess Layla continued her perilous exploration of the castle's magical artifacts, Malik sought to further entangle Tariq in his web of intrigue. He decided to share with Tariq the legend of Al-Qamar, a tale full of fantastical elements and mystical machinations, designed to pique Tariq's curiosity and distract him from the princess's plight.

One evening, Malik invited Tariq to his chambers, offering him a seat by the fire. The room was dimly lit, the flickering flames casting shadows that danced across the walls. Malik leaned back in his chair, his expression one of practiced nonchalance. "Tariq," Malik began, his voice low and compelling, "have you ever heard the legend of Al-Qamar?" Tariq shook his head, intrigued. "No, I haven't. What is this legend?"

Malik's eyes gleamed as he began to weave the tale. "Al-Qamar is said to be a legendary city of unparalleled beauty and magic, hidden somewhere in the vast expanse of the desert. The city is said to appear only once every hundred years, bathed in the light of a rare lunar eclipse. It is a place where the impossible becomes possible, where the laws of nature are bent to the will of the city's inhabitants." Tariq leaned forward, captivated. "What kind of magic exists in Al-Qamar?" Malik continued, his voice filled with a mixture of awe and reverence. "The streets of Al-Qamar are paved with shimmering silver, and its buildings are constructed from crystal that glows with an inner light. The city is home to creatures from the farthest reaches of imagination— dragons with scales of emerald, phoenixes that burst into flames only to rise anew, and unicorns with horns that can heal any wound."

Tariq's eyes widened. "How is it possible? Such creatures, such wonders..." Malik smiled. "In Al-Qamar, nothing is impossible. The city's inhabitants are said to possess incredible powers. They can manipulate time and space, create illusions so real they become reality, and wield artifacts of immense power. It is a place where dreams and nightmares coexist, where one's deepest desires and darkest fears are brought to life."

Tariq's mind raced with questions. "Who built this city? And why does it appear only once every hundred years?" "The city was built by a council of ancient sorcerers, powerful beings who sought to create a sanctuary of magic and wonder," Malik explained. "They hid it from the world to protect its secrets and to prevent its power from being misused. The lunar eclipse serves as a gateway, allowing the city to reveal itself briefly before vanishing once more." Tariq was enthralled. "Has anyone ever found it?" Malik nodded. "There are tales of travelers who stumbled upon Al-Qamar, only to be forever changed by their experiences. Some returned with extraordinary gifts, while others were never seen again, lost to the city's enigmatic allure."

Tariq's curiosity was insatiable. "What kind of artifacts exist in Al-Qamar? And what powers do they hold?" Malik leaned in, his voice a conspiratorial whisper. "It is said that the city holds artifacts of unimaginable power. The Scroll of Ages contains knowledge and wisdom from centuries past. The Elemental Amulet, a relic that allows its bearer to harness the power of the four elements. The Crystal of Clarity is said to possess the ability to reveal hidden truths and dispel illusions. These are but a few of the wonders that lie within the city."

As Malik spoke, he could see the growing fascination in Tariq's eyes. The legend of Al-Qamar had taken hold of him, filling his mind with visions of magic and adventure. Malik knew that Tariq's curiosity would lead him deeper into the mysteries of

Al-Qamar, distracting him from the dangers facing the princess. "Malik," Tariq said, his voice filled with determination, "I must find this city. I must see it with my own eyes, experience its wonders, and uncover its secrets." Malik nodded, hiding his satisfaction. "I understand, Tariq. But be warned, the journey to Al-Qamar is fraught with peril. Many have sought it and few have returned. You must be prepared for anything." Tariq nodded, resolute. "I will be ready. Thank you, Malik, for sharing this legend with me. It has given me a new purpose." As Tariq left Malik's chambers, his mind ablaze with thoughts of Al-Qamar, Malik watched him go, his plan unfolding perfectly. The legend had ensnared Tariq, leading him on a quest that would divert his attention from the princess and the true dangers lurking within the castle.

CHAPTER 31: THE NATURE OF POWER AND PROTECTION

Princess Layla had been deeply engrossed in her exploration of the castle's magical artifacts, despite the growing sense of unease that accompanied her discoveries. One evening, while perusing an ancient tome in the castle's vast library, she came across a reference to a powerful relic said to possess extraordinary protective abilities.

The passage described the relic as an amulet imbued with ancient magic, capable of shielding its bearer from harm and warding off dark forces. Intrigued, Layla read further, learning that the amulet was hidden somewhere within the castle, waiting to be claimed by one worthy of its power.

As she closed the book and leaned back in her chair, Layla's thoughts turned inward. She pondered the nature of power and protection, reflecting on what she had learned and experienced, and if she had encountered this amulet before. "Power is a double-edged sword," Layla mused. "It can be used to protect and uplift, but it can also corrupt and destroy. Those who seek power must tread carefully, for it can easily become a burden rather than a gift." She thought about the magical artifacts she had encountered, each one a testament to the incredible potential of magic. Yet, many of these items also carried dire warnings and dark histories.

Layla's mind turned to the concept of protection. "True protection comes not just from strength, but from wisdom and compassion. To shield others from harm, one must understand their fears and vulnerabilities. It is not enough to simply wield power; one must also have the heart to use it wisely."

She thought, the Sultan, and the heavy burden of responsibility he carried. His role was to protect the kingdom and its people, a task that required both strength and benevolence. Layla wondered if she was capable of bearing such a burden, and if the relic could help her fulfill her duties.

Determined to find the relic, Layla decided to embark on a quest within the castle. She knew that the path would not be easy, but she felt a sense of purpose and resolve. The relic could provide the protection she needed, not just for herself, but for those she loved and for the kingdom. As she rose from her chair and prepared to leave the library, Layla whispered to herself, "I will find this relic and use its power to protect those who cannot protect themselves. I will learn from the past and ensure that my actions are guided by wisdom and compassion."

Layla's journey through the castle began in earnest. She visited hidden chambers and secret vaults, deciphering clues and unraveling mysteries. With each step, she felt a growing sense of determination. The relic was within her reach, and she was ready to face whatever challenges lay ahead. In the midst of her search, Layla encountered Tariq in one of the castle's dimly lit corridors. His face lit up with a smile when he saw her. "Layla, what brings you here at this hour?" Tariq asked, his voice filled with warmth. Layla hesitated for a moment, then decided to share her quest. "I have learned of a relic, said to possess great protective power. I believe it can help us, Tariq. But I must find it first." Tariq's eyes widened with interest. "A relic of protection? That sounds incredible. Let me help you. Together, we can uncover its secrets and ensure it is used wisely."

With Tariq by her side, Layla felt a renewed sense of hope and strength. Their bond, forged in the oasis and deepened by their shared experiences, gave her the courage to continue her quest. Together, they ventured deeper into the castle, guided by the promise of the relic and the hope that it could protect them from the dark forces that threatened their world. As they delved into the castle's depths, Layla's thoughts remained focused on the nature of power and protection. She knew that the journey ahead would test her resolve and her character, but with Tariq's support, she felt ready to face whatever challenges awaited them.

CHAPTER 32: TARIQ'S FASCINATION

After Malik had shared the legend of Al-Qamar with Tariq, the wanderer found himself captivated by the tale. The idea of a hidden city, filled with magical wonders and treasures beyond imagination, sparked his curiosity and ignited his adventurous spirit.

That night, as Tariq lay in his bed, he couldn't stop thinking about the magical city. He imagined its streets paved with silver, the air shimmering with enchantment. He pictured the fantastic creatures Malik had described—emerald-scaled dragons, flaming phoenixes, and majestic unicorns—all inhabiting this mystical place.

Tariq's mind wandered through the legendary city. He envisioned towering spires made of crystal that glowed with an ethereal light, casting a rainbow of colors across the city. He imagined markets filled with artifacts of immense power, each with its own story and magical properties. Tariq fantasized about the many wonders that would await him. The Scroll of Ages, the Elemental Amulet and the Crystal of Clarity. Tariq's heart raced at the thought of uncovering these treasures and the potential they held. As dawn approached Tariq decided he would seek out the city of Al-Qamar. He knew the journey would be perilous, filled with unknown dangers, but his adventurous spirit and thirst for discovery pushed him forward.

The next morning, Tariq found Princess Layla in the gardens, her face brightening when she saw him. He took her hand, his eyes shining with excitement. "Layla, I've decided to search for the city of Al-Qamar," he announced. "The legend Malik told me has sparked something within me. I believe that finding this city could answer many questions and uncover wonders beyond our wildest dreams." Layla looked at him with a mix of admiration and concern. "Tariq, the journey to Al-Qamar is fraught with danger. Many have sought it and never returned. Are you sure this is the path you want to take?" Tariq nodded, his resolve firm. "I must, Layla. The possibility of discovering such a place, of seeing its magic and learning its secrets, is something I cannot ignore. And I believe that what we find there could help protect Al-Madina and its people."

Layla sighed but saw the determination in his eyes. "Then I will support you, Tariq. But promise me you will be careful. And if you need help, you will not hesitate to ask." Tariq smiled and embraced her. "I promise, Layla. I will return with tales of wonder and, hopefully, the means to protect our people."

With Layla's blessing and his heart filled with anticipation, Tariq began preparing for his journey. He gathered supplies and sought out maps and information that might guide him to the elusive city. The legend of Al-Qamar had become more than just a story; it was now a beacon, guiding him towards a new adventure.

As Tariq set out for the castle, his mind was filled with visions of the magical city. The wonders and treasures of Al-Qamar awaited him, and he was ready to face whatever challenges lay ahead. With each step, the dream of uncovering the hidden city's secrets grew stronger, propelling him forward into the unknown.

CHAPTER 33: THE SULTAN'S COURT

As Tariq approached the Sultan's throne, he could feel the weight of the majestic hall bearing down on him. The Sultan, a figure of immense authority and presence, sat atop his golden throne, surrounded by advisors and courtiers. Tariq knew that his request was bold, but he was determined to see it through.

The grand hall of the Sultan's palace was a tapestry of opulence and power, adorned with intricate mosaics and glistening chandeliers. The air was thick with the scent of incense, weaving through the hall like an ethereal veil. At the far end, upon a throne encrusted with jewels, sat Sultan a man of wisdom and might, whose gaze was as piercing as the desert sun. Into this realm of splendor and scrutiny stepped Tariq, the wanderer, his heart a storm of hope and trepidation. His journey had been long and fraught with peril, yet his resolve remained unbroken. He sought an audience with the Sultan, to plead his case and secure the funds necessary to continue his quest—a mission born of destiny and shrouded in mystery.

Tariq bowed deeply before the Sultan. "Your Majesty, I come before you with a request. I have learned of a legendary city, Al-Qamar, said to be filled with unimaginable treasures and ancient magic. I seek your permission to embark on a journey to find this city and uncover its secrets." The Sultan raised an eyebrow, intrigued. "Al-Qamar, you say? A city of legend and magic. Tell me more, Tariq. What makes you believe this city exists, and why should I grant you this permission?"

Tariq recounted the legend Malik had shared with him, describing the wonders and potential benefits of finding Al-Qamar. He spoke of the artifacts and the magic that could protect and strengthen Al-Madina. The Sultan listened intently, his eyes narrowing as he considered Tariq's words. The idea of uncovering such a powerful and magical city was tempting, not just for the potential protection it could offer, but for the power it might bring to his rule.

Tariq bowed deeply, his voice steady yet filled with the passion of his cause. "Great Sultan, I seek the means to embark on a journey that will uncover secrets lost to time, treasures that lie beyond the horizon. My quest is not for personal gain but for the glory and prosperity of Al-Madina, and your great kingdom. With your support, I shall bring back riches and knowledge that will benefit us all." As Tariq finished his explanation, the Sultan leaned back in his throne, deep in thought. "If Tariq succeeds," he mused to himself, "the treasures and artifacts of Al-Qamar could solidify my rule and secure the future of Al-Madina. Such power would not only protect the kingdom but also extend my influence far beyond its borders."

The Sultan considered the risks. If Tariq succeeded, the Sultan's position would be unassailable. If Tariq failed, it would be one less threat to his power. The Sultan leaned back, contemplating the wanderer's words. "Your ambition is bold, Tariq. Many have come before you with promises of greatness, only to falter in the face of adversity. What makes you different?" The courtiers whispered among themselves, their eyes flickering with curiosity and doubt. Yet amidst the sea of skepticism, one voice rose in his defense. Princess Layla, stepped forward, her presence a beacon of grace and determination. Before Tariq could respond, Princess Layla interjected, her eyes shining with conviction.

"Sultan…" she began, her voice a melodic harmony that silenced the hall, "this man, Tariq, is no ordinary wanderer. His journey speaks of courage and purpose. I believe his quest, though veiled in mystery, holds the promise of great fortune and honor for our kingdom." The Sultan's gaze softened. "Layla, your words carry weight in this court. Tell me, why should I entrust Tariq?"

"Sultan, I have seen the fire in his eyes, the unyielding spirit that drives him. Tariq is not driven by greed, but by a sense of duty and honor. He has my faith, and I stand by his side in this endeavor." The hall fell silent, the weight of Layla's endorsement echoing through the chamber. The Sultan's gaze shifted between Layla and Tariq, seeing the unwavering determination in both their eyes. Finally, he spoke, his voice resonant and commanding. "Tariq, I shall grant you the resources you seek. But know this—your success will not only be a testament to your resolve but to the trust Layla and I place in you. Return with the treasures and wisdom you promise, and you shall be honored as a hero. Fail, and the burden of disappointment will be yours to bear."

Tariq bowed deeply, his heart swelling with gratitude and determination. "I shall not fail you, great Sultan. Your faith and generosity will be rewarded." As he left the grand hall, accompanied by the whispers of the courtiers and the hopeful gaze of Princess Layla, Tariq knew that the journey ahead would be fraught with challenges. Yet, with the support of the Sultan and the faith of the princess, he felt a renewed strength within him—a promise to fulfill his destiny and honor those who believed in him. As the doors closed behind Tariq, the Sultan turned to his advisors. "Keep a close eye on him," he commanded. "This journey could bring us great power, but it could also bring unforeseen consequences. We must be prepared for both outcomes." The advisors nodded, understanding the gravity of the situation. The Sultan's mind was filled with visions of the power and influence he could wield with the treasures of Al-Qamar. His ambition burned brighter than ever, and he was willing to take the necessary risks to secure his rule.

As Tariq prepared for his journey, he was unaware of the Sultan's deeper motives. His thoughts were consumed with the possibilities that lay ahead—the wonders of Al-Qamar and the promise of its ancient magic. With the Sultan's support, Tariq felt more confident than ever, ready to face whatever challenges awaited him on the path to the legendary city.

CHAPTER 34: ECHOES OF THE PAST

As Tariq stepped out of the Sultan's court, the grand doors closing behind him with a soft thud, he felt a mixture of relief and apprehension. The golden light of the afternoon sunbathed the castle courtyard in a warm glow, and the gentle hum of the bustling city beyond the palace walls reached his ears. He paused for a moment, letting the reality of his new mission settle within him. The support of Sultan and the heartfelt endorsement of Princess Layla had given him the resources and hope he needed. Yet, with this new beginning, memories of his past journey flooded his mind, each step that led him to this crucial juncture. Tariq shook off the weight of his memories and focused on the path ahead. With the Sultan's resources and Princess Layla's faith in him, he felt a renewed sense of purpose. The journey to Al-Qamar awaited, and with it, the answers he had sought for so long.

As he walked through the castle gates, the city of Al-Madina spread out before him, alive with possibilities. The sun dipped lower in the sky, casting long shadows that danced with the promise of adventure. Tariq took a deep breath and set forth, ready to face whatever challenges lay ahead with courage and determination.

CHAPTER 35: SHADOWS IN THE SQUARE

The main square of Al-Madina bustled with life as merchants hawked their wares, children chased each other in playful glee, and townsfolk went about their daily routines. Tariq navigated through the throng, his eyes scanning the vibrant stalls and listening to the melodic hum of the city. His mind, though focused on the quest ahead, remained alert to his surroundings. As he reached the center of the square, where a grand fountain sprayed cool mist into the air, Tariq felt a prickling at the back of his neck— a sense of being watched. Before he could react, a group of rough-looking men emerged from the crowd, their faces shadowed by hooded cloaks. Their leader, a burly figure with a scar running down his cheek, stepped forward, blocking Tariq's path. "Well,

well, what do we have here?" the leader sneered, his voice dripping with menace. "A wanderer with a purpose, perhaps?" Tariq met the man's gaze steadily, his hand instinctively moving to the hilt of his dagger. "I am merely a traveler passing through," he replied calmly, though his heart beat faster with caution. The bandit leader chuckled darkly, his companions closing in around Tariq. "We've heard whispers of a man seeking a treasure beyond imagination. And where there's treasure, there's opportunity." Tariq's eyes narrowed. "What do you want?"

The leader leaned in, his breath hot and foul. "Your coins, wanderer. Hand it over, and we might let you leave with your life." A murmur of agreement rippled through the bandits. Tariq tightened his grip on his dagger, ready to defend himself, but he knew he was outnumbered and outmatched. Just as he calculated his next move, a commanding voice rang out from the edge of the square. "Leave him be!"

The crowd parted to reveal a young women, flanked by a squad of cloaked men. Her presence was both dominating and formidable, and her eyes blazed with determination. The bandits hesitated, their bravado wavering under her fierce gaze. "This man is under my protection," the young woman declared, stepping forward. "If you value your lives, you will leave now."

The bandit leader scowled, but he knew better than to challenge this woman and her cadre. With a grunt, he signaled his men to retreat. "This isn't over, wanderer," he spat before disappearing into the crowd. Tariq released a breath he hadn't realized he was holding. "Thank you. Your timing was impeccable." The woman offered him a warm smile. "It seems your journey is more perilous than anticipated. You must be careful. There are those who would stop at nothing to possess what you seek." He nodded, his gratitude evident. "I will be. But why did you come here?" "I had a feeling you might need assistance," she said softly. "And besides, I wanted to see you the wanderer. Your quest is important to the people of Al-Madina

As the tension in the square eased and the townsfolk resumed their activities, Tariq and the woman walked towards the edge of the square, discussing the path ahead. The encounter with the bandits served as a stark reminder of the dangers that lay in wait, Tariq felt more resolved than ever to continue his journey.

CHAPTER 36: WHISPERS OF THE HEART

Princess Layla watched from the shadows of the bustling market square, her heart a tumultuous sea of emotions. She had come to ensure Tariq's safety, to see him off on his journey with the Sultan's blessing, but what she witnessed left her feelings in disarray.

As the bandits closed in on Tariq, a young woman from the crowd had bravely intervened, her eyes fierce and determined as she stood beside him. Layla's chest tightened with a feeling she rarely experienced—envy. The woman had spoken with a confidence and familiarity that suggested a deep connection with Tariq, one that Layla couldn't ignore.

When the bandits had dispersed, Layla approached, her royal guards flanking her. She saw the gratitude in Tariq's eyes, but behind his thanks, there was a flicker of something else when he glanced at the other woman. Layla's smile faltered slightly as she addressed him, ensuring he knew she was there to protect him. She had hoped her presence would reassure him, but the sight of the woman's comforting hand on his arm gnawed at her heart. As she walked alongside Tariq towards the city gates, Layla's thoughts churned. She had always been the one to advocate for him, to see the potential in his quest and support his journey. Yet, seeing another woman by his side, offering support and protection, made her feel strangely vulnerable. She had always been the one in control, the princess who could command respect and loyalty with a mere word. Now, she felt like an outsider in Tariq's world, a world where other bonds were just as strong, if not stronger.

The other woman, introduced as Yasmin, had a quiet strength that Layla couldn't dismiss. She had helped Tariq without hesitation, her actions driven by a deep, unspoken bond. Layla envied the ease with which Yasmin connected with Tariq, the unspoken understanding that seemed to pass between them. Tariq's gratitude was evident, but his gaze lingered on Yasmin for a moment too long, and Layla felt a pang of jealousy. She turned away, hiding her turmoil behind a mask of regal composure.

As Tariq mounted his horse and set off on his journey, Layla remained at the gates, watching him disappear into the horizon. The wind whispered around her, carrying with it the promise of adventure and the weight of unspoken feelings.

Yasmin approached her, sensing the princess's inner conflict. "He will be safe, Your Highness. Tariq is strong and determined. He will succeed." Layla nodded, her voice steady but her heart aching. "I know he will. He carries the hopes of many, including mine." Yasmin's eyes softened with understanding. "Your support means everything to him, Princess. He values it more than you know." Layla forced a smile, her mind awash with conflicting thoughts. "Thank you, Yasmin. I trust you will watch over him."

As the sun dipped below the horizon, casting long shadows across the city, Layla walked back towards the palace, her heart heavy with unspoken emotions. She had always been strong, always been the pillar others leaned on, but now she felt a vulnerability she hadn't known before. The journey ahead was not just Tariq's; it was hers too, a journey of the heart, where she would have to confront her own feelings and find a way to navigate the complex web of love, jealousy, and duty.

In the quiet solitude of her chambers, Layla sat by the window, gazing at the stars. She whispered a silent prayer for Tariq's safety, her heart echoing with the longing and uncertainty that now defined her world. She had given him her protection, but in doing so, she had also given him a piece of her heart. And as the night enveloped Al-Madina, Layla knew that her journey was just beginning.

CHAPTER 37: THE ENCHANTED ENCOUNTER

Princess Layla sat in her chambers, the moonlight casting a silver glow through the intricate lattice of her window. Her thoughts drifted back to the first time she met Tariq, a meeting shrouded in mystery and enchantment that had left an indelible mark on her heart. It was a night much like this one, the air thick with the scent of jasmine and the soft hum of crickets. Layla had been restless, her soul yearning for something beyond the confines of the palace walls. She had slipped out quietly, her feet leading her to the edge of the ancient oasis that bordered Al-Madina. As she wandered deeper into the oasis, the trees seemed to whisper secrets, their leaves rustling with a life of their own. The moonlight filtered through the canopy, creating an ethereal path that beckoned her forward. It was there, in a small clearing bathed in silver light, that she first saw him.

Tariq stood at the center of the clearing, his eyes closed, his face serene. He seemed to be in communion with the very essence of the oasis, his presence a harmonious blend of strength and tranquility. Layla watched, captivated, as he raised his hands, and the moonlight around him intensified, creating a soft, glowing aura.

She stepped forward, unable to resist the pull of his presence. The sound of her approach made Tariq open his eyes, and their gazes locked. In that moment, Layla felt a connection that transcended words, a silent understanding that they were bound by fate. "You," Tariq said softly, his voice a soothing balm in the night. "You are the woman in my dreams."

Layla nodded, her heart pounding in her chest. "And you… who are you?" "I am Tariq, a wanderer seeking the truth hidden within these lands," he replied, his eyes reflecting the moonlight. "And you, what brings you here on this enchanted night?" Layla took a step closer, drawn by the gentle strength in his voice. "I seek something beyond the walls of the palace. A purpose, a meaning… something more."

Tariq smiled, a warm, inviting smile that eased the turmoil in her heart. "Then perhaps our paths were meant to cross. For I too seek something greater, a truth that lies beyond the horizon." They spent the night talking, sharing stories of their lives and dreams under the watchful gaze of the moon. Layla learned of Tariq's aspirations that resonated deeply with her own yearning for purpose.

As dawn approached, Tariq took Layla's hand, his touch gentle yet firm. "Our paths are intertwined. There is a reason we met here tonight. I feel it in my soul." Layla's heart swelled with a mixture of hope and fear. "But how can we know for sure?"

Tariq looked into her eyes, his gaze steady and reassuring. "Sometimes, we must trust in the whispers of our hearts. They lead us to where we are meant to be."

The memory of that night brought a soft smile to Layla's lips. She had known then, in that mystical moment, that Tariq was someone special. His presence had awakened something within her, a sense of destiny and purpose that had guided her ever since.

Now, as she sat in her chambers, the weight of recent events pressed upon her. The jealousy she felt was a shadow of the deeper connection she had with Tariq, a bond forged under the silver light of the moon. She knew she had to trust in that connection, to believe in the path they were meant to walk together.

Rising from her seat, Layla moved to the window and looked out at the stars. "Tariq," she whispered, her voice a soft prayer carried on the night breeze. "May your journey be safe, and may the truth you seek bring us both the answers we need."

With that, she closed her eyes, letting the memories of their first meeting comfort her. She would wait, with faith and patience, for the day when their paths would cross again, and the whispers of destiny would guide them to their shared fate.

CHAPTER 38: MIRAGES AND MYSTERIES

The desert stretched out before Tariq, an endless sea of golden dunes under a blazing sun. Each step forward was met with a gust of hot, dry wind, carrying with it the whispers of the ancient sands. Tariq, though weary, pressed on, driven by the mission that lay ahead and the memory of the promise he had made to his father.

As the sun climbed higher, casting harsh shadows and blinding light, Tariq began to notice strange things in the periphery of his vision. At first, it was nothing more than flickers—shimmering shapes that danced just beyond his understanding. But as the day wore on, these fleeting visions grew more vivid, their forms more defined.

He saw a caravan of camels, laden with treasures and guided by large figures, their faces hidden in the shadows of their hoods. Yet, as he approached, the vision dissolved into a mirage, leaving only the empty desert behind. Tariq paused, his heart pounding, a mixture of curiosity and unease tearing at him.

Continuing his journey, Tariq's eyes caught sight of a grand oasis, lush and vibrant with towering palm trees and clear, sparkling water. The sound of laughter and music filled the air, inviting him to rest and partake in its bounty. But as he neared, the oasis flickered and vanished, leaving only the relentless sand.

Tariq's mind raced with questions. Were these visions mere tricks of the desert sun, or something more? He recalled the tales his father used to tell him of the desert spirits, ethereal beings that guarded ancient secrets and treasures. Could these visions be a sign, a message from beyond?

As evening approached, the air grew cooler, and the desert took on a surreal beauty under the setting sun. Tariq's steps slowed as he saw another vision—this one more distinct and compelling. A figure, cloaked in white, stood atop a distant dune, their silhouette outlined against the crimson sky. The figure raised an arm, beckoning him forward.

With renewed determination, Tariq climbed the dune, his eyes fixed on the mysterious figure. But as he reached the top, the figure was gone, leaving behind an intricate pattern etched into the sand. Tariq knelt down, tracing the lines with his fingers, recognizing them as ancient symbols, similar to those scrawled on some artifacts in the castle.

His heart pounded with excitement and trepidation. The symbols seemed to form a map, pointing towards a distant location. Tariq quickly sketched the pattern into his journal, ensuring he would not forget. He stood, looking out over the vast expanse of the desert, a sense of purpose solidifying within him.

As night fell, the desert transformed under a blanket of stars, each one twinkling with ancient wisdom. Tariq set up camp, the visions of the day lingering in his mind. He wondered what awaited him on this journey—whether he would find the answers he sought or be consumed by the mysteries of the desert.

Lying under the stars, Tariq thought of Princess Layla and the mystical night they first met. Her belief in him gave him strength, and he knew he had to press on, not just for himself but for everyone who believed in his quest. The strange visions of the day felt like a guiding force, urging him forward on a path of destiny.

As sleep claimed him, Tariq's dreams were filled with images of the ancient city of Al-Qamar, a place of legend and wonder. He saw its grand towers and hidden treasures, felt the weight of its secrets calling to him. The journey ahead was fraught with danger and uncertainty, but Tariq's resolve was unwavering. He would uncover the truth, no matter the cost.

In the stillness of the desert night, beneath the watchful gaze of the stars, Tariq's heart beat with the promise of adventure and discovery. The journey to Al-Qamar awaited, and with it, the answers that had eluded him for so long.

CHAPTER 39: THE MIRAGE OF AL-QAMAR

The first light of dawn painted the desert in hues of gold and rose. Tariq awoke with a start, the images of his dreams still vivid in his mind. As he packed his belongings and continued his journey, a sense of urgency pushed him forward. The visions and symbols he had encountered in the desert seemed to converge, guiding him toward an unseen destination.

Hours passed, and as the sun reached its zenith, Tariq saw something on the horizon. At first, it was a shimmering blur, but as he drew closer, the outline of a city began to form. His heart raced with excitement and disbelief. Could this be Al-Qamar, the legendary city his father had sought?

The city rose majestically from the sands, its towers gleaming like jewels in the sunlight. Intricate archways and domes adorned the skyline, and the air was filled with the faint sound of distant bells. Tariq approached with a sense of awe, but as he neared the gates, a strange force stopped him. It was as if an invisible barrier blocked his path, preventing him from entering the city.

Frustration gnawed at him. He could see the wonders of Al-Qamar, yet he was denied entry. Tariq walked along the perimeter of the city, searching for a way in, but the barrier remained impenetrable. He sat down in the shadow of the grand gates, his mind racing with thoughts of how he might solve this problem.

He recalled the ancient symbols he had seen in the desert, the ones he had sketched into his journal. They seemed to form a map, pointing towards this very city. Perhaps they held the key to entering Al-Qamar. Tariq pulled out his journal and studied the symbols carefully, trying to decipher their meaning.

Hours passed, and as the sun dipped towards the horizon, casting long shadows over the desert, an idea began to take shape in Tariq's mind. The symbols were not just a map; they were a riddle, a test of understanding and wisdom. He needed to align the symbols with the city's layout, finding the right combination to unlock the barrier.

Tariq stood up and walked to the gates, his fingers tracing the intricate carvings. He whispered the ancient words. As he spoke, the symbols in his journal seemed to glow faintly, resonating with the carvings on the gate.

He arranged the symbols in the sand before the gate, aligning them with the patterns he had seen. As he placed the final symbol, a low rumble echoed through the desert, and the barrier shimmered before vanishing. Tariq's heart leapt with hope as the gates of Al-Qamar slowly opened, revealing the wonders within.

He took a deep breath and stepped through the gates, feeling a sense of triumph and awe. The city was even more magnificent up close, with its streets lined with lush gardens and fountains that sparkled like liquid diamonds. The air was filled with the scent of exotic flowers and the sound of birds singing melodious tunes.

Tariq wandered through the streets, marveling at the beauty and mystery of Al-Qamar. He knew that his journey was far from over, but this was a significant step towards uncovering its secrets. The city held many wonders and many dangers, but with the support of Princess Layla guiding him, Tariq felt ready to face whatever lay ahead.

As night fell and the city was bathed in the soft glow of lanterns, Tariq found a quiet spot to rest. He closed his eyes, the memory of his journey filling him with a sense of purpose. The path ahead was uncertain, but he was determined to see it through, and uncover the truths hidden within the legendary city of Al-Qamar.

CHAPTER 40: WONDERS OF AL-QAMAR

The city was a living tapestry of colors, sounds, and scents, a place that seemed to pulse with a magic all its own. Every building was a masterpiece, adorned with intricate mosaics and delicate carvings that shimmered in the light.

The streets were paved with polished stones that reflected the sky above, creating a mirror-like effect that made it feel as though he was walking among the clouds. Gardens filled with exotic plants and flowers lined the pathways, their vibrant hues a feast for the eyes. Fountains of crystal-clear water bubbled and sang, casting rainbows in the air as the sunlight danced through the mist.

As he wandered deeper into the city, Tariq marveled at the harmonious blend of nature and architecture. Trees with golden leaves arched over the streets, their branches woven together to form natural canopies that provided shade and comfort. Birds of every color and song flitted about, their melodies blending into a symphony that filled the air with joy.

He came upon a marketplace, bustling with activity yet imbued with a sense of calm and order. Stalls overflowed with goods from distant lands— silks that shimmered like liquid moonlight, spices that filled the air with their intoxicating aromas, and gems that sparkled with an inner fire. The merchants greeted him with warm smiles, their eyes twinkling with the wisdom of ages.

Tariq's eyes were drawn to a grand palace at the heart of the city, its towers reaching towards the heavens, crowned with domes of sapphire and gold. He felt an inexplicable pull towards it, as if it held the answers to the mysteries he sought. As he approached, the palace gates opened, revealing a courtyard filled with lush gardens and flowing streams.

A figure emerged from the palace, a tall and graceful woman with an aura of serenity and power. Her robes flowed like water around her, and her eyes held the depth of the cosmos. "Welcome, Tariq," she said, her voice like the whisper of the wind. "I am Amara, the guardian of Al-Qamar. We have awaited your arrival."

Tariq bowed respectfully. "Guardian Amara, it is an honor to be here. This city is beyond anything I could have imagined." Amara smiled, a gesture that radiated warmth. "Al-Qamar is a place of wonders and secrets, a sanctuary for those who seek the truth, and now it is your turn to uncover the mysteries that lie within."

She led him through the palace, each room more magnificent than the last. There were libraries filled with ancient tomes, laboratories where alchemists worked their magic, and halls adorned with tapestries that told the history of the city. Tariq felt a sense of belonging, as if he had finally found the place he was meant to be.

In a grand hall, Amara showed him a map of Al-Qamar, its intricate lines and symbols glowing softly. "This map will guide you," she said. "But remember, the true path lies within your heart. Trust in your instincts." Tariq nodded, his resolve strengthening. "I will honor your legacy and uncover the secrets of this city. Thank you, Guardian Amara."

As night fell, the city of Al-Qamar transformed into a realm of dreams. Lanterns of every color illuminated the streets, casting a magical glow that turned the city into a wonderland. The stars above seemed to mirror the lights below, creating a breathtaking tapestry of celestial beauty.

Tariq stood on a balcony, gazing out over the city. His heart was filled with hope and determination. The journey ahead was still fraught with challenges, but he knew that he was on the right path. The magic and wonder of Al-Qamar were now a part of him, and he would carry their light into the darkness, uncovering the truths that had eluded him for so long.

CHAPTER 41: THE BIRTH OF AL-QAMAR

As Tariq stood on the balcony, overlooking the shimmering city of Al-Qamar, Guardian Amara joined him. She sensed his curiosity and the questions that lingered in his mind. With a gentle smile, she began to recount the tale of Al-Qamar's creation, a story woven into the very fabric of the city's magic.

Long ago, in an era shrouded in myth, a powerful seer had a vision of a city that would stand as a beacon of knowledge and enlightenment, a place where the realms of magic and reality intertwined. This seer, known as Qamar, foresaw a sanctuary where wisdom from across the world would converge, a city that would be a testament to the boundless potential of human and mystical collaboration. Qamar's prophecy spoke of a land untouched by time, hidden within the heart of the desert. It was said that those with pure intentions and a thirst for knowledge would be drawn to this sacred place, guided by the stars and the whispers of the wind.

Centuries passed, and Qamar's prophecy remained a legend, until a group of scholars, mystics, and artisans embarked on a pilgrimage to find this fabled land. Led by Nezzera, a wise and compassionate leader, they journeyed through deserts and mountains, following the celestial signs foretold by Qamar.

After years of searching, they stumbled upon a hidden oasis in the heart of the desert. It was a place of unparalleled beauty, where crystal-clear waters flowed and verdant flora thrived. The group knew that they had found the destined site for their city.

They named the city Al-Qamar, in honor of the seer whose vision had guided them. With reverence and determination, they began to build, infusing their knowledge of architecture, magic, and nature into every stone and structure. The city's foundations were laid with the intention of creating a harmonious blend of the mystical and the mundane.

The magic of Al-Qamar was not merely in its construction but in the very essence of its being. The scholars and mystics who founded the city were well-versed in ancient spells and enchantments. They wove protective charms into the city's walls, ensuring that only those deemed worthy could enter.

They called upon elemental spirits to bless the land, infusing the soil, water, and air with a vitality that would sustain the city for eternity. The waters of the oasis were enchanted to provide healing and rejuvenation, while the trees and plants were imbued with the essence of life, allowing them to flourish even in the harshest of conditions.

The city's founders established great libraries and academies, attracting sages, alchemists, and explorers from distant lands. They shared their knowledge freely, creating a repository of wisdom that spanned the ages. The magic of Al-Qamar grew with each passing generation, as new discoveries and spells were added to its archives.

To protect this treasure trove of knowledge and magic, the founders appointed guardians—wise and powerful individuals chosen for their dedication to the city's principles. These guardians, like Amara, were entrusted with the duty of maintaining the balance and ensuring that Al-Qamar remained a place of learning and harmony.

The guardians could communicate with the elemental spirits and draw upon the city's ancient magic to ward off threats and guide those who sought the city's wisdom. Over time, the guardianship became a sacred lineage, passed down through the ages to those who demonstrated both the strength and the purity of heart necessary to uphold Al-Qamar's legacy.

As Amara finished her tale, Tariq felt a deep sense of awe and reverence for the city he had finally entered. Al-Qamar was not just a place of physical beauty but a living testament to the power of vision, collaboration, and the boundless possibilities of magic. "This city," Amara said softly, "is a sanctuary for those who seek to understand the mysteries of the world. It is a place where dreams and reality converge, and where the legacy of those who came before us continues to thrive." Tariq nodded, his heart swelling with a renewed sense of purpose. He had come to Al-Qamar seeking answers, and now he understood that his journey was part of a much larger tapestry—a story of hope, wisdom, and the enduring magic that connected all who sought the truth.

With Amara by his side, Tariq felt ready to delve deeper into the mysteries of Al-Qamar, to uncover the secrets that lay within its enchanted walls and to honor the legacy of his father and all who had come before him. The path ahead was filled with challenges and wonders, but Tariq knew he was where he was meant to be.

CHAPTER 42: THE GUARDIAN'S PATH

As the moon rose high over Al-Qamar, casting a silvery glow over the enchanted city, Tariq and Amara walked through the palace gardens. The air was filled with the scent of blooming flowers and the gentle hum of nighttime creatures. Tariq's mind buzzed with questions, and he turned to Amara, seeking to understand the enigmatic guardian who had welcomed him.

"Amara," Tariq began softly, "how did you come to be the guardian of this magnificent city?" Amara smiled, her eyes reflecting the moonlight. "It is a tale intertwined with destiny and duty, much like your own journey, Tariq."

She paused by a fountain, its waters glistening like liquid silver. "I was born in a distant village, far from the splendor of Al-Qamar. My parents were scholars, deeply versed in ancient lore and magic. From a young age, I was drawn to the mysteries of the world, always seeking knowledge and understanding."

Tariq listened intently, captivated by the serene strength in her voice. "One night, when I was but a child, I had a dream. In it, I saw a city bathed in light, a sanctuary of wisdom and magic. The dream was so vivid, so real, that I knew it was a vision, a calling. My parents, wise as they were, recognized the significance of my dream. They knew of Al-Qamar from the ancient texts and understood that I was destined to be part of its legacy."

Amara's eyes grew distant, lost in the memories of her past. "They guided me, taught me everything they knew. As I grew older, my abilities with magic became more pronounced. I could communicate with the spirits of nature, heal with a touch, and see beyond the veil of reality. When I came of age, my parents sent me on a pilgrimage to find Al-Qamar, much like the founders had done centuries before."

She walked slowly around the fountain, her fingers trailing in the cool water. "The journey was arduous, filled with trials and challenges. But every step brought me closer to my destiny. The visions continued to guide me, leading me through deserts, forests, and mountains. Finally, I arrived at the hidden oasis where Al-Qamar stood, its beauty surpassing even my dreams."

Tariq marveled at her story, understanding the depth of her commitment and the strength it took to fulfill her destiny. "When I entered the city," Amara continued, "I was welcomed by the guardians of the time. They saw the potential within me and began my training. I learned the ancient spells that protect the city, the wisdom contained within the libraries, and the responsibilities of a guardian."

She looked at Tariq, her gaze steady and filled with a quiet power. "Becoming a guardian is not just about possessing magic or knowledge. It is about understanding the delicate balance between the seen and unseen worlds, about protecting and nurturing the essence of Al-Qamar. It is a path of lifelong learning and unwavering dedication."

Tariq nodded, his respect for Amara deepening. "You have dedicated your life to this city and its people. It is a noble path."

Amara's smile was gentle. "And now, Tariq, your path has brought you here. The city recognizes your potential, just as it did mine. You have the strength and heart needed to uncover the secrets that lie within. Remember, the journey is as important as the destination. Every step you take, every challenge you face, is a part of your growth."

The night deepened, and the stars above Al-Qamar seemed to shine brighter, as if in acknowledgment of their conversation. Tariq felt a renewed sense of purpose, inspired by Amara's story and her unwavering dedication. "Thank you, Amara," he said, his voice filled with gratitude. "Your journey gives me hope and strength. I will do my best to honor the legacy of Al-Qamar and those who have come before me."

Amara placed a reassuring hand on his shoulder. "I believe in you, Tariq. Trust in yourself and in the wisdom of this city. Together, we will uncover the truths that have been hidden for so long." The city around Tariq began to fade away, and turn to mist, Tariq in his heart knew that Al-Qamar was truly a city of mirage and he had fell victim to one of its many reflections. Amara stood beside him, and gestured towards to mountains. The true nature of Al-Qamar lay ahead and the journey to uncover its secrets would test his resolve.

As he stood beneath the starlit sky, Tariq felt a profound connection to Al-Qamar and its guardian. The journey ahead was still uncertain, but with Amara's guidance and the city's ancient magic, he knew he was ready to face whatever challenges lay in wait. The path of discovery and enlightenment stretched out before him, filled with endless possibilities. The morning sun rose over the desert, casting its golden light on the sand dunes and valleys. Tariq stood in the sunlight, contemplating his next move. He felt a strong pull towards the high desert mountains, convinced that they held more answers to his quest. The ancient map and the symbols he had deciphered hinted at hidden knowledge buried within the rugged peaks.

Tariq set up camp, his thoughts filled with the journey ahead. As night fell, he gazed up at the stars, feeling a deep connection to the world around him. The path was uncertain, but his purpose was clear. In the stillness of the night, Tariq felt a sense of peace and determination. The wisdom of Al-Qamar guiding him, he was ready to face the challenges of the high desert mountains. The journey was far from over, but each step brought him closer to the truth.

CHAPTER 43: THE MOUNTAINS

As Tariq ventured deeper into the high desert mountains, the terrain became increasingly rugged and wild. The mountains were silent, but there was a sense of ancient magic in the air, a feeling that Tariq could not shake.

As the sun began to set, casting long shadows over the rocky peaks, Tariq reached a secluded valley. To Tariq's surprise, the valley was not empty. Strange, mystical creatures gathered around a large bonfire, their forms shimmering in the twilight. There were beings with features of animals and humans, some with wings, others with horns, and all possessing an aura of enchantment.

Among them was a tribe of tall, elegant figures with eyes that glowed like embers. They were the Guardians of the Mountains, ancient guardians who had lived in these highlands for centuries. Their leader, a majestic figure named Elyon, stood at the center, addressing the gathered creatures.

"The city of Al-Qamar has reappeared," Elyon said, his voice resonant and filled with authority. "This is a sign, a momentous event that has not occurred in generations. It signifies the convergence of powerful forces and the potential for great change." Tariq, feeling a mix of curiosity and caution, approached the gathering. Elyon noticed his presence and gestured for him to come closer. The creatures parted, allowing Tariq to step into the circle of light cast by the bonfire.

"Welcome, wanderer," Elyon said, his eyes piercing yet kind. "We sensed your arrival. You come for Al-Qamar, do you not?" Tariq nodded, his voice steady. "Yes, I do. I am on a quest to uncover the secrets of the city."

Elyon nodded thoughtfully. "The reappearance of Al-Qamar is a rare event, and it has drawn the attention of many. The city holds great power and knowledge, but it also attracts those who would seek to exploit it. You must be careful, Tariq. The path you walk is fraught with both opportunity and peril."

A murmur of agreement rippled through the crowd. One of the mystical creatures, a being with the body of a lion and the wings of an eagle, spoke up. "The city's magic is ancient and potent. It calls to those who have the strength to wield it and the wisdom to understand it. We have seen many come and go, but few are chosen." Tariq felt a sense of urgency. "What do you know of the city's secrets? How can I uncover the truth?"

Elyon motioned for Tariq to sit by the fire. "Patience, young one. The answers you seek will not come easily. The high desert mountains hold many clues, remnants of ancient civilizations that once thrived here. You must explore, listen, and learn. The mountains will reveal their secrets to those who are worthy."

As the night deepened, the Guardians of the Mountains shared stories of Al-Qamar, tales passed down through generations. They spoke of a time when the city was a beacon of enlightenment, attracting scholars and mystics from all corners of the world. They told of the powerful enchantments that protected the city and the trials that awaited those who sought to enter its inner sanctum. Tariq listened intently, his resolve strengthening with each story. He realized that his journey was not just about finding answers but about proving himself worthy of the knowledge he sought. The high desert mountains were a crucible, a place where he would be tested and transformed.

As the first light of dawn touched the peaks, Elyon stood and addressed Tariq once more. "You are welcome to stay with us and learn from our wisdom. The mountains have much to teach, and we will guide you as best we can. Remember, the journey is as important as the destination. Embrace the challenges and grow from them." Tariq bowed in gratitude. "Thank you, Elyon, and all of you. I will do my best to honor your guidance and the legacy of Al-Qamar."

With the support of the Guardians of the Mountains, Tariq felt more prepared than ever to face the trials ahead. The mystical creatures and their ancient knowledge would be invaluable allies on his quest. As he set out to explore the high desert mountains, he carried with him the hope and determination to uncover the truths that lay hidden in the shadows of time.

CHAPTER 44: THE GUARDIANS OF THE MOUNTAINS

As the first rays of dawn filtered through the peaks, casting a golden light over the valley, the mystical creatures gathered around the fire once more. Tariq, feeling both humbled and honored, listened as each member of the tribe introduced themselves, sharing their origins and roles in the guardianship of the high desert mountains.

Elyon, the Eldest

Elyon, the tribe's leader, stood tall and imposing, his eyes reflecting the wisdom of centuries. "I am Elyon, the eldest of the Guardians. My lineage traces back to the first guardians who settled these mountains. We have always been the protectors of ancient secrets, ensuring that only those with pure intentions can access the hidden knowledge. I come from a lineage of seers and mystics, and it is my duty to guide and protect those who seek the truth."

Aria, the Winged Messenger

Next to speak was Aria, a graceful figure with the body of a human and the wings of an eagle. Her feathers shimmered in the early light. "I am Aria, the Winged Messenger. My ancestors were sky spirits, tasked with delivering messages between realms. I can travel swiftly across great distances, bringing news and wisdom from far-off lands. The winds and skies are my domain, and I watch over the movements of the heavens."

Kael, the Elemental Guardian

A being with the form of a lion and the wings of an eagle, Kael, stepped forward. His mane flowed like molten gold. "I am Kael, the Elemental Guardian. My lineage is tied to the very earth and sky. I come from a line of protectors who harness the power of the elements. Fire, water, earth, and air are at my command. We ensure the balance of nature in these mountains, maintaining harmony between the realms."

Liora, the Keeper of Lore

A slender, ethereal figure with a crown of flowers adorning her head introduced herself. Her voice was melodic, like a gentle stream. "I am Liora, the Keeper of Lore. My people are the storytellers and historians of the mystical realms. We preserve the knowledge and tales of our ancestors, ensuring that the wisdom of the past is not lost. I come from a village hidden in the heart of the forest, where the trees themselves whisper stories of old."

Thorne, the Shadow Walker

A figure cloaked in shadows, with eyes that glowed like embers, stepped forward. His presence was both unsettling and intriguing. "I am Thorne, the Shadow Walker. My lineage is tied to the realm of shadows, where we navigate the thin veil between light and dark. My people are the watchers of the night, ensuring that the balance between good and evil is maintained. We see what others cannot and protect against the unseen threats that lurk in the darkness."

Mira, the Water Weaver

A being with flowing hair that shimmered like water and eyes as deep as the ocean spoke next. Her voice was calm and soothing. "I am Mira, the Water Weaver. My ancestors were the guardians of the seas and rivers, controlling the flow of water and ensuring its purity. I come from an underwater kingdom, where we live in harmony with the creatures of the deep. Water is my element, and I use its power to heal and protect."

Eryn, the Forest Guardian

Finally, a tall, majestic figure with antlers adorned with vines and flowers introduced himself. His voice was resonant and earthy. "I am Eryn, the Forest Guardian. My lineage is tied to the ancient groves and woodlands. My people are the protectors of the trees and all living creatures within the forest. We ensure that the balance of life is maintained and that the forest remains a sanctuary for all who dwell there."

With the introductions complete, Elyon addressed Tariq once more. "Now you know us, Tariq. Each of us holds a piece of the knowledge you seek. Together, we will guide you through these mountains, helping you uncover the truths hidden within. Your journey is not just yours alone; it is a path that intertwines with all of ours."

Tariq bowed deeply, his heart filled with gratitude and respect. "Thank you, Elyon, and all of you. I am honored to be in your presence and to receive your guidance. I will do my best to honor the legacy of Al-Qamar and the wisdom you have shared with me."

As the sun climbed higher, casting its warm light over the valley, Tariq felt a renewed sense of purpose. With the support of the Guardians of the Mountains, he was ready to face whatever challenges lay ahead.

CHAPTER 45: SHADOWS IN THE VALLEY

As the sun climbed higher, casting warm light over the valley, the Guardians of the Mountains and Tariq prepared for the journey ahead. The atmosphere was filled with a sense of purpose and camaraderie. However, the tranquility of the moment was soon shattered by a sudden chill in the air, a foreboding presence that made the hairs on Tariq's neck stand on end.

From the shadows at the edge of the valley, several figures emerged. Cloaked in darkness, their forms seemed to shift and waver as if they were made of the very shadows they commanded. The leader of these shadowy figures, a tall and menacing being with eyes like burning coals, stepped forward.

"So, the guardians and their new companion are planning to uncover the secrets of Al-Qamar," the leader hissed, his voice a sinister whisper that echoed through the valley. "We cannot allow that." Elyon stepped forward, his posture unwavering. "Who are you, and what do you want?"

The shadowy leader sneered. "We are the Shadow Sentinels, the keepers of the darkest secrets. We have protected the hidden truths of these mountains for centuries, ensuring that only those worthy may proceed. Your quest threatens to disrupt the balance we have maintained." Tariq felt a surge of anger and determination. "We seek knowledge and truth. Our intentions are pure." The leader's eyes narrowed. "Intentions mean nothing. Actions do. We have seen many who claimed purity, only to succumb to greed and power. You will not proceed."

Elyon raised his hand, a gesture of peace and authority. "We are not here to fight. We seek to restore balance and uncover the wisdom that has been lost. Stand aside and let us pass." The Shadow Sentinels did not move. Instead, they drew closer, their presence oppressive and menacing. "You speak of balance, yet you bring chaos. We cannot let you pass," the leader declared, his voice growing colder. Aria, the Winged Messenger, stepped forward, her wings flaring in defiance. "We will not be deterred by your threats. The journey to the mountain depths is crucial, and we will see it through."

Kael, the Elemental Guardian, summoned a swirl of fire and wind around his form. "Stand aside or face the consequences." The tension in the air was palpable, the valley charged with the impending clash of powerful forces. The Shadow Sentinels seemed unfazed, their forms blending with the encroaching darkness. As the confrontation reached its peak, a soft, melodic voice broke through the tension. Liora, the Keeper of Lore, stepped forward, her presence calming. "There is no need for conflict," she said gently. "We are all guardians of something greater. Perhaps we can find a way to coexist."

The leader of the Shadow Sentinels seemed to hesitate, the fiery intensity in his eyes dimming slightly. "What do you propose?" he asked, his voice still wary. Liora smiled, her eyes filled with ancient wisdom. "Tariq shall travel alone. Let him prove his intentions. He will undergo the trials, face the challenges, and show us all that he is worthy. He will succeed.

The Shadow Sentinels conferred among themselves, their voices a hushed whisper. Finally, the leader turned to Liora. "Very well. Tariq will face his trials alone. But be warned, what lies ahead is not for the faint of heart." Tariq felt a mixture of relief and apprehension. The path ahead was still fraught with danger, but at least now he had a chance to prove himself.

As the guardians helped prepare Tariq for the trials he would face, the valley seemed to hold its breath, the outcome of his journey hanging in the balance. Tariq knew that the journey ahead would test his strength, resolve, and wisdom, but he was ready to face whatever challenges lay ahead.

CHAPTER 46: THE
ARTIFACTS OF POWER

With the agreement in place to face the Guardians of the Mountains gathered around the fire once more. Tariq sensed that this moment was pivotal. The guardians began to discuss various artifacts that might aid him on his journey, each one imbued with ancient magic and powerful abilities.

Elyon's Wisdom

Elyon, the eldest of the guardians, was the first to speak. "There are several artifacts in these mountains that could prove invaluable to your quest, Tariq. Each one holds a unique power that can help you overcome the trials ahead and unlock the secrets of Al-Qamar."

The Crystal of Clarity

Aria, the Winged Messenger, stepped forward, her wings shimmering in the firelight. "One such artifact is the Crystal of Clarity. It is said to possess the ability to reveal hidden truths and dispel illusions. With this crystal, you can see beyond the deception of the shadows and uncover the true nature of things."

The Elemental Amulet

Kael, the Elemental Guardian, conjured a small flame in his palm. "There is also the Elemental Amulet, a relic that allows its bearer to harness the power of the four elements—fire, water, earth, and air. This amulet can protect you from natural dangers and empower you to manipulate the elements to your advantage."

The Scroll of Ages

Liora, the Keeper of Lore, produced an ancient scroll from her robes. "The Scroll of Ages contains knowledge and wisdom from centuries past. It can guide you through the most complex of challenges, providing insight and understanding. This scroll has been passed down through generations of guardians, and its wisdom is boundless."

The Cloak of Shadows

Thorne, the Shadow Walker, emerged from the darkness, his presence both eerie and comforting. "The Cloak of Shadows is a powerful artifact that allows its wearer to blend into the shadows and move

177

unseen. It can protect you from prying eyes and enable you to navigate through the most perilous situations undetected."

The Chalice of Life

Mira, the Water Weaver, spoke next, her voice like the gentle flow of a stream. "The Chalice of Life is a sacred artifact that holds the essence of life itself. It can heal wounds, restore vitality, and even purify tainted water. This chalice is a gift from the spirits of the water, and it holds great healing power."

The Staff of the Forest

Eryn, the Forest Guardian, stepped forward with a staff made of twisted wood and adorned with leaves and vines. "The Staff of the Forest connects its bearer to the heart of nature. It can summon the strength of the trees and the wisdom of the ancient woods. This staff can guide you through the wilderness and protect you from its dangers."

The Decision

Tariq listened intently, feeling a sense of awe and gratitude for the guardians' generosity and wisdom. Each artifact held incredible power, and he knew that choosing the right ones would be crucial for his journey.

Elyon spoke again, his voice filled with solemnity. "Tariq, you must choose which artifacts to take with you. Consider their powers carefully, for they will aid you in different ways. The trials ahead will test your strength, wisdom, and resolve. These artifacts can help you, but ultimately, it is your heart and spirit that will guide you."

Tariq nodded, his mind racing as he weighed the options. The Crystal of Clarity could reveal the true path, the Elemental Amulet could grant him control over the elements, and the Scroll of Ages could provide invaluable wisdom. The Cloak of Shadows offered stealth, the Chalice of Life provided healing, and the Staff of the Forest connected him to nature.

"I will take the Crystal of Clarity," Tariq decided, "to see through the deceptions that lie ahead. The Elemental Amulet will help me harness the power of the elements, and the Scroll of Ages will guide me with its wisdom."

The guardians nodded in approval, each one stepping forward to present the chosen artifact to Tariq. As he accepted each one, he felt a surge of power and a deep sense of responsibility. "Thank you," Tariq said, his voice filled with gratitude. "I will honor these gifts and use them wisely on my journey."

Elyon placed a reassuring hand on Tariq's shoulder. "You have chosen well, Tariq. May these artifacts guide and protect you. Remember, you are not alone. The spirit of Al-Qamar and the wisdom of the guardians are with you." As Tariq prepared to set out, he felt a renewed sense of purpose. With the artifacts in his possession and the support of the guardians, he was ready to face whatever challenges lay ahead. The journey to uncover the secrets of Al-Qamar continued, and Tariq knew that he was on the path to fulfilling his destiny.

CHAPTER 47: THE ENCHANTED LAKE

With the artifacts secured and the guardians' blessings, Tariq continued his journey deeper into the high desert mountains. The terrain grew more rugged, the air crisper, and the sense of ancient magic more palpable with each step.

As the sun began its descent, casting long shadows over the rocky landscape, Tariq noticed a shimmering light in the distance. Curious, he made his way toward the source, the path winding through narrow passes and over jagged rocks. The light grew brighter, reflecting the last rays of the setting sun, until finally, Tariq emerged into a hidden valley.

At the center of the valley lay a pristine lake, its waters clear and still, reflecting the sky above like a perfect mirror. The air around the lake was cool and refreshing, a stark contrast to the harsh desert climate. Intrigued, Tariq approached the water's edge, feeling an inexplicable pull towards the serene body of water.

The lake was surrounded by lush vegetation, vibrant flowers, and towering trees whose leaves whispered secrets in the gentle breeze. It was a place of peace and tranquility, seemingly untouched by time. As Tariq knelt to drink from the lake, he noticed something extraordinary—a faint glow emanating from beneath the surface.

Curiosity piqued, Tariq peered into the water, straining to see what lay below. The glow grew brighter, revealing the outline of an ancient structure submerged beneath the lake. The sight took his breath away—columns and archways of a lost temple, their details obscured by the depths but still magnificent in their silent grandeur.

Tariq felt a sense of urgency. He knew that this temple, hidden beneath the enchanted lake, held secrets that could be crucial to his quest. But how could he reach it? He glanced at the artifacts he carried, considering their potential uses.

He decided to use the Elemental Amulet, hoping its power over water could help him access the submerged temple. Holding the amulet tightly, he focused his thoughts, feeling the energy of the elements flow through him. The water around him began to stir, rippling and parting as if responding to his silent command.

Slowly, a path of dry ground formed through the lake, leading directly to the temple's entrance. Tariq marveled at the power of the amulet, grateful for its guidance. He stepped onto the path, his heart pounding with anticipation as he made his way to the temple.

As he approached the entrance, he saw intricate carvings adorning the columns—symbols and runes like those he inscribed in the desert. The temple seemed to resonate with a faint, melodic hum, as if it were alive with ancient magic. Tariq felt a sense of awe and reverence as he crossed the threshold, entering the sacred space.

Inside, the temple was a marvel of ancient craftsmanship. The walls were lined with murals depicting the history of Al-Qamar and its connection to the elemental spirits. Statues of guardians stood watch, their eyes seeming to follow Tariq as he moved through the hallways. At the center of the temple, a grand altar stood, bathed in the soft glow of the crystal light.

As Tariq stood in the ancient temple, the weight of the Scroll of Ages in his hands, a creeping sense of doubt began to gnaw at him. The grandeur of the temple, the power of the artifacts, and the enormity of his quest all seemed overwhelming. He felt small and insignificant in the face of such ancient and powerful forces.

Tariq's mind was clouded with uncertainty. Was he truly the one destined to uncover the secrets of Al-Qamar? Could he live up to the legacy of his father and the expectations of the guardians?

Tariq sank to his knees before the altar, the scroll still clutched in his hands. "Am I truly worthy of this?" he whispered, his voice barely audible. "What if I fail? What if I'm not strong enough?"

The melodic hum of the temple seemed to soften, as if in response to his doubts. The carvings on the walls, the statues of the guardians, and the glow of the crystal light all seemed to watch him, their silent presence both comforting and unnerving. Tariq closed his eyes, seeking solace in the quiet of the temple.

A gentle voice broke the silence, filled with wisdom and compassion. "Tariq, your doubts are natural. Every great journey is fraught with uncertainty. But remember, it is not the absence of fear that defines a hero, but the courage to move forward despite it."

Tariq opened his eyes to see Elyon, the eldest of the Guardians, standing before him. The guardian's eyes were kind, his presence a beacon of reassurance. "You are not alone in this journey, Tariq. The guardians, the spirits of Al-Qamar, are all with you. Trust in yourself and the path you have chosen."

Aria, the Winged Messenger, stepped forward, her wings shimmering in the soft light. "You have been chosen for a reason, Tariq. The journey is not about perfection, but about perseverance. Each step you take, each challenge you face, brings you closer to the truth."

Kael, the Elemental Guardian, placed a hand on Tariq's shoulder, his grip firm and supportive. "The elements are with you, guiding and protecting you. Draw strength from the earth, the sky, the fire, and the water. They are your allies."

Liora, the Keeper of Lore, knelt beside him, her presence calming. "The Scroll of Ages holds the wisdom of the ancients, but it is your heart and mind that will unlock its secrets. Trust in your instincts and let the knowledge guide you."

Thorne, the Shadow Walker, emerged from the darkness, his eyes glowing softly. "Even in the shadows, there is light. Embrace your doubts, for they are a part of your journey. Use them to grow stronger, to understand yourself better."

Mira, the Water Weaver, smiled gently. "The waters of life flow through you, Tariq. Let them cleanse your doubts and fears. You are capable of great things."

Eryn, the Forest Guardian, added his voice to the chorus of support. "Nature itself believes in you. The trees, the flowers, the very earth beneath your feet—they all resonate with your purpose. Draw strength from them."

Tariq felt a surge of warmth and gratitude, the words of the guardians filling him with renewed confidence. "Thank you," he said, his voice stronger. "I will do my best to honor your faith in me and to fulfill my father's legacy."

Elyon nodded, his eyes filled with pride. "Remember, Tariq, you are never alone. The journey may be difficult, but it is one you are destined to undertake. Trust in yourself, and trust in the wisdom of Al-Qamar."

With the support of the guardians, Tariq rose to his feet, the Scroll of Ages held firmly in his hands. The doubts that had clouded his mind began to fade, replaced by a sense of purpose and determination. The path ahead was still uncertain, but he knew that he had the strength and support to face whatever challenges lay ahead.

On the altar lay an ancient tablet, bound in gold and adorned with precious gems. Tariq felt a surge of recognition—this was a map to Al-Qamar. But why was it here, in this hidden temple?

He approached the altar, reaching out to touch the tablet. As his fingers brushed against it, a vision flooded his mind—images of the guardians, standing in this very temple, deciphering the ancient runes and unlocking the secrets of Al-Qamar. Tariq felt a deep connection with their legacy, a sense of purpose and destiny intertwined.

With newfound determination, Tariq canvased the tablet, the ancient stone crackling softly. The symbols and runes glowed faintly, revealing their hidden wisdom. He knew that this knowledge was the key to unlocking the full potential of the artifacts he carried and understanding the true nature of Al-Qamar.

As he studied the tablet, the melodic hum of the temple grew louder, resonating with the beating of his heart. Tariq felt a profound sense of clarity and enlightenment, knowing that his journey was far from over but that he was on the right path.

With the Scroll of Ages, the power of the Elemental Amulet guiding him, Tariq left the temple with the tablet in hand. The path through the lake closing behind him. As he stood on the shore, he looked out over the serene waters, feeling a deep sense of peace and purpose. The journey to uncover the secrets of Al-Qamar continued, and Tariq knew that he was closer than ever to fulfilling his destiny.

As he left the temple, the melodic hum followed him, a reminder of the wisdom and magic that guided him. The journey to uncover the secrets of Al-Qamar continued, and Tariq knew that he was ready to face the trials and tribulations ahead with courage and conviction.

CHAPTER 48: REFLECTIONS OF RESOLVE

As Tariq exited the ancient temple, his renewed confidence wavered. Despite the guardians' reassurances, the enormity of his quest loomed large, and the shadows of doubt crept back into his mind. He found himself standing by the edge of the lake, the still waters reflecting the sky and mountains around him.

Kneeling by the water's edge, Tariq stared at his reflection. The face that looked back at him seemed burdened, the weight of the expectations of the guardians heavy on his shoulders. He dipped his fingers into the cool water, sending ripples across the surface. As the ripples settled, the image in the water shifted, and Tariq saw not his own face but that of Princess Layla.

Her eyes, warm and wise, gazed back at him with a look of encouragement and understanding. Tariq's breath caught in his throat, his heart aching with the memory of her support and the strength she had always given him. "Layla," he whispered, his voice trembling with emotion. The vision of Layla in the water smiled gently, her presence a balm to his troubled soul. "Tariq," she said, her voice soft yet firm, "you have come so far, and you carry the hopes and dreams of many. The wisdom of Al-Qamar, and the faith of the guardians—they all rest upon your shoulders, but you are strong enough to bear it."

Tariq's eyes filled with tears. "But what if I'm not? What if I fail?" Layla's reflection grew more resolute. "Failure is not the end, Tariq. It is a part of the journey. Every step you take, every challenge you face, brings you closer to your goal. Trust in yourself and the path you are on. You have the strength, the wisdom, and the heart to succeed." Tariq closed his eyes, letting Layla's words wash over him. He could almost feel her presence beside him, a comforting warmth that chased away the chill of doubt. "I miss you, Layla," he murmured. "Your belief in me has always given me strength."

The reflection in the water shimmered, Layla's eyes filled with unwavering faith. "And I will always believe in you, Tariq. Remember, you are never alone. The guardians, the spirits of Al-Qamar, and I are with you every step of the way. Trust in yourself, for you are capable of great things."

Tariq took a deep breath, feeling the weight of his doubts lift, replaced by a sense of determination and resolve. "Thank you, Layla," he said, his voice steady. "I will honor your faith in me. I will see this journey through."

The vision of Layla in the water smiled one last time before fading away, leaving Tariq staring at his own reflection once more. But now, the face that looked back at him was different—stronger, more resolved, and filled with a quiet confidence.

Rising to his feet, Tariq felt a renewed sense of purpose. He knew that the path ahead would be challenging, but he also knew that he had the strength and support to face whatever lay in wait. The journey to uncover the secrets of Al-Qamar continued, and with the encouragement of Princess Layla and the guidance of the guardians, Tariq felt ready to meet his destiny.

With the Scroll of Ages in his possession and the power of the Elemental Amulet guiding him, Tariq set out from the lake, his steps sure and his heart filled with determination. The mountains, with all their secrets and challenges, awaited him, and Tariq knew that he was prepared to face them.

CHAPTER 49: THE
GUARDIAN'S SECRET

As Tariq ventured further into the high desert mountains, the guardians voices accompanied him, each lending their unique strengths and wisdom to guide him. Unbeknownst to Tariq, one of the guardians, Thorne the Shadow Walker, watched him with a growing sense of inner turmoil.

Thorne had always been the most enigmatic of the guardians, his presence often unsettling yet crucial. His ability to navigate the shadows and see what others could not made him invaluable. But beneath his calm exterior, Thorne harbored a secret that gnawed at him—a secret that now threatened to disrupt his focus.

Thorne's Hidden Past

Long ago, Thorne had not been a guardian of shadows but a human. His name had been Elias, a scholar and healer in a distant land. Elias had fallen deeply in love with a woman named Arina, a fellow scholar whose beauty and intelligence had captivated him from the moment they met. Their love had been passionate and profound, a bond that seemed unbreakable.

However, fate had been cruel. Arina had fallen gravely ill, and despite Elias's extensive knowledge of healing, he could not save her. In his desperation, Elias had sought out ancient magic, hoping to find a way to bring her back. His quest led him to the high desert mountains and the hidden city of Al-Qamar. There, he discovered the power of shadows and the offer of immortality in exchange for becoming a guardian.

Desperate to save Arina and consumed by grief, Elias accepted the offer, becoming Thorne, the Shadow Walker. But the transformation came at a cost—he could no longer return to his human life. His existence as a guardian was eternal but empty, haunted by the memory of the love he had lost.

As Thorne observed Tariq, he couldn't help but see echoes of his former self. Tariq's determination, his quest for knowledge, and the love he had for Princess Layla reminded Thorne of the life he had once lived and the love he had lost. A pang of jealousy stirred within him, a feeling he had not experienced in centuries. One evening, as they camped by a small stream, Thorne appeared before Tariq. The shadows danced around them, casting flickering patterns on the ground. Tariq was engrossed in the Scroll of Ages, studying its ancient runes and seeking guidance. "Tariq," Thorne said, his voice a low whisper. "Do you ever fear that your quest might lead to loss, rather than the answers you seek?"

Tariq looked up, surprised by the question. "I have my doubts, yes. But I must try. For my father, for Layla, and for myself. I cannot let fear stop me." Thorne nodded, the shadows deepening around him. "Once, I was much like you. Driven by love and a desire to protect. But the path I chose led to unforeseen consequences. I lost the person I loved and became something else entirely." Tariq listened intently, sensing the weight of Thorne's words. "What happened?" Thorne's eyes glowed faintly in the darkness. "I was human once, in love with a woman who was my world. When she fell ill, I sought ancient magic to save her. It led me here, to Al-Qamar. I became a guardian, hoping to gain the power to bring her back. But in doing so, I lost my humanity and my chance to be with her."

Tariq's heart ached for Thorne's loss. "I'm sorry. That must have been incredibly painful." Thorne's voice grew softer, tinged with regret. "It was. And now, I see you, with your determination and the love you hold for Layla. It stirs memories I thought long buried. I fear for you, Tariq. I fear you might face a similar fate."

Tariq placed a reassuring hand on Thorne's arm. "I appreciate your concern, Thorne. But I believe our paths, while similar, are not the same. I have the guidance of the guardians, the wisdom of the Scroll of Ages, and the support of Layla. I will be careful, and I will honor your warnings." Thorne nodded, his expression unreadable. "Perhaps you are right. But know this, Tariq: the shadows can be both friend and foe. Use them wisely."

As Tariq returned to his studies, Thorne retreated into the darkness, his thoughts conflicted. The jealousy he felt was a reminder of his lost humanity, a reminder of what he had sacrificed. Yet, seeing Tariq's determination gave him a glimmer of hope—a hope that perhaps, through Tariq, he might find redemption for the choices he had made.

The journey to uncover the secrets of Al-Qamar continued, each step bringing new challenges and revelations. With the guardians by his side, and the support of those who believed in him, Tariq pressed on, his resolve strengthened by the knowledge that he was not alone.

CHAPTER 50: THE CHAINED SHADOW

Tariq, with the Scroll of Ages and the Elemental Amulet securely in his possession, wandered deeper into ruins of the mountains. The corridors were dimly lit by the faint glow of magical runes etched into the walls, guiding his path. The air grew cooler, and a sense of profound silence enveloped him as he descended further into the depths.

As he turned a corner, he noticed a faint, eerie light emanating from a chamber ahead. Intrigued and cautious, he approached the source of the light. The chamber was vast, its ceiling disappearing into darkness. At the center, chained to a large stone pillar, was a shadowy figure. The creature's form was insubstantial, constantly shifting and swirling, its eyes glowing with a deep, malevolent light.

Tariq hesitated at the threshold, unsure of what he was encountering. The creature sensed his presence and looked up, its eyes locking onto his with an intensity that sent a chill down his spine. "Who are you?" Tariq asked, his voice echoing through the chamber. The creature's voice was a low, resonant whisper, filled with a mix of bitterness and sorrow. "I am Nerezza, once a guardian of Al-Qamar, now condemned to this eternal imprisonment."

Tariq stepped closer, curiosity overcoming his fear. "Why are you chained here, Nerezza? What did you do to deserve this?" Nerezza's form flickered, the chains rattling as it shifted. "Long ago, I was one of the guardians, entrusted with the protection and wisdom of this sacred city. But I grew ambitious, my heart corrupted by the desire for power. I sought to harness the darkest magics, to control the very essence of shadows."

Tariq listened intently, sensing there was more to the story. "What happened then?" Nerezza's eyes flared with a mix of anger and regret. "My actions brought great peril to Al-Qamar. I unleashed forces beyond my control, endangering the city and its people. The other guardians, in their wisdom and mercy, did not destroy me. Instead, they bound me here, in the depths of this chamber, to atone for my transgressions and to serve as a warning to others who might be tempted by the same dark path."

Tariq felt a pang of sympathy for the creature. "Is there no way for you to find redemption?" Nerezza's form seemed to sag, the chains clinking softly. "Redemption is a distant dream for one such as I. The chains that bind me are forged from the very essence of my misdeeds. To break them would require a purity of heart and a strength of will that I no longer possess."

Tariq thought for a moment, then spoke with determination. "Perhaps redemption is not beyond your reach, Nerezza. The guardians believed in mercy and wisdom. If you truly seek to atone, there may yet be a way."

Nerezza's eyes glimmered with a faint hope. "Why would you, a stranger, seek to help me?" Tariq stepped closer, his voice filled with compassion. "Because I believe in second chances. Because I know what it means to seek redemption and understanding. If there is a way to help you, I will find it."

The shadow creature regarded Tariq with a newfound respect. "You are different, Tariq. There is a light within you that shines even in the darkest of places. If you truly wish to help, there is an ancient ritual, a rite of purification, that may break these chains. It is a perilous task, requiring the combined power of the guardians magic and the purest of intentions."

Tariq nodded, his resolve firm. "Tell me what I must do." Nerezza explained the ritual, detailing the ancient runes and incantations needed to summon the purifying light. It would require strength and resolve, as well as Tariq's unwavering faith and determination.

As Tariq absorbed the instructions, he felt a renewed sense of purpose. The journey to uncover the secrets of Al-Qamar had taken an unexpected turn, but he knew that helping Nerezza could be a crucial step in understanding the full extent of the city's ancient wisdom.

With a promise to return, Tariq left the chamber, his mind set on the task ahead. He would gather the guardians and perform the ritual, not only to free Nerezza but also to strengthen his own resolve and understanding of the path he walked.

The journey continued, each step bringing new challenges and revelations. With the support of the guardians and the strength of his convictions, Tariq felt ready to face whatever lay ahead, determined to bring light to even the darkest corners of the ancient city of Al-Qamar.

CHAPTER 51: THE NATURE OF GOOD AND EVIL

Tariq felt a profound weight as he returned to the chamber where Nerezza, the shadow creature, remained chained. The instructions for the purification ritual echoed in his mind, but another, deeper question lingered as well. He wanted to understand more about the nature of good and evil from Nerezza's perspective.

He approached the creature, its shadowy form still shifting and swirling, and sat down cross-legged in front of the stone pillar. "Nerezza, before we attempt the ritual, I need to understand more about you and the choices that led you here. Can we talk about the nature of good and evil?"

Nerezza's glowing eyes fixed on Tariq, and a slow, thoughtful hum emanated from its form. "A profound question, Tariq. Good and evil are concepts that have plagued the hearts and minds of beings since the dawn of time. They are not as clear-cut as one might hope." Tariq nodded, leaning forward. "What do you mean?"

Nerezza's voice was tinged with melancholy. "I was once a scholar and healer. My intentions were pure, driven by love and a desire to save. But in my desperation, I sought power through dark means, believing that the end justified the means. It is here that the lines between good and evil blurred." Tariq's eyes widened. "So, do you believe that your intentions were good, but your actions were evil?"

Nerezza seemed to ponder this. "Intentions and actions are two sides of the same coin. One can have the purest intentions but take actions that bring about great harm. Conversely, sometimes actions perceived as harsh or cruel can lead to greater good. It is a delicate balance, one that I failed to maintain."

Tariq considered this, recalling his own struggles and doubts. "I've always thought that good and evil were clear—doing good means helping others and doing evil means causing harm. But I'm starting to see that it's more complex than that."

Nerezza's form flickered, its voice growing softer. "Indeed, Tariq. Good and evil are often defined by perspective. What one person sees as an act of kindness, another might see as interference or even cruelty. My downfall was not in seeking power, but in letting my desire for it overshadow my empathy and wisdom."

Tariq's heart ached for Nerezza's plight. "So, how do we navigate this complexity? How do we ensure that our actions align with our intentions?" Nerezza's eyes glowed with a mix of sadness and hope. "By seeking balance and always questioning our motives. By surrounding ourselves with those who challenge us to stay true to our values. And by understanding that we are fallible, capable of both great good and profound evil. Redemption lies in acknowledging our mistakes and striving to do better."

Tariq felt a surge of determination. "I will take your words to heart, Nerezza. Your experience has taught me a valuable lesson. I will strive to balance my intentions with my actions and seek the wisdom of those around me." Nerezza nodded, a faint smile in its eyes. "You have a good heart, Tariq. I see the potential for great things in you. Remember, even in the darkest times, there is always a path to redemption."

As Tariq stood, he felt a renewed sense of clarity. The conversation with Nerezza had given him a deeper understanding of the complexities of good and evil, and the importance of self-reflection and balance. He was more determined than ever to face the trials ahead and uncover the secrets of Al-Qamar.

With a final nod to Nerezza, Tariq left the chamber, his mind and heart aligned with a new purpose. The journey continued, each step guided by the wisdom he had gained and the resolve to walk the path of balance and redemption.

CHAPTER 52: THE REVELATION

As Tariq left the chamber, the weight of his conversation with Nerezza lingered heavily on his mind. He had taken only a few steps when a sudden burst of light erupted from the chamber, casting away the shadows and illuminating the chamber he had just left. Startled, Tariq turned back, his heart pounding with both fear and curiosity.

He hurried back into the chamber, where Nerezza had been imprisoned. The chains that had once bound the shadow creature lay shattered on the ground, and in the center of the room stood a figure bathed in light. As the light dimmed, Tariq realized with a shock that he was looking at a version of himself.

The figure, a reflection of Tariq, stepped forward, the glow around him fading to reveal familiar features. His eyes, though identical to Tariq's, held centuries of wisdom and sorrow. The realization struck Tariq like a thunderbolt—Nerezza had been a twisted version of himself all along, a manifestation of his darkest fears and desires. Tariq's heart raced as he approached the figure. "What... what is this? How can you be me?"

The figure smiled gently, a hint of sadness in his eyes. "I am the part of you that you fear most, the part that was consumed by doubt and ambition. The guardians' magic and your own inner struggle created me, an embodiment of what you could become if you let your darker impulses rule you." Tariq's mind reeled. "But why? Why imprison you here?"

The figure's expression softened. "To teach you a lesson, to show you the importance of balance and self-awareness. Our discussion on good and evil, the acknowledgment of our flaws and the commitment to redemption—those are the keys to freeing yourself from your darkest fears." As the words sank in, Tariq felt a profound sense of understanding. The chains that had bound Nerezza, his shadow self, were not physical but symbolic. By confronting his inner darkness and discussing the nature of good and evil, he had found the strength to break free.

Tariq took a deep breath, his resolve strengthening. "So, by understanding and accepting my inner struggles, I can prevent myself from becoming consumed by them." The figure nodded. "Exactly. You have the power to choose your path. Remember, it is not about being perfect but striving to balance your intentions with your actions. The guardians believed in you, and now you must believe in yourself."

With a final, reassuring smile, the figure began to fade, the light around him growing brighter until it filled the entire chamber. When the light finally receded, Tariq found himself alone, but with a newfound sense of clarity and purpose.

He turned and left the chamber, the lessons he had learned guiding his steps. As he emerged from the chamber, the guardians awaited him, their expressions filled with anticipation and pride.

Elyon stepped forward, his eyes reflecting the wisdom of ages. "You have faced your inner darkness and emerged stronger, Tariq. This is but one step on your journey, but it is a crucial one."

Aria, the Winged Messenger, smiled. "Your resolve and courage have shown us that you are indeed worthy of the task ahead."

Kael, the Elemental Guardian, placed a hand on Tariq's shoulder. "Remember, the balance you seek within yourself is the same balance you will need to uncover the secrets of Al-Qamar."

Liora, the Keeper of Lore, nodded approvingly. "You carry the wisdom of the ancients and the strength of your own heart. Use them wisely."

Thorne, the Shadow Walker, his own eyes reflecting a hint of newfound peace, said, "Even in the shadows, you found light. That is your true power."

Mira, the Water Weaver, and Eryn, the Forest Guardian, added their blessings, each one reaffirming Tariq's purpose and strength.

With the support and guidance of the guardians, Tariq felt ready to continue his journey. The revelation within the chamber had given him a deeper understanding of himself and the nature of his quest. He knew that the path ahead would be challenging, but he was prepared to face it with courage and wisdom.

The journey to uncover the secrets of Al-Qamar continued, each step bringing Tariq closer to fulfilling his destiny. And as he moved forward, the lessons of balance, self-awareness, and redemption guided him, lighting his way through the darkness.

CHAPTER 53: THE SULTAN'S DECEPTION

Back in the opulent palace of the Sultan, the air was thick with tension. The Sultan paced restlessly in his grand chamber, his mind occupied with thoughts of the mysterious city of Al-Qamar. News of its reappearance had reached his ears, igniting a burning curiosity and an even stronger desire for the treasures and knowledge it promised.

The Sultan, a man of ambition and cunning, had initially seen Tariq as a means to an end—a tool to uncover the secrets of Al-Qamar. But as time passed and no word came from Tariq, his patience wore thin. He began to doubt Tariq's capabilities and questioned whether he had made the right decision in entrusting such a valuable mission to an outsider.

The Sultan's advisors stood by, silent and watchful. They knew better than to interrupt their ruler's musings. Finally, the Sultan turned to them, his eyes cold and calculating. "Tariq has been gone for too long," the Sultan said, his voice laced with impatience. "I fear he may have either failed or decided to keep the treasures of Al-Qamar for himself. We cannot sit idly by while such power remains out of our grasp."

One of his advisors, a shrewd and conniving man named Malik, stepped forward. "Your Majesty, perhaps it is time to consider other options. We could send a party of our own to retrieve the treasures of Al-Qamar. With your permission, I can assemble a team of our best warriors and scholars."

The Sultan nodded slowly, his mind racing with possibilities. "Yes, Malik, that is a wise suggestion. But we must be cautious. Tariq may still prove useful. If he succeeds and brings back the treasures, we can reward him appropriately. If not, our own party will ensure that we do not leave empty-handed."

Malik bowed, a cunning smile playing on his lips. "As you command, Your Majesty. I will see to it that the preparations are made immediately."

The Sultan dismissed his advisors, returning to his private thoughts. He could not shake the feeling of unease that had settled over him since hearing of Al-Qamar's reappearance. The city was said to be a place of immense power and wisdom, and the idea of possessing such knowledge was intoxicating. But it also meant facing unknown dangers and potentially powerful adversaries.

The Sultan walked to the window of his chamber, looking out over the sprawling city below. The thought of Tariq uncovering the secrets of Al-Qamar and returning a hero gnawed at him. He could not allow an outsider to gain such glory and power, especially not if it meant overshadowing his own reign.

As the sun set, casting a golden glow over the palace, the Sultan made his decision. He would send his own expedition to Al-Qamar, ensuring that no matter what, the treasures of the ancient city would fall into his hands. Tariq's success or failure would be irrelevant—what mattered was securing the power for himself.

That night, as the palace buzzed with the secret preparations for the expedition, the Sultan sat alone, a cold smile on his lips. He had always believed that power and cunning would prevail over all else, and this would be no different. The journey to Al-Qamar would be fraught with challenges, but he was confident in his ability to manipulate events to his advantage.

In the depths of the high desert mountains, Tariq remained unaware of the Sultan's machinations. His journey, guided by the wisdom of the guardians and the strength of his own convictions, continued forward. But as he delved deeper into the mysteries of

Al-Qamar, he would soon find that the greatest
threats were not just the ancient trials but the betrayal
brewing back home.

CHAPTER 54:
CONFRONTATION IN THE
PALACE

Princess Layla moved swiftly through the grand corridors of the palace, her heart pounding with a mixture of anger and determination. She had overheard Malik and the Sultan discussing their plans to send another expedition to Al-Qamar, effectively undermining Tariq's mission. She could not stand by and allow such treachery to go unchallenged.

As she approached the Sultan's chamber, the guards stepped aside, recognizing the fierce resolve in her eyes. She entered without hesitation, finding the Sultan seated at his desk, poring over maps and documents. He looked up, surprised to see the princess standing before him with such intensity.

"Sultan," Layla began, her voice steady but filled with conviction, "I must speak with you about your plans regarding Al-Qamar and Tariq." The Sultan leaned back in his chair, his expression guarded. "Layla, this is a matter of state. It is not your place to interfere."

Layla's eyes flashed with defiance. "It is my place when it concerns treachery against a man who has risked his life for us. Tariq is out there, following the path we set for him, and you are already planning to double-cross him."

The Sultan's face hardened. "You do not understand the complexities of ruling, Layla. As Sultan, I must ensure the security and prosperity of our kingdom. Tariq's mission is uncertain, and we cannot afford to put all our hopes on a single person."

Layla took a step closer, her voice rising. "You speak of ruling, but where is your honor? Where is your integrity? Tariq believes in the promise you made to him. By sending another party, you betray not only him but also the values of leadership and trust."

The Sultan's eyes narrowed. "Leadership requires making difficult decisions, Layla. Sometimes, it means taking actions that seem harsh for the greater good. Al-Qamar holds immense power and knowledge—power that could secure our kingdom's future. I cannot gamble on the success of one man, no matter how capable."

Layla's voice softened, but her determination remained. "I understand the burdens of leadership, Sultan. I know that ruling is not always black and white. But this is not just about power or knowledge. It is about faith, trust, and the bonds we create. Tariq's journey is about more than just treasure—it is about honoring the legacy of Al-Qamar and our own integrity."

The Sultan sighed, the weight of his decisions visible on his face. "You speak with the passion of youth, Layla, but you lack the experience to understand the true cost of ruling. Every decision I make carries consequences, not just for me but for our people. I cannot afford to be sentimental."

Layla stepped closer, her eyes pleading. "And what will be the cost of this betrayal? How will it affect our people when they see that their ruler cannot be trusted? How will it affect you, knowing that you sacrificed honor for expedience? Tariq has the potential to succeed, and he deserves our support, not our duplicity."

The Sultan remained silent for a moment, contemplating her words. Finally, he spoke, his voice heavy with the weight of his office. "Perhaps you are right, Layla. Perhaps I have been too focused on securing power and not enough on the values that should guide us. But understand, the burdens of leadership are heavy, and sometimes, we must make choices that others cannot comprehend."

Layla placed a hand on his arm, her voice gentle but firm. "True leadership lies in balancing those burdens with honor and trust. Tariq's journey is a test not just for him but for all of us. Let us show that we can lead with integrity and faith."

The Sultan nodded slowly, a flicker of understanding in his eyes. "Very well, Layla. I will reconsider my decision. But know this—the path of leadership is fraught with challenges, and there will be times when we must make difficult choices."

Layla smiled, her heart filled with hope. "I understand, Sultan. And I will stand by you, just as I stand by Tariq. Together, we can navigate these challenges and emerge stronger."

As the Sultan returned to his maps and documents, Layla felt a sense of relief. She had planted a seed of doubt in his plans, and she hoped that it would grow into a commitment to honor and trust. The journey ahead was still uncertain, but with faith and integrity, they could face whatever challenges lay in wait.

CHAPTER 55: THE ESSENCE OF POWER

Princess Layla's heartfelt words had planted a seed of doubt in the Sultan's mind, but their conversation was far from over. As they stood in the opulent chamber, the Sultan leaned against his desk, contemplating the nature of power and what truly gave someone the right to rule.

"Layla," the Sultan began, his voice tinged with both weariness and curiosity, "you speak of honor and trust, but what truly gives someone the right to rule? Is it not the ability to wield power effectively and to ensure the prosperity and security of our people?"

Layla met his gaze, her eyes filled with determination. "Power alone does not grant the right to rule, Sultan. It is the manner in which one wields that power that defines a ruler. A ruler must possess wisdom, compassion, and integrity. Without these qualities, power becomes nothing more than a tool for tyranny." The Sultan raised an eyebrow, intrigued. "And what, in your view, defines true power?"

Layla took a deep breath, choosing her words carefully. "True power lies in the ability to inspire and uplift others. It is the strength to make difficult decisions with empathy and fairness. A ruler should be a servant to their people, guiding them with a steady hand and an open heart. It is not about domination but about fostering trust and unity."

The Sultan considered her words, his expression thoughtful. "But what of those who seek to challenge our rule? What of the threats that constantly loom over our kingdom? Does a ruler not need to be strong and unyielding to protect their people?"

Layla nodded. "Strength is indeed necessary, but it must be tempered with justice and mercy. A ruler who rules through fear and coercion may maintain control for a time, but such a reign is brittle and doomed to fall. True strength comes from earning the respect and loyalty of your people, from creating a bond that cannot be easily broken."

The Sultan sighed, running a hand through his graying hair. "You speak with the idealism of youth, Layla. But the world is a harsh place, filled with those who would exploit any sign of weakness."

Layla stepped closer, her voice soft yet firm. "And that is why it is all the more important to lead with integrity. Power used wisely can unite and strengthen. When people see a ruler who is fair, who listens, and who genuinely cares for their well-being, they will stand by that ruler through any storm."

The Sultan's eyes softened, a flicker of emotion crossing his face. "You remind me of your mother, Layla. She too believed in the power of compassion and integrity. Perhaps I have lost sight of those ideals in my quest to protect our kingdom."

Layla smiled gently. "It is never too late to return to those ideals, Sultan. To rule is to carry the weight of countless lives, and with that comes the responsibility to lead with honor. Our strength lies not just in our ability to wield power, but in our ability to inspire and uplift those we lead."

The Sultan nodded slowly, a sense of clarity washing over him. "You are wise beyond your years, Layla. Perhaps it is time I listened more to the voices of compassion and integrity. Tariq's journey is a testament to those values, and we should honor that."

Layla felt a surge of hope. "Thank you, Sultan. Together, we can guide our kingdom with the strength of our convictions and the wisdom of our hearts. Let us support Tariq and ensure that our actions reflect the true nature of leadership."

The Sultan embraced Layla, a gesture of both reconciliation and renewed purpose. "You have given me much to ponder, Layla. Let us move forward with a commitment to honor, trust, and the true essence of power."

As the night deepened, the palace seemed to breathe a sigh of relief, the tension easing with the newfound understanding between the Sultan and Layla. The journey ahead was still fraught with challenges, but with a renewed sense of integrity and purpose, they were ready to face whatever came their way.

CHAPTER 56: THE RELIC OF AL-TAHIRA

Princess Layla's conversation with the Sultan had given her hope, but also a deep sense of urgency. She knew that Tariq's journey was fraught with dangers, and while the guardians offered their wisdom and protection, she felt compelled to do more. The tales of an ancient relic, hidden deep within the Sultan's castle, came to mind—a relic that might hold the power to protect Tariq.

The relic, known as the Heart of Al-Tahira, was said to contain the essence of a powerful being. Legends spoke of its incredible protective capabilities, but also of the potential dangers that came with unleashing the being within. Despite the risks, Layla felt she had no choice. She had to find the relic and ensure Tariq's safety.

As the palace slumbered under the veil of night, Layla donned a simple cloak and slipped through the silent corridors, heading towards the deepest parts of the castle. She moved with determination, her heart pounding with each step. The path to the relic was fraught with obstacles, and only a few knew of its exact location.

Layla descended narrow, winding staircases, the air growing cooler and damper as she ventured deeper into the ancient structure. The walls, lined with old, faded tapestries, seemed to whisper secrets of times long past. She finally reached a heavy, iron-bound door, hidden behind a tapestry depicting a great battle.

She hesitated for a moment, then pushed the door open, revealing a dimly lit chamber. The room was filled with old scrolls, tomes, and artifacts, but at its center stood a pedestal, upon which rested a small, ornate box, housing an amulet, The Heart of Al-Tahira.

Layla approached the pedestal with reverence, her fingers trembling as she opened the box. Inside lay a amulets adorned with a gem, glowing with an otherworldly light. The air around it seemed to hum with energy, and Layla felt a mix of awe and fear.

As she reached out to touch the relic, a voice echoed in the chamber, soft yet commanding. "Who dares disturb the Heart of Al-Tahira?" Layla's breath caught in her throat. "I am Princess Layla. I seek the power of this relic to protect someone dear to me, who is on a perilous quest."

The voice seemed to sigh, a sound filled with ancient weariness. "The Heart of Al-Tahira holds great power, but it also binds a being of immense strength and complexity. To wield this power, you must understand the risks. The being within is neither wholly good nor evil, but a blend of both. Its essence can protect, but it can also corrupt."

Layla's resolve did not waver. "I understand the risks. But Tariq's journey is too important. If there is a chance that this relic can help him, I must take it." The voice grew softer, almost contemplative. "Very well, Princess Layla. The Heart of Al-Tahira shall be yours. But remember, to wield its power wisely, you must balance its dual nature. It is a heavy burden to bear."

With those words, the gem's light intensified, and Layla felt a surge of energy as the relic's power flowed into her. She closed the box, securing the Heart of Al-Tahira, and carefully placed it in her satchel. With the relic in her possession, she felt a mix of hope and apprehension.

As she made her way back to her chambers, Layla's thoughts were consumed by the warnings she had received. She would need to find a way to harness the relic's power without succumbing to its potential for corruption. But for now, she focused on the immediate goal—getting the Heart of Al-Tahira to Tariq.

Morning light filtered into the palace as Layla prepared for her journey to the high desert mountains. She knew the path would be dangerous, but her determination to protect Tariq and support his quest gave her strength. With the relic in hand and a heart full of resolve, she set out, ready to face whatever challenges lay ahead.

CHAPTER 57: A HEART HEAVY WITH DOUBT

As Princess Layla journeyed towards the high desert mountains, the weight of her decision to use the Heart of Al-Tahira grew heavier with each step. The morning sun bathed the rugged landscape in golden light, but her mind was clouded with uncertainty and doubt.

She rode on her swift horse, the relic secure in her satchel. The warnings of the mysterious voice echoed in her thoughts: the Heart of Al-Tahira held the essence of a powerful being, capable of great good but also prone to corruption. Layla had little knowledge of the relic's history or the nature of the being within. The risks were immense, and she feared that she might inadvertently bring harm to Tariq and his quest.

As she ascended the rocky paths, Layla's mind wandered back to the palace and her conversations with the Sultan. She had argued for honor and integrity, yet now she faced a dilemma that challenged those very principles. Was it prudent to use a power she did not fully understand, especially when the stakes were so high?

She found a shaded spot beneath a cluster of ancient trees and dismounted, letting her horse graze nearby. Sitting on a flat rock, she pulled the box containing the Heart of Al-Tahira from her satchel and opened it once more. The center gem of the amulet glowed with a mesmerizing light, and Layla could feel its energy pulsing in her hand.

"What am I to do?" she whispered to herself. "I want to protect Tariq, but at what cost?"

The forest seemed to listen, the leaves rustling gently in the breeze as if whispering their own counsel. Layla closed her eyes and took a deep breath, trying to center herself. She needed to think clearly, to weigh the potential benefits against the grave risks.

The being within the Heart of Al-Tahira was neither wholly good nor evil, but a blend of both. It could provide immense protection, but it could also bring unforeseen consequences. The essence of the relic's power was a double-edged sword, and Layla feared she might not be able to control it.

As she sat in contemplation, the image of Tariq's face filled her mind—his determination, his courage, and the love they shared. She knew that his journey was perilous, and that any advantage could make the difference between success and failure. But was she willing to gamble with such a volatile power?

Layla's thoughts turned to the guardians and their wisdom. They had placed their trust in Tariq and his ability to balance strength with compassion. Perhaps she could seek their guidance, or find a way to use the relic's power in a controlled manner.

As the sun climbed higher in the sky, Layla made her decision. She would continue her journey to Tariq, but she would not use the Heart of Al-Tahira recklessly. Instead, she would seek counsel from the guardians and learn more about the relic's true nature. Only then would she decide how to wield its power.

With a renewed sense of purpose, Layla secured the relic in her satchel and mounted her horse. The path ahead was still uncertain, but she felt a small measure of clarity. She would not let fear dictate her actions, but neither would she rush into using a power she did not fully understand.

As she rode towards the high desert mountains, Layla's heart was heavy with doubt but also filled with hope. She trusted that the journey would bring her the wisdom she needed, and that together with Tariq and the guardians, they would find a way to uncover the secrets of Al-Qamar and fulfill their destiny.

CHAPTER 58: THE RELEASE

Princess Layla continued her journey towards the high desert mountains, her heart filled with a mix of determination and trepidation. The decision to use the Heart of Al-Tahira weighed heavily on her mind, but she knew that time was running out. Tariq needed all the help he could get, and the relic might be their only hope.

As she reached a secluded clearing, surrounded by ancient rocks and a clear stream, Layla decided it was time. She dismounted her horse and took out the ornate box containing the relic. The gem inside glowed with an intense, mesmerizing light, pulsing with a rhythm that seemed almost alive.

Taking a deep breath, Layla opened the box and held the Heart of Al-Tahira in her hands. The air around her crackled with energy, and she felt a powerful surge coursing through her. She whispered a silent prayer, hoping she was making the right choice, and then spoke the incantation she had learned from the ancient texts in the palace.

A sudden burst of light erupted from the gem, and a figure began to materialize before her. The entity that emerged was a strange mix of shadow and red, its form constantly shifting and swirling. Its eyes, however, were what caught Layla's attention—they were filled with a profound sadness.

The entity looked around, taking in its surroundings, and then fixed its gaze on Layla. "Why have you released me?" it asked, its voice a melancholic whisper. "Do you understand the consequences of your actions?"

Layla swallowed hard, her heart pounding. "I released you to protect someone dear to me. He is on a perilous quest, and I believed you could help."

The entity sighed, its form flickering with each breath. "My release comes at a great cost. For every being freed from the Heart of Al-Tahira, another must take its place. This relic was created to balance the forces of light and darkness, to contain those who could not be allowed to roam freely."

Layla's eyes widened in horror. "I… I didn't know. I'm so sorry. Who will be imprisoned now?"

The entity's eyes grew even sadder. "It is not for me to say. The relic's magic is ancient and complex. It seeks balance, and it will choose someone who holds great power or potential. This is the burden of the Heart of Al-Tahira."

Layla felt a wave of guilt and sorrow wash over her. "Can you still help Tariq? Can you protect him on his journey?"

The entity nodded slowly. "I can offer my protection and guidance, but know that my powers are tied to the very balance of the world. Use my abilities wisely, for the consequences of imbalance are severe."

Tears welled up in Layla's eyes. "I never meant to cause harm. I only wanted to help."

The entity moved closer, its shadowy form comforting despite its eerie appearance. "Your intentions were pure, Princess. But the path of power is fraught with unintended consequences. Learn from this, and strive to understand the deeper forces at play in our world."

Layla nodded, her resolve strengthening. "I will. And I will do everything in my power to restore balance and make things right."

The entity placed a shadowy hand on her shoulder, a gesture of reassurance. "Then let us go to Tariq. Together, we may still achieve great things."

As they prepared to continue their journey, Layla couldn't shake the feeling of dread about who might be imprisoned within the Heart of Al-Tahira now. But she knew she couldn't turn back. With the entity's guidance, she hoped to find a way to protect Tariq and ensure that their quest would not lead to further harm.

With renewed determination, Layla mounted her horse, the entity following like a protective shadow. The path ahead was uncertain and filled with dangers, but she was ready to face whatever challenges lay ahead. The journey to uncover the secrets of Al-Qamar continued, each step guided by the wisdom she had gained and the lessons she had learned.

CHAPTER 59: THE NATURE
OF FREEDOM

As Princess Layla continued her journey towards Tariq, the entity released from the Heart of Al-Tahira followed closely, a constant reminder of the power and responsibility she now carried. The landscape around them was harsh and rugged, the high desert mountains looming ever closer. Layla's mind was heavy with thoughts about the entity's words and the nature of freedom, sacrifice, and choice.

They rode in silence for a time, the only sound the rhythmic clopping of hooves on the rocky ground. Finally, Layla turned to the entity, her curiosity and concern compelling her to speak. "May I ask you something?" she began, her voice tentative. The entity's shadowy form flickered as it nodded. "Of course, Princess. What is it you wish to know?" Layla hesitated for a moment, then asked, "You spoke of the consequences of your release and the balance that must be maintained. It made me think about the nature of freedom and sacrifice. Is freedom truly an illusion?"

The entity's eyes, filled with ancient wisdom and sadness, regarded her thoughtfully. "Freedom is a complex and multifaceted concept, Layla. In many ways, it is both real and illusory. True freedom often requires sacrifice, and the choices we make can bind us in ways we do not foresee." Layla pondered this. "So, our choices and the sacrifices we make can limit our freedom?"

The entity nodded. "Indeed. Every choice carries with it consequences and responsibilities. By choosing to release me, you have taken on a great burden, one that limits your own freedom in certain ways. Similarly, my release required the imprisonment of another, a sacrifice that maintains the balance of power."

Layla's heart ached at the thought. "But is there no way to achieve true freedom without such sacrifices?" The entity's form shifted slightly, its voice contemplative. "True freedom is a rare and precious thing, often found not in the absence of constraints, but in the acceptance and understanding of them. It is about finding balance and harmony within the choices we make and the responsibilities we bear."

Layla nodded slowly, absorbing the entity's words. "I see. So, freedom is not just about being unbound, but about making conscious choices and understanding the sacrifices involved." The entity smiled, a faint, melancholic expression. "Yes, Princess. Freedom is intertwined with responsibility and sacrifice. It is a journey of self-discovery and understanding, of learning to navigate the complexities of life and power."

Layla felt a sense of clarity and resolve. "Thank you for sharing your wisdom. I will do my best to honor the responsibilities that come with my choices and strive to maintain the balance." The entity's eyes softened. "You have a good heart, Layla. Your willingness to seek understanding and your commitment to balance will serve you well. Remember, the journey is as important as the destination, and the choices you make along the way define your path."

As they continued their journey, Layla felt a renewed sense of purpose and determination. The conversation with the entity had given her a deeper understanding of the nature of freedom and the importance of conscious choice and sacrifice. She was more resolved than ever to support Tariq and ensure that their quest would be guided by wisdom and integrity.

The landscape around them grew more rugged and foreboding, but Layla's heart was lightened by the knowledge she had gained. With the entity's guidance and the lessons she had learned, she felt ready to face whatever challenges lay ahead.

The journey to uncover the secrets of Al-Qamar continued, each step bringing Layla and Tariq closer to their destiny. Together, they would navigate the complexities of power, freedom, and sacrifice, striving to bring light and balance to the ancient mysteries they sought to unravel.

CHAPTER 60: A HEART HEAVY WITH SACRIFICE

Princess Layla rode on with the entity, her mind awash with the revelation of the true nature of the Heart of Al-Tahira. The entity had been a protector, but its release required the imprisonment of another, a balance that must be maintained. Layla realized with a heavy heart that the relic had chosen her as the one to take the entity's place.

As they reached a secluded plateau overlooking the high desert mountains, Layla dismounted her horse and faced the entity. The realization of her fate was clear in her eyes, but she held herself with a quiet dignity. "Is it true?" she asked, her voice barely a whisper. "Am I the one who must be imprisoned now?"

The entity nodded, its eyes filled with sorrow. "Yes, Princess Layla. The balance must be maintained. My release from the Heart of Al-Tahira means that another must take my place. The relic has chosen you, sensing your strength and your willingness to sacrifice for the greater good."

Layla's heart ached, but she accepted her fate with grace. "If this is what it takes to protect Tariq and ensure the success of his quest, then I accept. My life has always been dedicated to serving my people and those I care about. This is just another way to do that."

The entity's form flickered, its sadness evident. "Your bravery and selflessness are truly remarkable, Layla. The relic chose wisely. But know that your sacrifice will not be in vain. I will protect Tariq with all the power I possess, ensuring that his journey continues and that the secrets of Al-Qamar are uncovered."

Tears welled in Layla's eyes, but she smiled through them. "Thank you. Please tell Tariq that I believe in him and that my spirit will be with him every step of the way." The entity bowed its head, a gesture of deep respect. "I will, Princess. Your sacrifice will be honored, and your strength will inspire us all." As Layla placed the Heart of Al-Tahira back into the ornate box, she felt a surge of energy surround her. The relic's power began to envelop her, the air shimmering with magic. Layla closed her eyes, embracing her fate with a heavy yet resolute heart.

The world around her faded into darkness, and she felt herself being drawn into the relic. The sensation was both overwhelming and strangely comforting, as if the essence of the Heart of Al-Tahira was welcoming her with open arms. She became one with the relic, her consciousness merging with its ancient power.

The entity watched with a mix of sadness and gratitude as Layla disappeared into the Heart of Al-Tahira. It then turned its gaze towards the mountains, its resolve strengthened by the princess's sacrifice.

CHAPTER 61: THE GUARDIAN'S OATH

Tariq continued his journey through the high desert mountains, unaware of the events unfolding miles away. He navigated the rugged terrain with determination, the wisdom of the guardians guiding his steps. As he approached a narrow pass, a sudden surge of energy filled the air, stopping him in his tracks.

From the shadows emerged the entity, now fully manifested in its protective form. Tariq stared in awe and confusion, recognizing the being from the tales of the Heart of Al-Tahira.

"Who are you?" Tariq asked, his voice filled with curiosity and caution.

The entity stepped forward, its eyes meeting Tariq's with a solemn expression. "I am the guardian released from the Heart of Al-Tahira, sent to protect you on your quest. Princess Layla has made a great sacrifice to ensure your safety and success." Tariq's heart sank. "Layla… what has happened to her?"

The entity's eyes were filled with sadness. "She has taken my place within the relic, maintaining the balance of its power. Her spirit remains strong, and she has asked me to convey her belief in you and her unwavering support."

Tariq's eyes welled with tears, but he stood tall, his resolve hardening. "I will honor her sacrifice. We will uncover the secrets of Al-Qamar and ensure that her bravery is not in vain." The entity nodded, its form glowing with renewed purpose. "Together, we will face whatever challenges lie ahead. The spirit of Princess Layla will guide us, and her strength will be our beacon."

As Tariq and the entity continued their journey, the high desert mountains loomed large, filled with ancient mysteries and trials. With the spirit of Layla watching over them, they pressed on, determined to uncover the secrets of Al-Qamar and fulfill their destiny.

CHAPTER 62: A RACE AGAINST TREACHERY

As Tariq and the entity moved deeper into the high desert mountains, the air grew colder, and the path more treacherous. The presence of the entity gave Tariq a strange comfort, knowing that Princess Layla's sacrifice had brought him this powerful guardian. However, the weight of her absence and the urgency of their mission pressed heavily on him.

The entity, sensing Tariq's thoughts, spoke in a low, resonant voice. "Tariq, there is something you must know. The Sultan, in his impatience and desire for the treasures of Al-Qamar, has made plans that may jeopardize your quest." Tariq's eyes widened in surprise and concern. "What do you mean? What has the Sultan done?"

The entity's form flickered as it continued. "The Sultan has grown weary of waiting for your return. He doubts your success and has decided to send his own party to retrieve the treasures of Al-Qamar. This party is not only a backup plan but also a potential threat to you. They are ordered to bring back the treasures at any cost, even if it means betraying you." Tariq felt a surge of anger and determination. "So, the Sultan is willing to betray me to secure the treasures for himself? I trusted him."

The entity's eyes softened with understanding. "The Sultan's actions are driven by fear and ambition. He believes that securing the treasures will ensure the prosperity and security of his kingdom. However, his lack of faith in you and his willingness to betray you are dangerous. We must hurry to find the treasures before his party does."

Tariq nodded, his resolve hardening. "Then we have no time to lose. We must reach Al-Qamar and uncover its secrets before the Sultan's men do. I will not let Layla's sacrifice be in vain, nor will I allow the Sultan's treachery to succeed."

The entity's form glowed with renewed energy. "I will guide you and protect you, Tariq. Together, we will navigate the challenges ahead and ensure that the treasures of Al-Qamar are used for the greater good."

As they continued their journey, Tariq felt a renewed sense of urgency. The landscape around them grew more rugged and foreboding, the path winding through narrow canyons and over steep cliffs. The sun dipped lower in the sky, casting long shadows over the mountains.

With each step, Tariq's determination grew. He thought of Layla, her bravery and sacrifice fueling his resolve. The Sultan's betrayal only strengthened his commitment to uncovering the secrets of Al-Qamar and ensuring that the treasures were used wisely.

They traveled through the night, the entity's presence guiding them through the darkness. As dawn approached, they reached a vast plateau overlooking a hidden valley. In the center of the valley lay the entrance to Al-Qamar, its ancient gates glimmering in the early morning light.

Tariq and the entity descended into the valley, their hearts pounding with anticipation. The path to the gates was lined with ancient statues and inscriptions, hinting at the city's powerful magic and wisdom. As they approached the gates, the entity spoke once more.

"Beyond these gates lie the treasures of Al-Qamar, guarded by powerful magic and ancient trials. We must proceed with caution and wisdom, for the challenges ahead will test your resolve and strength."

Tariq nodded, his eyes fixed on the gates. "I am ready. Let us uncover the secrets of Al-Qamar and ensure that the treasures are used for the greater good."

With the entity by his side and the spirit of Princess Layla guiding him, Tariq stepped forward, ready to face whatever challenges lay ahead. The journey to uncover the secrets of Al-Qamar continued, each step bringing him closer to fulfilling his destiny and ensuring that the treasures were safeguarded from those who sought to misuse them.

CHAPTER 63: THE PIT OF SHADOWS

As Tariq and the entity ventured further into the hidden valley, the ancient gates of Al-Qamar loomed closer. The air grew thick with an otherworldly energy, and the ground beneath their feet seemed to hum with latent magic. Every step Tariq took felt heavier, the weight of the journey pressing down on him.

Suddenly, the path narrowed, leading to a vast pit that stretched across the valley floor. Tariq halted at the edge, peering into the darkness below. The pit seemed to pulse with a malevolent energy, and from its depths came a chorus of unsettling sounds—hisses, growls, and whispers that sent chills down Tariq's spine.

The entity moved closer, its shadowy form flickering with concern. "This is the Pit of Shadows," it explained, its voice filled with gravity. "It is a barrier designed to prevent intruders from reaching Al-Qamar. Within it dwell creatures born of dark magic and ancient curses. We must find a way to cross without falling prey to them."

Tariq nodded, his eyes scanning the pit for any possible route across. As he did, the creatures within began to emerge, crawling and slithering up the walls of the pit. They were monstrous, nightmarish beings that defied description.

The first creature to appear was a massive, serpentine beast with scales as black as obsidian and eyes that glowed with an eerie green light. Its body was covered in jagged spines, and it moved with a sinuous, predatory grace. As it reared up, it let out a bone-chilling hiss, revealing rows of razor-sharp teeth.

Following the serpent came a swarm of smaller, but no less menacing, creatures. These were twisted, humanoid figures with elongated limbs and twisted features. Their skin was a sickly gray, and their eyes were empty, soulless voids. They moved with a disturbing, unnatural agility, clambering over each other in their eagerness to reach Tariq and the entity.

From the depths of the pit also emerged enormous, bat-like creatures with leathery wings and talons that gleamed in the dim light. They swooped and circled above, their screeches echoing through the valley like a cacophony of nightmares. Their eyes burned with a fiery red intensity, and their jaws snapped hungrily at the air.

Tariq's heart pounded in his chest as the creatures closed in, their menacing presence making it clear that they would not allow him to pass without a fight. He looked to the entity, seeking guidance and reassurance.

The entity's form glowed brighter, its voice calm and resolute. "These creatures are born of darkness and fear, but they can be overcome with light and courage. We must use the power of the artifacts and your own inner strength to push through."

Tariq took a deep breath, his resolve hardening. He drew the Elemental Amulet from his satchel, its power thrumming in his hand. As he held it aloft, the amulet began to glow with a brilliant light, casting long shadows across the valley.

The light seemed to repel the creatures, causing them to recoil and hiss in fury. The serpentine beast writhed in pain, its scales sizzling where the light touched them. The humanoid figures shielded their eyes, their soulless voids reflecting the fear they had instilled in others. The bat-like creatures screeched and flapped their wings, struggling to maintain their aerial dominance.

With the entity's guidance, Tariq began to channel the power of the amulet, directing beams of light towards the creatures. The light cut through the darkness, creating a path across the pit. The creatures shrieked and retreated, unable to withstand the purity of the light.

Tariq and the entity moved forward, the light protecting them as they crossed the pit. The creatures continued to claw and snap at the edges of the light, but they could not breach its protective barrier. Step by step, Tariq advanced, his determination unwavering. As they reached the far side of the pit, the light from the amulet began to dim, its power spent for the moment. The creatures, sensing an opportunity, surged forward once more, but the entity stepped in front of Tariq, its form expanding to shield him.

"We have crossed the first barrier," the entity said, its voice filled with a mixture of relief and caution. "But the journey is far from over. Al-Qamar's secrets lie ahead, and we must be prepared for whatever challenges come next." Tariq nodded, his heart still pounding but his spirit unbroken. "Thank you for your guidance and protection. We will face whatever comes together."

With the Pit of Shadows behind them, Tariq and the entity continued their journey towards the gates of Al-Qamar. The path ahead was still fraught with danger, but Tariq's resolve was stronger than ever. With the spirit of Princess Layla watching over them and the wisdom of the guardians guiding his steps, he was ready to uncover the secrets of the ancient city and fulfill his destiny.

CHAPTER 64: THE CONDEMNED CREATURES

As Tariq and the entity stood at the edge of the Pit of Shadows, the light from the Elemental Amulet dimming, Tariq felt a pull of curiosity. The creatures, now kept at bay by the residual light, seemed more than just mindless beasts. There was an air of tragedy about them, a sense of stories untold. Tariq took a deep breath and decided to speak to them, hoping to understand their plight.

"Who are you?" Tariq called out, his voice echoing in the vastness of the pit. "What brought you to this place?" The creatures hissed and growled, their initial aggression giving way to a murmur of whispers. Finally, the massive serpentine beast, its green eyes glowing with a melancholic light, slithered closer and began to speak. "We were once noble

249

beings," the serpent said, its voice a deep, resonant rumble. "Guardians, scholars, and warriors of Al-Qamar. We dedicated our lives to the protection and prosperity of the ancient city." Tariq's eyes widened in surprise. "How did you end up here, condemned to this pit?"

The serpentine beast sighed, its scales rippling with sorrow. "Our aspirations were noble, but over time, ambition and desire for power corrupted us. We sought to harness the darker magics of Al-Qamar, believing we could control them and use them for good. But we were wrong."

Another creature, one of the twisted humanoid figures, stepped forward. Its voice was softer, filled with regret. "We fell prey to our own hubris. The dark magic we sought to control consumed us, twisted our forms, and poisoned our minds. In our desperation to atone for our mistakes, we attempted to destroy the source of the corruption, but it was too late." The bat-like creature swooped down, its eyes burning with a mix of anger and sadness. "The guardians of Al-Qamar could not bring themselves to destroy us, for we were once their kin. Instead, they bound us to this pit, a perpetual reminder of the consequences of our folly. We are condemned to guard the path to Al-Qamar, preventing others from making the same mistakes." Tariq's heart ached with empathy. "I'm sorry for your suffering. Is there no way to free you from this fate?"

The serpent shook its head slowly. "Our punishment is eternal, a necessary balance for the dark powers we unleashed. But your compassion is appreciated, young wanderer. Perhaps, through your actions, you can prevent others from falling into the same trap." The humanoid figure nodded. "Remember our story, Tariq. Power is a double-edged sword. It can achieve great things, but it can also corrupt and destroy. Seek wisdom and balance in your quest."

Tariq bowed his head in respect. "I will honor your advice and carry your story with me. Thank you for sharing your wisdom. The creatures slowly retreated into the shadows, their forms blending with the darkness. The pit fell silent once more, but the echoes of their words lingered in Tariq's mind. He felt a renewed sense of purpose and a deeper understanding of the perils that lay ahead.

Turning to the entity, Tariq spoke with determination. "We must continue. Al-Qamar holds the answers we seek, but we must tread carefully and remember the lessons we've learned." The entity nodded, its eyes filled with approval. "You have shown compassion and wisdom, Tariq. Let us proceed with caution and resolve." With the path now clear, Tariq and the entity resumed their journey towards the ancient gates of Al-Qamar. The city's secrets awaited them, and with the knowledge they had gained from the condemned creatures, they were better prepared to face the challenges ahead.

CHAPTER 65: THE WEIGHT OF MEMORIES

As Tariq and the entity continued their journey towards the gates of Al-Qamar, the air grew colder and more charged with magic. The path ahead was still fraught with dangers, but the lessons learned from the pit of creatures gave them a newfound understanding and caution. The entity, sensing Tariq's deep contemplation, decided to share more of its own experiences. "Tariq," the entity began, its voice carrying a somber tone, "there is something I need to share with you. The creatures we encountered in the pit were not just strangers to me. Many of them were once my friends, comrades, and fellow guardians." Tariq looked at the entity, his eyes filled with empathy and curiosity. "You knew them? How did they come to be in such a state?" The entity's form flickered with a mix of sorrow and regret. "Long ago, Al-Qamar was a city of great wisdom and power, protected by noble beings who dedicated their lives to its preservation. I was among them, and I witnessed the gradual corruption of many who sought to wield the darker magics of the city."

Tariq listened intently, his heart heavy with the weight of the entity's memories. "It must have been difficult to watch your friends and comrades fall into darkness." The entity nodded, its eyes glowing with a deep sadness. "It was a time of great turmoil. We were all tempted by the promise of greater power and knowledge. Some believed that by mastering the dark arts, they could achieve greater good. But the darkness is insidious; it corrupts slowly, making noble intentions twisted and malevolent." Tariq sighed, the enormity of the entity's past weighing on him. "And you? How did you resist the temptation?"

The entity's form steadied, a faint light flickering within. "I was fortunate to see the warnings in time. I chose to embrace the balance of light and shadow, understanding that true power lies not in domination but in harmony. But my efforts to save my friends were in vain. Many of them succumbed to the darkness, and I was powerless to stop their descent." Tariq's voice was filled with compassion. "I'm sorry you had to go through that. It must have been incredibly painful."

The entity's eyes softened. "It was, but it also taught me the importance of vigilance and the strength of the heart. Watching my friends become creatures of darkness was a constant reminder of the fine line we walk between light and shadow. It is a struggle we must all face, and one that requires constant self-awareness and discipline."

As they walked, the entity continued to share its memories, painting a vivid picture of a once-glorious city now shrouded in mystery and darkness. Tariq felt a profound connection to the entity, understanding that their journey was not just about uncovering ancient treasures but also about confronting the very nature of power and its potential for corruption.

"The guardians of Al-Qamar," the entity continued, "were not just protectors but also stewards of its wisdom. We were entrusted with the city's secrets, and it was our duty to ensure that they were used for the greater good. But the temptation of absolute power was too great for many, leading to their downfall."

Tariq nodded, his resolve strengthening. "I will honor their memory by ensuring that our quest remains true to the values of wisdom and balance. The treasures of Al-Qamar must be safeguarded and used wisely, not for personal gain or domination."

The entity smiled, a sense of pride and hope emanating from its form. "You have a noble heart, Tariq. Your determination and compassion will guide you well. Together, we will face the challenges ahead and uncover the secrets of Al-Qamar with integrity and wisdom."

As they approached the ancient gates of Al-Qamar, the weight of their journey and the memories shared deepened Tariq's understanding of the path he walked. The city's secrets awaited them, and with the entity's guidance and the lessons of the past, he felt prepared to face whatever lay ahead.

CHAPTER 66: THE NATURE OF POWER

Tariq and the entity continued their journey through the ancient gates of Al-Qamar, the path ahead filled with an aura of ancient magic and mystery. As they walked, the conversation turned to the nature of power, a topic that weighed heavily on both their minds.

"Tariq," the entity began, its voice thoughtful, "we have encountered many who sought power for noble purposes, only to be consumed by it. The nature of power is complex, and its use demands great responsibility. It is essential to understand this as we move forward."

Tariq nodded, his thoughts drifting to the lessons he had learned from the guardians and the condemned creatures. "Power can be a force for good, but it can also corrupt if not wielded with wisdom and integrity. How can one stave off corruption while holding power?"

The entity's form flickered with a gentle light. "Power itself is neither good nor evil; it is the intent and actions of those who wield it that determine its nature. To stave off corruption, one must constantly reflect on their motives and remain grounded in their values. Surrounding oneself with wise and honest advisors is also crucial, as they can offer perspectives and guidance."

Tariq considered this, thinking of the guardians who had guided him thus far. "So, it's about maintaining a balance and staying true to one's principles, even when faced with difficult choices?"

"Exactly," the entity affirmed. "Power should be used to uplift and protect, not to dominate or control. It is a tool for service, not for personal gain. This requires humility and a commitment to the greater good."

The conversation reminded Tariq of the actions of the Sultan, and he couldn't help but draw a contrast. "The Sultan... he wields power but seems to have lost sight of these principles. His impatience and desire for control have led him to betray trust and consider actions that serve his interests, rather than the well-being of his people."

The entity's eyes glowed with understanding. "The Sultan's actions reflect the dangers of unchecked ambition and fear. His desire to secure the treasures of Al-Qamar has blinded him to the true purpose of power. He sees it as a means to solidify his rule, rather than as a responsibility to protect and serve his people."

Tariq's resolve hardened. "I must ensure that the treasures of Al-Qamar are used wisely. They must not fall into the hands of those who seek power for selfish reasons. I must honor the lessons we've learned and the sacrifices that have been made."

The entity's form shimmered with approval. "Your commitment to these principles is what sets you apart, Tariq. Remember, the true measure of a leader is not in their ability to wield power, but in their capacity to use it with wisdom, compassion, and integrity."

As they walked, Tariq reflected on the importance of these values. The path to Al-Qamar was not just a physical journey but a moral and philosophical one as well. He knew that maintaining his commitment to these principles would be crucial in navigating the challenges ahead and in safeguarding the treasures of the ancient city.

The conversation with the entity deepened Tariq's understanding of the nature of power and the responsibilities that came with it. He felt a renewed sense of purpose, determined to use the knowledge and treasures of Al-Qamar to benefit the greater good.

With the entity by his side and the lessons of the past guiding his steps, Tariq pressed on, ready to face whatever challenges awaited them within the ancient city. The journey was far from over, but with wisdom and integrity as his compass, he felt prepared to navigate the complexities of power and ensure that the legacy of Al-Qamar was honored and preserved.

CHAPTER 67: THE SHADOW OF DOUBT

As Tariq and the entity delved deeper into the ancient city of Al-Qamar, the weight of their mission pressed heavily upon them. The ruins around them whispered of a once-great civilization, now shrouded in mystery and magic. Despite the progress they had made, a shadow of doubt began to creep into the entity's mind.

The entity had been released from the Heart of Al-Tahira with a solemn vow to protect Tariq and aid him in his quest. However, the burden of its own past and the sacrifices it had witnessed began to gnaw at its resolve. The memories of noble beings turned to darkness and the endless cycle of power and corruption weighed heavily on its ethereal shoulders.

As they reached a grand hall filled with intricate carvings and ancient symbols, Tariq paused to study the surroundings. The entity, sensing an opportunity, floated nearby, its thoughts clouded with uncertainty.

"Tariq," the entity began, its voice hesitant, "do you ever wonder if our efforts are truly worth the sacrifices we've made?" Tariq looked up from the carvings, a look of surprise on his face. "What do you mean?"

The entity's form flickered, its voice filled with a deep melancholy. "I have seen so many noble beings succumb to darkness, their aspirations twisted by the power they sought to wield. Sometimes I wonder if it's possible to truly remain uncorrupted. The cycle of power and corruption seems never-ending."

Tariq's expression softened. "I understand your concerns. The nature of power is indeed complex and fraught with danger. But I believe that with wisdom, integrity, and the right intentions, it is possible to use power for good."

The entity sighed, a soft, echoing sound. "But what if even the purest of intentions are not enough? What if we are destined to repeat the same mistakes, to fall into the same traps?"

As Tariq continued to explore the grand hall, the entity's thoughts grew darker. It began to question its devotion to Tariq and the mission. The memories of its friends and comrades, once noble beings now condemned to darkness, haunted it. The entity started to entertain thoughts of betrayal or escape, considering whether it could break free from its own cycle of servitude and find a different path.

"Perhaps," the entity mused aloud, "there is another way. A way to break free from this cycle, to escape the burdens we carry."

Tariq turned to face the entity, concern etched on his features. "What are you saying? Are you thinking of leaving?"

The entity's eyes glowed with a mix of sadness and determination. "I do not know. I have devoted myself to this mission, to protecting you and uncovering the secrets of Al-Qamar. But the weight of the past, the endless cycle of power and corruption, makes me question whether it is worth it. What if I could be free from these burdens?"

Tariq stepped closer, his voice gentle but firm. "I cannot pretend to understand the full extent of your struggles, but I believe in our mission. We have the opportunity to learn from the past, to ensure that the treasures of Al-Qamar are used wisely. Your guidance has been invaluable, and I need you by my side."

The entity's form flickered, the internal conflict evident. "Your faith in me is heartening, Tariq. But the temptation to escape, to seek a different path, is strong. I fear that if I stay, I might fall into the same traps that ensnared so many before me."

Tariq reached out, his hand passing through the entity's ethereal form but conveying a sense of solidarity. "We face this journey together. Your wisdom and experience can help us navigate the dangers ahead. If you leave, I will lose more than just a guardian—I will lose a friend and a guide."

The entity's eyes softened, the flickering light stabilizing. "Perhaps you are right, Tariq. The path of power and responsibility is fraught with peril, but it is also a path that offers hope and redemption. I will stay, for now, and see this journey through. But know that the shadow of doubt remains, and I will need your support to stave off the temptations of darkness."

Tariq nodded, his heart filled with gratitude and determination. "Together, we will uncover the secrets of Al-Qamar and ensure that the treasures are safeguarded. We will honor the sacrifices made and strive to break the cycle of corruption."

With a renewed sense of purpose, Tariq and the entity continued their journey through the ancient city, each step guided by the lessons of the past and the hope for a brighter future. The road ahead was still uncertain, but with the bond they shared, they were ready to face whatever challenges lay in wait.

CHAPTER 68: THE CRYSTAL SHIMMERS

As Tariq and the entity ventured deeper into the ancient city of Al-Qamar, the air around them seemed to hum with a strange energy. The ruins whispered secrets of the past, and the shadows cast by the crumbling walls danced with an unsettling life of their own.

Tariq's attention was drawn to the artifact he had carried since the beginning of his journey—a small, intricately carved crystal with ancient symbols etched into its surface. It had been a gift from one of the guardians, intended to dispel illusion and protect one from deceit. But now, the crystal was behaving erratically, pulsing with an intense light and emitting a low, vibrating hum.

"What's happening?" Tariq asked, his voice filled with confusion and concern as he held the crystal in his hand. "Why is the crystal acting like this?"

The entity, floating nearby, watched with a mixture of apprehension and understanding. It recognized the crystal of clarity and its reaction for what it truly was: a warning. The crystal had detected the entity's thoughts of betrayal and was focusing its energies to protect Tariq from potential harm.

"It's… it's reacting to the energies around us," the entity said, its voice carefully measured to conceal the full truth. "This place is filled with ancient magic. The artifact must be sensitive to it."

Tariq frowned, studying the crystal's glowing symbols. "But it's never acted this way before. It feels like it's trying to tell me something." The entity's form flickered as it moved closer, trying to project an aura of calm. "The artifact is a powerful tool, Tariq. It could be sensing any number of things in these ruins. Ancient wards, residual magic… there are many possibilities."

But deep down, the entity knew the artifact was reacting to its own inner turmoil. The thoughts of escape and betrayal had triggered the crystal's protective mechanisms, and it was trying to shield Tariq from the perceived threat. The entity had to tread carefully to avoid revealing its true intentions. "Perhaps it's trying to guide us," the entity suggested, hoping to divert Tariq's suspicions. "Let's follow its lead and see where it takes us. There may be something important it wants us to find."

Tariq nodded, though his concern was evident. "Alright. Let's see where it leads." They continued through the ancient corridors, the artifact's light growing stronger and more focused. It seemed to be pointing them towards a specific direction, its energy pulsing in rhythm with their steps. Tariq felt a strange mix of anticipation and unease, but he trusted the artifact's guidance.

As they ventured deeper into the heart of Al-Qamar, the ruins became more elaborate, the walls lined with intricate carvings and ancient texts. The air grew thicker with magic, and the shadows seemed to move with a life of their own.

The entity remained silent, its thoughts racing. It needed to keep Tariq's trust, to ensure that its own doubts and fears did not jeopardize their mission. But the artifact's relentless focus on it was a constant reminder of the potential consequences of its wavering loyalty. "Tariq," the entity said, its voice filled with a forced calm, "be prepared for anything. This place holds many secrets, and we must be vigilant."

Tariq nodded, his grip tightening on the artifact. "I will. And thank you for your guidance." They reached a large chamber, its walls adorned with glowing symbols and ancient inscriptions. The artifact's light pulsed brightly, illuminating a pedestal in the center of the room. On the pedestal rested another artifact, a staff, large and ornate. "This must be it," Tariq said, his voice filled with awe. "The crystal has led us here for a reason."

The entity floated closer, studying the room with a keen eye. It felt the power emanating from the staff and knew that it could hold the key to their quest. But the crystal in Tariq's hand continued to hum, its light casting suspicious glances at the entity.

"Be cautious, Tariq," the entity warned, hiding its own turmoil. "This crystal is powerful. We must approach it with respect and care."

Tariq nodded, stepping forward to examine the pedestal. As he did, the crystal in his hand pulsed one last time, its light dimming as if satisfied that it had fulfilled its purpose. Tariq felt a sense of reassurance, though the underlying tension remained.

With the entity by his side, Tariq reached out to the staff, ready to uncover its secrets. The path ahead was still fraught with challenges, but with the guidance of the artifacts and the lessons learned along the way, they pressed on, determined to fulfill their destiny and protect the treasures of Al-Qamar.

CHAPTER 69: THE
SULTAN'S MERCENARIES

Under the cloak of night, the Sultan's mercenaries trudged through the desolate expanse of the desert mountains. The air was thick with an eerie silence, broken only by the occasional howl of the wind and the crunch of sand beneath their boots. The shadows cast by the rugged terrain seemed to shift and dance, playing tricks on their weary eyes.

Khalid, the leader of the mercenary group, signaled for a halt. His men, hardened warriors all, gathered around him with a mixture of wariness and unease. The desert mountains were known for their treacherous paths and ancient magic, and even these seasoned fighters could not shake the feeling of dread that hung in the air. "We need to stay vigilant," Khalid said, his voice low but firm. "These mountains hold many secrets, and we're not the first to seek the treasures of Al-Qamar. We must be ready for anything." One of the mercenaries, a burly man named Farid, glanced around nervously. "The stories say these mountains are cursed, filled with ancient spirits and dark magic. Do you think the Sultan knows what he's sending us into?"

Khalid's eyes narrowed. "The Sultan is desperate for the treasures of Al-Qamar. He's willing to risk anything to get them, including our lives. But remember, we're here for a reason. The reward for success will be great." Another mercenary, a lithe woman named Zhara, shivered despite the warmth of the night. "I've heard tales of guardians and monstrous creatures that roam these lands. We must tread carefully. This is not just about treasure—it's about survival." Khalid nodded, his grip tightening on his sword. "Agreed. We'll move in formation and keep our eyes and ears open. Any sign of danger, we regroup immediately. Understood?"

The mercenaries murmured their assent, their faces grim and determined. As they resumed their march, the darkness seemed to press in around them, the shadows growing longer and more menacing. Every rustle of the wind, every distant sound, set their nerves on edge.

The path ahead was treacherous, winding through narrow canyons and over jagged rocks. The moon cast an otherworldly glow on the landscape, illuminating strange symbols carved into the stone.

The mercenaries felt as though they were being watched, unseen eyes tracking their every move.

Khalid's thoughts turned to the stories he had heard as a child, tales of ancient guardians who protected the secrets of Al-Qamar with fierce determination. He wondered if those stories held any truth, and if so, what lay in wait for them in the heart of the mountains.

As they continued their journey, the sense of unease grew stronger. The air seemed to hum with a strange energy, and the mercenaries could feel the weight of ancient magic pressing down on them. It was as if the very mountains themselves were alive, whispering secrets and warnings to those who dared to venture within. Farid, ever the skeptic, grumbled under his breath. "I don't like this. We should have turned back when we had the chance." Zhara shot him a sharp look. "And go back to the Sultan empty-handed? You know what he does to those who fail him. We have no choice but to press on." Khalid listened to their exchange, his own doubts gnawing at him. He had pledged loyalty to the Sultan, but the cost of that loyalty was becoming increasingly clear. The treasures of Al-Qamar might bring wealth and power, but at what price?

As they neared a particularly steep and narrow pass, Khalid held up a hand to signal another halt. "We'll rest here for a moment. Keep your weapons ready and your senses sharp. We're entering the heart of the mountains now."

The mercenaries settled in, their eyes scanning the darkness for any sign of movement. The air was thick with tension, and Khalid could almost feel the weight of the ancient magic around them. He knew that the true test lay ahead, and that they would need all their skill and courage to survive what was to come.

In the silence of the desert mountains, the mercenaries waited, their hearts heavy with anticipation and fear. The journey to uncover the secrets of Al-Qamar had only just begun, and the path ahead was filled with unknown dangers and ancient mysteries.

CHAPTER 70: THE SHADOW SENTINELS

As the mercenaries settled in the narrow pass for a brief rest, the air grew colder, and the shadows around them seemed to deepen. The eerie silence was broken by a low, haunting whisper that sent shivers down their spines. Khalid, ever alert, stood up, his eyes scanning the darkness. "What was that?" Zhara asked, her voice tense.

Before Khalid could respond, figures began to materialize from the shadows, their forms ethereal and menacing. The mercenaries instinctively drew their weapons, but Khalid held up a hand, signaling them to wait. The shadowy figures, known as the Shadow Sentinels, approached with an air of ancient authority. "Lower your weapons," one of the Sentinels said, its voice a cold whisper. "We mean you no immediate harm." Khalid, sensing the power radiating from these beings, motioned for his men to comply. "Who are you?" he demanded. "What do you want?"

The leading Sentinel stepped forward, its eyes glowing faintly in the darkness. "We are the Shadow Sentinels, guardians of the ancient magic of Al-Qamar. You seek the treasures of the city, but you cannot claim them without our aid." Farid, unable to contain his curiosity, spoke up. "Why should we trust you? What do you gain from helping us?"

The Sentinel's eyes narrowed. "We seek to change the course of this land, to reshape it with the power we possess. But our powers are bound by the ancient magic that created us. To wield our full strength, we require human hosts."

Khalid's eyes widened. "Human hosts? What does that mean?"

Another Sentinel stepped forward, its voice equally chilling. "We need your bodies to channel our magic. In return, you will gain immense power, enough to control the treasures of Al-Qamar and reshape the world as you see fit. Together, we can achieve greatness."

Zhara looked skeptical. "And what happens to us if we agree? Do we become like you, bound to the shadows?" The leading Sentinel shook its head. "No. You will retain your consciousness and free will. Our power will amplify yours, but you will remain in

274

control. The only price is that our essence will be intertwined with yours." Khalid considered the offer, weighing the risks and rewards. "If we agree, what guarantees do we have that you won't betray us once you have what you want?"

The Sentinel's gaze was steady. "Our interests align, mortal. We seek to break free from the confines of this ancient magic and restore balance to the land. With your help, we can achieve this. Betrayal is not in our interest."

Farid, ever the skeptic, muttered under his breath. "This sounds too good to be true."

Khalid turned to his men, seeing the mix of fear and curiosity in their eyes. He knew the dangers were great, but the promise of power was tempting. "We need to decide together. The treasures of Al-Qamar could bring us immense wealth and influence, but the risks are high."

Zhara stepped forward, her expression resolute. "I say we take the chance. We're already deep into this. Turning back now means facing the Sultan's wrath empty-handed. With the power of the Sentinels, we stand a chance."

The other mercenaries murmured their agreement, the lure of power outweighing their fears. Khalid turned back to the Sentinels. "Very well. We accept your offer. How do we proceed?"

The leading Sentinel's eyes gleamed with satisfaction. "Come closer, and we shall bind our essence to yours. The process will be quick, and you will feel our power flow through you."

The mercenaries stepped forward, their hearts pounding with a mixture of anticipation and dread. The Sentinels extended their shadowy hands, touching each mercenary lightly. A surge of energy coursed through them, filling them with a sense of strength and power they had never known.

Khalid felt the darkness intertwine with his own essence, a cold yet invigorating presence. He looked at his men and saw the same realization in their eyes. They had taken a dangerous step, but the power they now possessed was undeniable.

The Sentinels, now bound to their human hosts, spoke in unison. "With our powers combined, we shall claim the treasures of Al-Qamar and reshape the destiny of this land. The path ahead is fraught with peril, but together, we are unstoppable."

With renewed determination and the power of the Sentinels coursing through them, the mercenaries continued their journey through the desert mountains. The treasures of Al-Qamar awaited, and with the ancient magic on their side, they were ready to face whatever challenges lay ahead.

CHAPTER 71: THE SHADOW KING'S EMERGENCE

As the last of the Shadow Sentinels bound their essence to the mercenaries, a palpable shift in the air occurred. The transformation was complete, and Khalid and his men felt a surge of unprecedented power coursing through their veins. They had become conduits for the ancient magic, their senses amplified and their strength magnified.

But with this newfound power came an unsettling realization. A massive shadow loomed over the mountain, growing larger and more defined with each passing moment. The darkness coalesced into a towering figure, its form taking on the shape of a giant. The ground trembled beneath its weight, and the air crackled with dark energy. Khalid's eyes widened in horror as he recognized the being before them. "What have we done?"

The giant shadow's eyes glowed with a malevolent light, its presence exuding an aura of ancient and terrible power. The mercenaries, now linked to the Sentinels, felt a cold dread settle in their hearts. They had unwittingly released a force far greater and more dangerous than they had anticipated.

The leading Sentinel, still bound to Khalid, spoke with a mixture of awe and fear. "This is the Shadow King, the ancient ruler imprisoned within the depths of these mountains. Our liberation has freed him from his prison."

The Shadow King's voice boomed across the landscape, a deep, resonant sound that seemed to shake the very foundations of the mountains. "You have freed me from my eternal bondage. For that, I am both grateful and bound to repay your actions."

Farid, his voice trembling, asked, "What does that mean for us?"

The Shadow King's gaze fell upon the mercenaries, and a cruel smile twisted his dark features. "It means that you have become my instruments. The power you now possess is a fraction of my own. Together, we will reclaim the treasures of Al-Qamar and reshape this land in my image."

Khalid felt a surge of defiance. "We didn't free you to become your slaves! We sought power and control, not subjugation." The Shadow King's laughter echoed ominously. "Power always comes with a price, Khalid. You sought to control forces beyond your understanding, and now you must bear the consequences. Serve me, and you will have power beyond your wildest dreams. Defy me, and you will be crushed under my might."

The mercenaries exchanged uneasy glances, the weight of their choice pressing heavily upon them. Zhara stepped forward, her voice steady despite her fear. "What do you want us to do?"

The Shadow King's eyes gleamed with dark ambition. "First, we must secure the treasures of Al-Qamar. They hold the key to restoring my full strength. Once that is done, we will reshape the kingdoms of this land, bending them to our will."

Khalid clenched his fists, the conflict within him evident. The power they had gained was intoxicating, but the cost was steep. "And if we refuse?"

The Shadow King's expression turned cold and menacing. "Then you will face a fate worse than death. But know this: resistance is futile. The power you wield binds you to me, and through it, I can control your very essence."

The realization of their predicament settled heavily upon the mercenaries. They had sought power and had found it, but in doing so, they had unleashed a force that threatened to consume them. Khalid's mind raced, searching for a way to turn this situation to their advantage.

With a resigned nod, Khalid spoke. "We will follow you, Shadow King. But know this—we seek the treasures for our own purposes as well. We are not mere pawns in your game." The Shadow King's smile widened, his eyes glittering with dark amusement. "Ambition and defiance—qualities I admire. Very well, Khalid. Serve me well, and you shall be rewarded beyond measure. Now, let us move forward. The treasures of Al-Qamar await."

As the Shadow King led the way, the mercenaries followed, their hearts heavy with the knowledge of what they had unleashed. The path ahead was fraught with peril and uncertainty, but they were bound by their choices and the power that now coursed through their veins. Together with the Shadow King, they would seek the treasures of Al-Qamar and confront the consequences of their ambition.

CHAPTER 72: THE SHADOW KING'S REVELATION

As the Shadow King led the mercenaries through the dark, winding paths of the desert mountains, the air grew colder and more oppressive. The night seemed to close in around them, amplifying the ancient power that radiated from the towering figure. The mercenaries, bound by the essence of the Shadow Sentinels, followed with a mix of awe and fear.

After a time, Khalid, unable to contain his curiosity and apprehension, spoke up. "Shadow King, you mentioned that you were imprisoned. Why were you bound, and what are your true intentions now that you are free?"

The Shadow King's eyes glowed with a deep, dark light as he turned to address the group. His voice was a resonant echo, filled with centuries of anger and sorrow. "Long ago, I was a ruler of this land, a being of immense power and ambition. I sought to harness the ancient magic of Al-Qamar to create a kingdom where my will reigned supreme. But my vision was deemed too dangerous, too corrupting, and the guardians of Al-Qamar conspired to imprison me."

Zhara, her eyes wide with intrigue, asked, "How were you imprisoned?" The Shadow King's expression darkened. "The guardians used their combined magic they tricked me, promising an alliance, then bound me within the mountain shadows, sealing me away for eternity."

Farid, ever skeptical, interjected, "And now that you are free, what is it that you seek to accomplish?" The Shadow King's eyes burned with a fierce determination. "My imprisonment gave me time to reflect on the nature of power and magic. I realized that magic, while a source of great strength, is also a source of endless corruption and conflict. It twists noble intentions and breeds chaos. My goal now is to destroy all magic in this land, to rid the world of its influence once and for all."

Khalid's brow furrowed. "Destroy all magic? But magic is intertwined with the very fabric of this land. How can you hope to achieve that?"

The Shadow King's gaze was unwavering. "The treasures of Al-Qamar hold the key. They contain the essence of ancient magic, and with them, I can create a spell powerful enough to sever the connection between magic and this world. It will be a cataclysmic event, but it is the only way to ensure that magic no longer corrupts and destroys."

The mercenaries exchanged uneasy glances. The power they had gained was tied to the magic of the Sentinels, and the thought of losing it filled them with dread. Zhara voiced their collective concern. "And what happens to us if magic is destroyed? We are bound to the Sentinels, linked to their power."

The Shadow King's smile was cold and calculating. "You will be freed from your bonds, returned to your mortal forms. The power you sought will be gone, but you will have played a crucial role in creating a new era, one free from the corrupting influence of magic."

Khalid's mind raced with the implications of the Shadow King's plan. The allure of power had brought them this far, but the cost was becoming increasingly clear. "And if we choose to oppose you?"

The Shadow King's eyes flashed with a dangerous light. "Opposition is futile. The power you possess binds you to me, and I can control your actions if necessary. But know this, Khalid—our goals align more than you realize. The treasures of Al-Qamar will grant you unimaginable power, even if it is fleeting. Use it wisely, and you will shape the future of this land."

The mercenaries fell silent, the weight of their choices pressing heavily upon them. They had sought power and had found it, but at a cost that now seemed almost too great to bear. Khalid looked at his men, seeing the fear and uncertainty in their eyes. "We will continue, Shadow King. But know that we do so with caution and a desire to see this through to the end."

The Shadow King nodded, his expression one of satisfaction and resolve. "Very well. The path ahead is fraught with danger and uncertainty, but together, we will reclaim the treasures of Al-Qamar and fulfill our destinies."

As they continued their journey, the shadow of the Shadow King loomed large, a constant reminder of the power and peril that lay ahead. The fate of the land hung in the balance, and with every step, the mercenaries were drawn deeper into a conflict that would reshape the very essence of their world.

CHAPTER 73: THE
ARGUMENT FOR MAGIC

As the Shadow King led the mercenaries further into the heart of the ancient city of Al-Qamar, Khalid's mind was a whirlwind of thoughts. The Shadow King's plan to destroy all magic in the land was a chilling prospect, one that Khalid knew could spell doom for countless lives. Summoning his courage, he decided to confront the Shadow King and plead for the necessity of magic.

"Shadow King," Khalid called out, his voice steady despite the fear gnawing at him. "We need to talk. Your plan to eradicate magic from this land—it will bring untold suffering to the people. Magic is not just a source of power; it is a vital part of life here."

The Shadow King paused, turning to face Khalid. His towering form cast an imposing shadow over the mercenaries, but Khalid stood his ground. "Explain yourself," the Shadow King commanded, his voice an echoing rumble.

Khalid took a deep breath. "Magic is woven into the very fabric of this land. It's not just a tool for power; it's essential for survival. The healers use magic to cure diseases, the farmers use it to grow crops in barren soil, and the artisans use it to create wonders that bring joy and prosperity. Without magic, entire communities would crumble."

The Shadow King's eyes narrowed, but he remained silent, allowing Khalid to continue. "Think about the balance you mentioned earlier. Magic, like any force, can be used for both good and ill. Destroying it entirely would tip the balance too far in the other direction, leading to chaos and destruction. The very thing you seek to prevent—corruption and conflict—would only be exacerbated by the absence of magic."

Zhara stepped forward, her voice adding weight to Khalid's argument. "He's right. We've seen firsthand how magic can heal and protect. It's a lifeline for many, especially those in the harshest parts of the land. Taking it away would doom them."

Farid, ever the skeptic, found his voice as well. "And let's not forget the natural disasters. Magic has been used to control floods, quell fires, and protect against storms. Without it, nature's wrath would be unchecked."

The Shadow King listened, his expression inscrutable. The mercenaries held their breath, waiting for his response. Finally, he spoke, his voice a low growl. "You argue well, Khalid. But you underestimate the corrupting influence of magic. It is a force that has led to countless wars and betrayals, even among those with the noblest intentions."

Khalid nodded, acknowledging the truth in the Shadow King's words. "I don't deny that magic can corrupt. But so can power, wealth, and ambition. The key is not to destroy magic, but to understand it, regulate it, and ensure that it is used wisely. We need to educate the people, to create systems that prevent misuse."

The Shadow King's eyes flickered with a hint of uncertainty. "And how do you propose to achieve this? How do you ensure that the cycle of corruption does not repeat itself?"

Khalid stepped closer, his voice earnest. "By learning from the past. The guardians of Al-Qamar sought to protect their knowledge and power, but they did so in secret, without involving the people. We need transparency, shared responsibility, and collective wisdom. The treasures of Al-Qamar can help us build a better future, but only if we use them wisely and inclusively."

The Shadow King's expression softened, though his eyes remained guarded. "You speak of ideals, Khalid. Noble ideals, but difficult to realize. I have seen the best intentions lead to the darkest outcomes."

Khalid met his gaze, unwavering. "So have I. But we cannot give up on the possibility of a better future. If we destroy magic, we destroy hope. Let us work together to find a way to harness magic's potential while mitigating its risks. We can create a new era, one where magic serves the people without corrupting them."

For a long moment, the Shadow King was silent, his thoughts hidden behind his dark, imposing exterior. Finally, he spoke, his voice softer but no less powerful. "Very well, Khalid. I will consider your words. But know this—if we fail to control the forces we seek to wield, the consequences will be dire. The balance must be maintained, and I will not hesitate to take drastic measures if necessary."

Khalid nodded, a sense of relief washing over him. "Thank you, Shadow King. Together, we will strive to create a future where magic is a force for good, not a source of corruption."

With the Shadow King's tentative agreement, the group pressed on, their mission now more complex and urgent than ever. The treasures of Al-Qamar awaited, holding the potential to shape the future of the land. Khalid and his mercenaries were determined to ensure that this future would be one of hope and balance, not destruction.

CHAPTER 74: SEEDS OF DISTRUST

As Khalid and his mercenaries continued their journey through the ancient city of Al-Qamar, the weight of their situation pressed heavily upon him. The Shadow King's tentative agreement to reconsider the eradication of magic had momentarily eased Khalid's fears, but doubts lingered in his mind. He knew that a being of such immense power and dark history could not be trusted so easily.

Khalid walked beside Zhara, his thoughts racing. The Shadow King's resolve to destroy all magic was clear, and while Khalid had managed to delay that plan, he could not shake the feeling that the Shadow King would ultimately follow through on his intentions. Khalid's mind began to formulate a plan, even if it meant risking his own life to undermine the Shadow King's agenda.

"Zhara," Khalid whispered, keeping his voice low to avoid drawing attention. "We need to be prepared. The Shadow King's agreement is fragile at best. I fear he will not hesitate to carry out his plan to destroy magic once he has the treasures of Al-Qamar." Zhara glanced at him, her eyes filled with concern. "What are you suggesting, Khalid? We are bound to him and the Sentinels. How can we oppose him?"

Khalid's jaw tightened. "We must find a way to undermine him from within. The treasures of Al-Qamar are powerful, and if we can secure them first, we might be able to turn the tide. We need to gather as much information as possible and find allies who can help us."

Farid, overhearing their conversation, stepped closer. "You're talking about a rebellion against the Shadow King? That's suicide." Khalid met Farid's gaze with unwavering determination. "It may be, but we cannot stand by and let him destroy everything. We have to try. The people of this land depend on magic for their survival. Without it, they will perish." Zhara nodded, her resolve hardening. "We need to find a way to weaken his influence. There must be something in the ancient texts and artifacts that can help us."

As they continued their journey, Khalid kept a watchful eye on the Shadow King, studying his every move. He knew that the Shadow King's power was immense, but he also believed that there must be a way to counteract it. The ancient city of Al-Qamar held many secrets, and Khalid was determined to uncover them.

In the depths of the city, they came upon a grand library, its shelves filled with dusty tomes and ancient scrolls. Khalid's heart quickened as he realized that this could be the key to their salvation. "Search the library," he instructed his men. "Look for anything that might give us an advantage—spells, artifacts, anything."

The mercenaries spread out, their hands quickly rifling through the ancient texts. Khalid focused on a particularly old and ornate book, its pages filled with intricate symbols and powerful incantations. As he read, a sense of hope began to grow within him. "Khalid," Zhara called softly, holding up a scroll. "I found something. It speaks of a binding spell that can weaken even the most powerful beings. If we can perform this spell, it might give us a chance against the Shadow King."

Khalid took the scroll, his eyes scanning the ancient script. "This could work. We need to gather the necessary components and perform the spell before the Shadow King realizes what we're up to." Farid looked uneasy. "And if he finds out?" Khalid's expression was grim. "Then we fight with everything we have. This is our only chance to protect the magic of this land and ensure its future."

With renewed determination, the mercenaries set about preparing for the spell. They knew the risks were great, but the alternative was unthinkable. As they worked, Khalid's mind raced with strategies and contingencies. He was prepared to face the Shadow King's wrath, even if it meant his own doom. The Shadow King, sensing a shift in the mercenaries' demeanor, approached Khalid. "What are you planning, Khalid? Do not think you can hide your intentions from me." Khalid met the Shadow King's gaze with a steely resolve. "We seek only to secure the treasures of Al-Qamar, as agreed. Our mission remains unchanged."

The Shadow King's eyes narrowed, but he said nothing more, turning away to continue their march. Khalid knew that time was running out. They had to act quickly and decisively.

As the night grew darker and the air colder, the mercenaries completed their preparations. Khalid held the scroll tightly, his heart pounding with anticipation and fear. The fate of the land rested on their shoulders, and they were ready to face whatever came next.

The Shadow King led them deeper into the heart of Al-Qamar, unaware of the rebellion brewing in their midst. The treasures awaited, and with them, the potential to change the course of history. Khalid and his mercenaries were prepared to risk everything to ensure that magic—and hope—would endure.

CHAPTER 75: A SENSE OF DREAD

As Tariq and the entity navigated the labyrinthine corridors of Al-Qamar, a sudden, overwhelming sense of dread washed over the entity. The air grew colder, and the shadows seemed to deepen, carrying with them an ancient malevolence. The entity halted, its form flickering with unease. "Tariq," the entity said, its voice trembling, "something is wrong. I sense a great power has awakened in these lands, something dark and ancient."

Tariq turned to the entity, concern etched on his face. "What do you mean? What kind of power?"

The entity's eyes glowed with a mix of fear and recognition. "It is the Shadow King. I can feel his presence. He has been freed from his prison, and his power is growing. This changes everything." Tariq's heart raced. "The Shadow King? But how? Who could have released him?" The entity's form steadied, its determination returning. "It must have been the mercenaries sent by the Sultan. They have been corrupted by the Shadow Sentinels and have unwittingly unleashed the Shadow King. His goal is to destroy all magic in this land, and if he succeeds, it will spell doom for countless lives."

Tariq clenched his fists, his resolve hardening. "We have to stop him. But how can we fight against such a powerful being?" The entity's eyes glowed with an inner light. "The treasures of Al-Qamar hold the key. If we can secure them before the Shadow King, we might be able to counteract his power. We must act quickly and with great caution." As they pressed on, the sense of dread continued to grow, weighing heavily on both Tariq and the entity. The ancient city seemed to pulse with dark energy, and the shadows cast by the crumbling walls appeared to move with a life of their own. They knew that time was running out, and the fate of the land rested on their shoulders. "Tariq," the entity said, its voice filled with urgency, "the Shadow King's power is formidable, but it is not invincible. We must use every resource at our disposal, including the knowledge and wisdom of the ancient guardians."

Tariq nodded, his mind racing with strategies and possibilities. "We need allies, those who understand the true nature of magic and are willing to fight to protect it. The guardians, the healers, the scholars—they all have a stake in this. We must unite them against the Shadow King." The entity's form flickered with approval. "Yes, unity is our greatest strength. Together, we can create a force capable of standing against the darkness. But we must move swiftly and decisively."

As they navigated the winding paths of Al-Qamar, they encountered ancient inscriptions and symbols that hinted at the city's powerful magic. The entity paused, studying the carvings with a keen eye. "These inscriptions speak of a binding spell, one that can weaken even the most powerful beings. If we can decipher it and gather the necessary components, it might give us the edge we need."

Tariq's eyes lit up with hope. "Let's do it. We'll gather the components and perform the spell. We'll stop the Shadow King and protect the magic of this land." With renewed determination, Tariq and the entity set about deciphering the ancient inscriptions and gathering the components for the binding spell. They knew the risks were great, but the alternative was unthinkable. The power of the Shadow King threatened to consume everything they held dear, and they were prepared to fight with everything they had.

As they worked, the sense of dread continued to loom over them, a constant reminder of the darkness they faced. But with each step, their resolve grew stronger. They would stand against the Shadow

King, protect the magic of Al-Qamar, and ensure a future filled with hope and light.

CHAPTER 76: THE REVELATION

As Tariq and the entity deciphered the ancient inscriptions and gathered the components for the binding spell, the air around them grew thick with the weight of unspoken truths. The entity's form flickered with an inner turmoil, the sense of dread intensifying. It was time to reveal a secret that had been buried deep within for centuries. "Tariq," the entity began, its voice heavy with emotion, "there is something you must know. My connection to the Shadow King is deeper than you realize. I am his son."

Tariq froze, his eyes wide with shock. "What? How is that possible?"

The entity's eyes glowed with a mixture of sorrow and resolve. "Long ago, before the rise of Al-

Qamar, this land was inhabited by a people who sought to understand and harness the power of magic. My father and I were among them, driven by a thirst for knowledge and a desire to wield the forces of magic." Tariq listened intently, his heart pounding with anticipation. "What happened?"

The entity's voice was filled with pain as it recounted their story. "Our people feared the power we sought to control. They saw it as a threat to their way of life and cast us out, branding us as outcasts. My father and I roamed the desert together, searching for a place where we could continue our studies in peace. Eventually, we came upon an oasis, a place of great beauty and tranquility." Tariq's eyes softened with empathy. "And what happened at the oasis?"

The entity's form flickered, the memories of that time overwhelming. "At the oasis, we discovered ancient texts and artifacts that spoke of powerful magic. My father believed that with this knowledge, we could create a new society, one where magic was understood and respected. But as we delved deeper into the magic, we began to change. The power we sought to control started to control us."

The entity paused, its voice trembling. "One fateful day, we were approached by the guardians of Al-Qamar. They saw the danger in the magic we wielded and sought to imprison us to prevent its spread. In a desperate bid to protect me, my father battled the guardians allowing himself to be gravely injured, hoping that his sacrifice would spare me."

Tariq's heart ached for the entity. "But he failed and was imprisoned instead?"

The entity nodded, its eyes filled with sorrow. "Yes. The guardians realized that my father's power alone was too great to contain. They used their combined magic to imprison him ensuring that he could not continue his studies or seek revenge. For centuries, I have been trapped, watching over this land and feeling the weight of my father's imprisonment."

Tariq took a deep breath, the enormity of the revelation sinking in. "Why didn't you tell me this before?"

The entity's form flickered with regret. "I feared that the truth would drive you away, that you would see me as a threat rather than an ally. But now, with the Shadow King free, you must know the full extent of our history. He seeks to destroy all magic, not just for power, but to exact revenge on those who imprisoned us and to free himself from the curse of our own making."

Tariq's resolve hardened. "We have to stop him. We must use the treasures of Al-Qamar to find a way to counteract his power and protect the magic of this land." The entity's eyes glowed with determination. "Yes. Together, we can find a way to restore balance and ensure that the mistakes of the past are not repeated. We must gather allies and use every resource at our disposal."

With a newfound understanding of the entity's past and the stakes of their mission, Tariq and the entity pressed on. The path ahead was fraught with danger, but they were united by a common goal: to protect the magic of Al-Qamar and ensure a future where knowledge and power were used wisely.

As they ventured deeper into the heart of the ancient city, the sense of dread loomed over them, a constant reminder of the Shadow King's malevolent presence. But with the entity's revelation and their shared determination, they were ready to face whatever challenges lay ahead.

CHAPTER 77: THE OASIS OF SACRIFICE

As Tariq and the entity pressed on through the ancient corridors of Al-Qamar, the entity felt compelled to share more of the dark history that bound it and the Shadow King. The story was one of desperation, sacrifice, and unintended consequences. "Tariq," the entity began, its voice heavy with the weight of centuries-old sorrow, "there is more you need to know. The oasis where my father and I sought refuge was a place of great beauty, but it also became a site of immense tragedy."

Tariq listened intently, his heart heavy with empathy. "What happened there?"

The entity's form flickered, the memories of the past overwhelming. "My father was gravely injured during our initial confrontation with the guardians of Al-Qamar. He fought valiantly to protect me, but their combined magic was too powerful. In my desperation, I used my own magic to create a relic, a powerful artifact designed to heal and protect him."

The entity paused, its eyes glowing with a mixture of regret and determination. "The relic succeeded in saving his life, but it came at a terrible cost. The magic I poured into the relic was so potent that it began to draw in all nearby energy, including my essence. It was trying to trap me within, preserving his life but also imprisoning me in a state of suspended animation." Tariq's eyes widened in shock. "So, the relic that saved him also became your prison?"

The entity nodded, its form trembling with the burden of its past actions. "Yes. I had hoped to find a way to save him from the guardians, to reverse the effects of his injuries, but the intense magic of the relic sealed my essence. They used the opportunity to bind him to the mountain, ensuring that he could not continue to save me." The entity continued, "The time he spent imprisoned, changed him, and warped him, surrounded and imprisoned with dark magic, over time in his imprisonment he became the Shadow King."

Tariq's heart ached for the entity. "You've carried this guilt for centuries. It's no wonder you feel such a deep connection to this land and its magic."

The entity's eyes softened with gratitude. "Your understanding means more than you know, Tariq. My father and I sought knowledge and power, but our ambitions led to our downfall. The relic became a symbol of my failure, a reminder of the price of unchecked ambition."

Tariq's resolve hardened. "We have to stop the Shadow King from repeating the same mistakes. We must use the treasures of Al-Qamar to protect the magic of this land and ensure that it is used wisely."

The entity's form glowed with determination. "Yes. Together, we can create a new legacy, one that honors the sacrifices of the past and paves the way for a brighter future. We must gather allies and use every resource at our disposal to counteract the Shadow King's power."

As they delved deeper into the heart of Al-Qamar, the sense of dread continued to loom over them, a constant reminder of the Shadow King's malevolent presence. But with the entity's revelation and their shared determination, they were ready to face whatever challenges lay ahead.

The ancient city of Al-Qamar held many secrets, and within its depths lay the potential to reshape the destiny of the land. Tariq and the entity pressed on, their mission clear: to protect the magic of Al-Qamar, to honor the sacrifices of those who came before, and to ensure that the future was one of balance and wisdom.

CHAPTER 78: THE SHADOW KING'S VENGEANCE

In the heart of Al-Qamar, the Shadow King strode with an air of dark authority. His presence, now fully manifested, exuded a sense of ancient power and malevolence. As he led the mercenaries through the treacherous paths, his mind wandered back to the pivotal moment that had defined his existence.

He remembered the oasis—a place that had once symbolized hope and sanctuary for him and his son. It was there, amidst the tranquility of the oasis, that he had watched his son, the entity, use powerful magic to create the relic. His heart had swelled with pride and fear as he saw his son's potential. But that pride had quickly turned to horror as the relic's magic had trapped his son, imprisoning him in an attempt to save his life.

The memory of that moment was seared into the Shadow King's mind. He could still see the look of desperation in his son's eyes, the way the magic had spiraled out of control, binding him to the relic. The guardians of Al-Qamar would use the opportunity to bind the Shadow King himself, but he had managed to break free, driven by a single, all-consuming desire: vengeance.

"I left the oasis," the Shadow King recalled, his voice a low growl, "with a heart full of rage. My son was trapped, and I could do nothing to save him. The tribesmen who had cast us out, who had branded us as outcasts, would pay for their betrayal."

The mercenaries around him listened with a mix of fear and fascination. The Shadow King's story was one of ancient magic and deep-seated revenge, and they knew they were following a being of immense power and dark ambition.

"I returned to the tribesmen," the Shadow King continued, his eyes burning with the memory of his rage. "I unleashed the full extent of my magic upon them. They had feared our power, and I showed them why. Their villages were consumed by shadows, their warriors fell before my might, and their leaders begged for mercy that I did not grant."

"The tribespeople had feared our power, and I showed them why," the Shadow King continued.

"They fell before me, one by one, their leaders begging for mercy that I did not grant. Their destruction was complete, and for a moment, I felt a dark satisfaction. But it was fleeting. My son remained imprisoned, and the guardians of Al-Qamar were not idle." Zhara's voice was cautious as she asked, "What did the guardians do?"

The Shadow King's expression hardened, his voice filled with bitterness. "The guardians, ancient protectors of the land's magic, intervened. They could not allow my rampage to continue. Their magic was formidable, their resolve unbreakable. They confronted me in the midst of my destruction, their combined power a formidable force."

He paused, his gaze distant as he remembered the confrontation. "The guardians used their magic to bind me, to imprison me within the mountain as a shadow. They channeled the very essence of the land's magic to create a prison that I could not escape. I became a formless entity, a being of shadow, bound to the mountain and unable to wreak further havoc." Farid's voice was filled with awe. "How did you endure such a fate?"

The Shadow King's eyes glowed with a fierce determination. "For centuries, I existed in that state, a shadow bound by magic, my rage and power contained but not extinguished. I bided my time, waiting for the moment when I could break free. The return of Al-Qamar and the actions of the Shadow Sentinels provided the opportunity I needed."

Khalid felt a chill run down his spine. The Shadow King's tale was one of relentless pursuit and unyielding vengeance. "And now that you are free, what do you intend to do?"

The Shadow King's gaze was unyielding. "I will complete what I started. The magic that imprisoned me must be destroyed. The treasures of Al-Qamar hold the key to severing the connection between magic and this world. Once that is done, I will ensure that the cycle of corruption and conflict ends." Zhara, her voice filled with resolve, spoke up. "But at what cost? The people of this land depend on magic for their survival. Destroying it would bring untold suffering."

The Shadow King's expression softened, but his resolve remained firm. "The path of destruction is the only way to break free from the cycle of corruption. Sacrifices must be made to ensure a future free from the taint of magic. It is a harsh truth, but one that must be faced."

As they continued their journey, the Shadow King's memories weighed heavily upon him. He remembered the faces of the tribespeople, the devastation he had wrought, and the relentless pursuit of power that had led to his downfall. Yet, amidst the darkness, a flicker of doubt remained. The memory of his son's desperate attempt to save him, the unintended consequences of their actions, and the realization that true power lay not in destruction but in understanding.

The Shadow King knew that his greatest challenge was yet to come. The treasures of Al-Qamar awaited, and with them, the potential to reshape the destiny of the land. But as he led the mercenaries forward, he could not shake the feeling that the path to true redemption lay not in the eradication of magic, but in its responsible and wise use. Khalid, listening closely, felt a chill run down his spine. "And what did you achieve through your vengeance?"

The Shadow King's gaze turned to Khalid, his expression unreadable. "I achieved satisfaction, but it was hollow. My son remained imprisoned, and the guardians of Al-Qamar grew more determined to contain my power. I realized that vengeance alone would not free my son or restore what we had lost. I needed a new plan, a way to harness the magic of Al-Qamar itself."

He paused, the weight of his centuries-old burden evident. "I sought to control the ancient magic, to bend it to my will. But the guardians were relentless. They trapped me within the mountains surrounding Al-qamar, using the very magic I sought to master against me. For ages, I have waited, studying the shadows I was imprisoned with, learning secret teachings from before this land and now that I am free, I will ensure that nothing stands in my way." Farid, ever the skeptic, spoke up. "And what of your son? Does he share your desire for vengeance?"

The Shadow King's eyes flickered with a mixture of pride and sorrow. "My son is bound by his own destiny. He has always sought knowledge and balance, but he is also driven by a desire to protect this land. He may not understand my methods, but he will come to see the necessity of my actions." Zhara's voice was cautious as she asked, "And if he opposes you?" The Shadow King's expression hardened. "Then he will be swept aside like all others who stand in my way. The destruction of magic is necessary to free us from the cycle of corruption and conflict. My son's imprisonment taught me that some sacrifices are unavoidable."

The mercenaries fell silent, the weight of the Shadow King's words pressing heavily upon them. They knew they were following a being of immense power and ruthless determination. Khalid, however, felt a growing resolve within him. The Shadow King's methods were extreme, and Khalid was determined to find another way.

As they continued their journey, the Shadow King's thoughts remained fixed on his goal. The treasures of Al-Qamar held the key to his plan, and with the mercenaries and the Shadow Sentinels by his side, he believed he would finally achieve his vision.

But deep within him, a flicker of doubt remained. The memory of his son's desperation, the unintended consequences of his actions, and the realization that true power lay not in destruction but in understanding. The path ahead was fraught with danger, and the Shadow King knew that his greatest challenge was yet to come.

As the Shadow King led the mercenaries deeper into the heart of Al-Qamar, he continued to recount his dark past, his voice resonating with the weight of ancient history and boundless rage.

"I unleashed my fury upon the tribes," the Shadow King began, his eyes burning with a cold fire. "Their villages were razed to the ground, their people consumed by the shadows I commanded. The air was filled with their cries, and the land itself seemed to tremble beneath the force of my vengeance."

Khalid and the other mercenaries listened in silence, their expressions a mix of fear and fascination. The Shadow King's tale was one of unchecked power and relentless wrath, a stark reminder of the dangers of ambition and retribution.

CHAPTER 79: A NEW BEGINNING

As the Shadow King recounted his past and the devastation he had wrought, his memories turned to the time after his imprisonment. For centuries, he had remained a shadow bound to the mountain, but the world outside continued to evolve. The people of the land, once fearful of magic, began to see its potential for good.

After the Shadow King's imprisonment, the devastation he had left behind was immense. Villages lay in ruins, and the people were left to rebuild from the ashes of their former lives. It was a time of great uncertainty and hardship, but also one of remarkable resilience and hope.

The guardians of the mountain, who had intervened to imprison the Shadow King, took on a new role in this changed world. They became protectors and guides, helping the people to understand and harness magic in ways that were constructive and beneficial. With their wisdom and guidance, the survivors began to rebuild their communities, using magic not as a tool of power and domination, but as a means to heal and nurture.

The guardians taught the people how to use magic to restore their lands, heal the sick, and create tools and structures that would improve their lives. Fields that had been scorched and barren flourished once more with the aid of magical irrigation and enchantments that enriched the soil. Healers used their knowledge to cure diseases and mend injuries, while artisans crafted wonders that brought joy and prosperity to their communities.

In recognition of their efforts and as a symbol of their commitment to using magic wisely, the people entrusted the guardians with ancient artifacts discovered within the oasis. These artifacts, imbued with powerful magic, were seen as both a gift and a responsibility. The guardians, understanding the potential and the dangers of these artifacts, set to work further augmenting them with protective magic.

Each artifact was carefully studied and enchanted with spells designed to protect the people and the land from future threats. Some were imbued with magic to ward off evil and shield communities from harm, while others were crafted to amplify the beneficial aspects of magic, ensuring that it could be used for healing and growth.

Over time, the guardians' efforts bore fruit. The land, once ravaged by the Shadow King's wrath, became a testament to the resilience and wisdom of its people. Communities thrived, bound together by a shared understanding of the importance of balance and the responsible use of magic. The artifacts, now symbols of hope and protection, stood as reminders of the lessons learned and the sacrifices made.

The guardians, revered as wise protectors, continued to guide the people, ensuring that the magic of Al-Qamar was used with respect and care. The story of the Shadow King and his son became a cautionary tale, a reminder of the dangers of unchecked ambition and the importance of unity and wisdom.

As the Shadow King led the mercenaries through the ancient city, these memories weighed heavily on his mind. He saw the transformation that had taken place during his imprisonment and understood the depth of the people's commitment to using magic wisely. Yet, his own resolve to destroy magic remained strong, driven by the belief that it was the only way to break the cycle of corruption.

Khalid, sensing the Shadow King's internal conflict, knew that their task was more urgent than ever. The treasures of Al-Qamar held the potential to shape the future of the land, and it was up to them to ensure that this power was used for good. With the knowledge of the past and the guidance of the guardians, they would strive to protect the magic of Al-Qamar and create a future where balance and wisdom prevailed.

CHAPTER 80:
CONVERSATIONS OF
SHADOWS

As Tariq and the entity delved deeper into the ancient city of Al-Qamar, the air grew denser with an eerie, palpable tension. The path they followed seemed to lead them to a part of the city that felt particularly ancient, a place where the walls whispered forgotten secrets and the shadows seemed to reach out with intangible hands.

In a secluded chamber, they stumbled upon another figure, bound in shadows much like the Nezzera once had been. This figure, though restrained and seemingly powerless, exuded an aura of sorrow and regret. Tariq approached cautiously, sensing a kindred spirit in this imprisoned shadow.

"Who are you?" Tariq asked, his voice soft but filled with curiosity.

The shadowy figure's eyes glowed faintly as it lifted its head. "I am Seraphis, a guardian of old, once a protector of these lands. Now, like many before me, I am a prisoner of my own making."

Tariq glanced at the entity, who nodded for him to continue. "Why are you imprisoned here, Seraphis? What crime led to your punishment?" Seraphis sighed, a sound that echoed with centuries of regret. "In our quest to harness and protect the magic of Al-Qamar, some of us fell victim to the allure of power. I was one such guardian. I sought to wield the magic for my own ends, believing that my intentions were pure. But as the Shadow King fell into darkness, so did I." Tariq felt a pang of empathy. "You sought to protect the land, but in doing so, you were consumed by the very power you wished to guard."

"Yes," Seraphis replied, his voice heavy with sorrow. "The guardians saw the corruption taking hold within me. To prevent further harm, they used their combined magic to imprison me, binding me within these shadows. It was a punishment, but also a mercy. They hoped that in confinement, I might reflect on my actions and find redemption."

The entity, who had been silent, now spoke. "Imprisonment is a double-edged sword. It can offer time for reflection and redemption, but it can also breed bitterness and despair. The nature of

319

punishment is complex, often serving as both a deterrent and a means of rehabilitation."

Seraphis nodded slowly. "Indeed. For centuries, I have pondered my actions, the choices that led to my downfall. The guardians believed that by binding me, they could contain the darkness within. In many ways, they were right. But the cost was great." Tariq's mind raced with thoughts of the Shadow King and his own journey. "Do you believe that true redemption is possible, even after such a fall?"

Seraphis's eyes glowed with a faint hope. "Redemption is always possible, Tariq, but it requires a willingness to confront one's own darkness and seek the light. It is a path fraught with challenges, but it is not impossible." The entity's form flickered as it added, "Punishment alone cannot lead to redemption. There must be an understanding of the underlying causes of one's actions and a genuine desire to change. The antiquities of Al-Qamar hold great power, but it is the intention behind their use that will determine their impact."

Tariq looked at Seraphis, seeing the reflection of his own struggles in the guardian's eyes. "What can we do to help you, Seraphis? Is there a way to free you from this imprisonment?"

Seraphis's expression softened with gratitude. "My imprisonment is a reminder of the dangers of unchecked ambition. To free me would require the combined magic of the guardians, a balance that is difficult to achieve. But perhaps, in your journey, you can learn from my mistakes and ensure that the power of Al-Qamar is used wisely."

With a heavy heart, Tariq nodded. "We will do our best. Your story is a reminder of the fine line between protection and domination, between wisdom and folly. We will strive to honor that balance."

As they left the chamber, Tariq's resolve hardened. The tales of the imprisoned guardians, the fallen protectors, and the dark history of Al-Qamar weighed heavily on his shoulders. Yet, with each step, he grew more determined to find a way to use the treasures of Al-Qamar for good, to restore balance, and to prevent the cycle of corruption from repeating.

The path ahead was uncertain, but Tariq and the entity knew that their journey was about more than just power. It was about redemption, understanding, and the hope of creating a future where magic was a force for healing and growth, not destruction.

CHAPTER 81: REFLECTIONS OF REALITY

As Tariq and the entity continued their journey through the ancient corridors of Al-Qamar, they came upon a tranquil chamber, its centerpiece a large, serene reflecting pool. The water was crystal clear, mirroring the surrounding architecture and casting an ethereal glow. Drawn to its calmness, the entity approached the pool and gazed into its depths.

For a moment, the entity saw only his current shadowy form. But as he focused, the water began to ripple, and a different image emerged—an image of himself as he once was, a human, filled with hope and determination. The sight took the entity by surprise, stirring memories long buried beneath centuries of imprisonment. Tariq, noticing the entity's reaction, stepped closer. "What do you see?"

The entity's voice was soft, almost wistful. "I see myself, as I once was—a human, not bound by shadows or ancient magic. It feels like a lifetime ago."

The reflection in the pool seemed to regard the entity with a calm, knowing expression. The entity's human form spoke, its voice an echo in the silence. "What is real in a world of illusion? How do we discern truth when our perceptions are clouded by magic and memory?"

The entity's shadowy form replied, "Reality is often shaped by our experiences and our choices. Magic can create illusions, but it can also reveal truths hidden beneath the surface. The challenge lies in understanding which is which."

The reflection's eyes glowed with a gentle wisdom. "Indeed. Our perceptions can deceive us, but they can also guide us. We must learn to see beyond the illusions, to seek the deeper truths that lie within."

Tariq listened intently, feeling the weight of their conversation. "But how do we distinguish between illusion and reality? How do we know what is truly real?"

The entity's human reflection smiled softly. "By looking within ourselves. Our intentions, our desires, our fears—they all shape our reality. To understand what is real, we must first understand ourselves. Only then can we see the world clearly, beyond the veils of illusion." The entity's shadowy form nodded. "I have spent centuries trapped by my own actions, my own ambitions. I sought power, but in doing so, I lost sight of what truly mattered. Now, I see the importance of balance, of wisdom. The path to redemption lies in recognizing our own flaws and striving to overcome them."

The reflection in the pool shimmered, its image growing clearer. "You have the power to shape your own destiny, to break free from the shadows that bind you. Remember that true power lies not in domination, but in understanding, in the willingness to see beyond the surface."

As the reflection faded, the entity felt a profound sense of clarity. The conversation with his past self had illuminated the path ahead, guiding him toward a deeper understanding of his own nature and the challenges they faced. Tariq placed a reassuring hand on the entity's shoulder. "We will face this together. The journey is not just about the treasures of Al-Qamar, but about understanding ourselves and the world around us."

The entity's form glowed with a renewed determination. "Yes, Tariq. Together, we will seek the truth, protect the magic of this land, and ensure that it is used wisely. The illusions of the past will not define our future."

With this newfound resolve, Tariq and the entity continued their journey, their bond strengthened by the revelations of the reflecting pool. The path ahead was still fraught with challenges, but they were ready to face them, guided by the understanding that reality is shaped not just by magic, but by the choices and intentions of those who wield it.

CHAPTER 82: THE AMBUSH

As Tariq and the entity pressed on with renewed resolve, the Shadow King and his mercenaries found themselves nearing a crucial juncture in the ancient city of Al-Qamar. The dark corridors and winding pathways led them to a hidden passageway that promised a strategic advantage—a way to intercept Tariq and the entity before they could secure the treasures of Al-Qamar.

The Shadow King's presence loomed large, his mind calculating the best way to ensure his victory. The air around him was thick with anticipation, and his mercenaries, now imbued with the dark power of the Shadow Sentinels, awaited his command. "Khalid," the Shadow King said, his voice a resonant whisper that echoed through the cavernous passageway. "We have a unique opportunity here. Tariq and the entity are close, but they are unaware of this pathway. We must use this to our advantage."

Khalid stepped forward, his mind racing with strategies. "We can set up an ambush here, in this narrow passage. It will be difficult for them to maneuver, and we can use the element of surprise to overwhelm them."

The Shadow King nodded, his eyes gleaming with dark intent. "Precisely. We will position ourselves along the walls, hidden in the shadows. When they pass through, we will strike swiftly and decisively. We cannot afford to let them reach the treasures before us." Farid, ever the skeptic, voiced his concern. "And what if they are stronger than we anticipate? What if the entity's power proves too great?"

The Shadow King's gaze hardened. "We have the element of surprise, and the power of the Shadow Sentinels at our disposal. We must trust in our strength and our resolve. Doubt will only weaken us." Zhara, her eyes scanning the passageway, added, "We should set traps along the path to slow them down and disorient them. That will give us an even greater advantage."

The Shadow King smiled, a cruel twist of his lips. "Excellent. Khalid, Farid, Zhara—prepare the traps and position the mercenaries. We must ensure that this ambush is flawless."

The mercenaries moved quickly, their training and newfound powers guiding their actions. They set traps—hidden snares, pressure-sensitive stones that would release a cloud of disorienting smoke, and enchanted barriers that would slow Tariq and the entity's progress. Meanwhile, they positioned themselves along the walls, their forms blending seamlessly with the shadows.

As they worked, the Shadow King's mind wandered. He knew that they were determined and resourceful, but he was equally determined to see his plan through to the end. The destruction of magic was not just a goal—it was a necessity, a way to break free from the cycle of corruption and conflict that had plagued the land for centuries.

Once the preparations were complete, the Shadow King signaled for silence. The air was thick with tension, and the shadows seemed to pulse with anticipation. They did not have to wait long. The sound of footsteps echoed faintly through the passageway, growing steadily louder.

Tariq and the entity approached, their voices low as they discussed their next steps. Unaware of the impending ambush, they moved cautiously, their senses attuned to the ancient magic of Al-Qamar.

The moment they entered the narrow passageway, the Shadow King gave the signal. The traps activated in quick succession, and the mercenaries sprang from the shadows, their weapons ready and their powers focused.

Chaos erupted as Tariq and the entity found themselves surrounded. The disorienting smoke filled the air, and the enchanted barriers slowed their movements. The mercenaries attacked with precision, their dark power clashing with the entity's ancient magic.

Tariq fought valiantly, his resolve unyielding. The entity, glowing with a fierce determination, unleashed spells to counter the traps and fend off the attackers. But the element of surprise had given the Shadow King and his forces a significant advantage.

Amidst the chaos, the Shadow King advanced, his eyes locked on Tariq. "You cannot win, Tariq. The power of the Shadow Sentinels is mine to command, and you are but a distraction on my path to victory."

Tariq's eyes burned with defiance. "We will not let you destroy everything we have fought to protect. The magic of this land is worth saving, and we will find a way to stop you."

The Shadow King's laughter echoed through the passageway. "You are brave, but misguided. This land must be purged of its magic to break the cycle of corruption. Your resistance is futile."

As the battle raged on, the outcome hung in the balance. Tariq and the entity knew that they faced overwhelming odds, but their resolve was unbroken. They fought not just for the treasures of Al-Qamar, but for the future of the land and its people.

CHAPTER 83: TREMORS OF POWER

The clash between Tariq, the entity, and the Shadow King's forces was fierce and unrelenting. Smoke and magical energy filled the narrow passageway, creating an intense and chaotic battlefield. Amidst the turmoil, the Shadow King's focus shifted to the entity, whose involvement seemed oddly restrained.

As the Shadow King advanced through the melee, he watched the entity closely. The entity's powers were formidable, and yet it had not unleashed its full potential. The Shadow King's eyes narrowed with suspicion and concern.

"Why does he hold back?" the Shadow King muttered to himself, his mind racing with possibilities.

"Is he biding his time, or is there something else at play?"

The entity, meanwhile, was engaged in a fierce but controlled defense, countering the traps and spells set by the mercenaries. It was clear that the entity's restraint was deliberate, a choice made with careful consideration.

In a rare moment of pause, the Shadow King caught the entity's eye. "Why do you not fight with your full strength?" he demanded, his voice filled with both anger and curiosity. "What are you hiding?"

The entity's gaze was steady, filled with a calm resolve. "My power is not a weapon to be unleashed recklessly. There is a greater purpose at stake, one that requires wisdom and restraint."

The Shadow King's expression darkened. "Your restraint could cost you dearly. Do you not understand the gravity of this battle? The magic of this land hangs in the balance."

The entity's form flickered with an inner light. "I understand more than you know. Power without control leads to destruction. We must find a way to balance our actions with the consequences they bring."

Frustration gnawed at the Shadow King. He could sense the immense power within the entity, a power that could easily tip the scales of the battle. Yet, the entity's deliberate restraint left him unsettled.

"You are a fool if you think restraint will save you. This is a battle for the future, and hesitation will lead to ruin."

Tariq, overhearing their exchange, seized the moment to speak. "The entity is right. Power must be wielded with wisdom. This land has seen enough destruction. We fight not just to win, but to ensure a future where magic is used responsibly."

The Shadow King's eyes blazed with a fierce determination. "Your idealism blinds you. The only way to break the cycle of corruption is to destroy magic entirely. You cannot see the bigger picture."

As the battle continued, the Shadow King's concern grew. He could feel the tremors of the entity's power, a force so vast and untapped that it threatened to overshadow even his own. The possibility that the entity could unleash this power at any moment made the Shadow King wary.

Determined to press his advantage, the Shadow King unleashed a surge of dark energy, directing it toward Tariq and the entity. The passageway shook with the force of his attack, the walls cracking under the strain. The entity reacted swiftly, raising a shield of light to protect Tariq and deflect the Shadow King's assault. The clash of their powers created a blinding flash, momentarily halting the battle.

As the light faded, the entity stood firm, its resolve unwavering. "We will not be swayed by fear or aggression. The true strength lies in understanding and balance." The Shadow King's frustration boiled over. "You speak of balance, yet you fail to grasp the necessity of sacrifice. If you will not fight with your full strength, you will fall."

But even as he spoke, doubt crept into the Shadow King's mind. The entity's power, held in check, represented a threat he could not ignore. The possibility that the entity might unleash its full potential in a decisive moment haunted him.

With a final, furious glance at the entity, the Shadow King renewed his assault. But the seeds of doubt had been sown, and he knew that this battle was more complex and dangerous than he had anticipated. As the struggle continued, Tariq and the entity remained united in their resolve, their actions guided by a deeper understanding of the power they wielded. The Shadow King, driven by his determination to destroy magic, could not shake the fear that the entity's restraint masked a greater, more profound threat.

The fate of Al-Qamar hung in the balance, and the outcome of this battle would determine the future of magic and the land itself. The Shadow King's concern for the entity's power grew, a constant reminder that true strength lay not just in might, but in the wisdom to wield it wisely.

CHAPTER 84: A DESPERATE ESCAPE

The battle raged on within the narrow passageway of Al-Qamar, a maelstrom of dark energy, magic, and determination. Tariq fought valiantly alongside the entity, but as the Shadow King's relentless assault intensified, it became clear that their position was becoming increasingly untenable.

Tariq's mind raced, weighing their options. The entity's power was immense, but its deliberate restraint was both their greatest strength and their most significant vulnerability. They needed to regroup, to find a way to turn the tide against the Shadow King. "Tariq," the entity said, its voice steady even amidst the chaos, "we cannot hold this position much longer. You must go. Find a way to secure the treasures of Al-Qamar. I will hold them off as long as I can." Tariq's eyes widened in shock. "I can't leave you behind! We need to face this together." The entity's gaze was resolute. "Your journey is not yet complete. The future of this land depends on your success. Trust me—I will manage here. Go, now!"

Reluctantly, Tariq nodded, understanding the gravity of their situation. He glanced around, searching for a path through the chaos. Spotting a narrow corridor that led deeper into the city, he made a swift decision. "I'll come back for you. Stay safe."

With one last look at the entity, Tariq turned and fled down the corridor. The sounds of battle faded behind him as he raced through the ancient passages, his heart pounding with a mix of fear and determination. He could only hope that the entity's formidable power would be enough to hold off the Shadow King and his forces.

As Tariq disappeared into the depths of Al-Qamar, the Shadow King's attention shifted. His eyes narrowed as he watched Tariq flee. "So, the boy runs," he muttered. "He will not escape my reach for long." The entity stood tall, its form glowing with a fierce light. "Your fight is with me now, Shadow King. Tariq will find a way to secure the treasures, and your plans will be thwarted."

The Shadow King's expression twisted into a cruel smile. "You underestimate my resolve. Tariq's escape will only delay the inevitable. And as for you, entity, your power is impressive, but it will not be enough to save you."

With a roar, the Shadow King unleashed another wave of dark energy, aiming to overwhelm the entity. The entity countered with a powerful shield of light, but the strain was evident. The mercenaries, sensing the entity's struggle, pressed their advantage, their attacks relentless.

Back in the depths of Al-Qamar, Tariq navigated the labyrinthine passages, his mind racing with thoughts of the treasures and the sacrifices being made. He knew he had to reach the heart of the city, where the most powerful artifacts were said to be hidden. There, he hoped to find something that could turn the tide against the Shadow King.

His path was fraught with danger, but Tariq's resolve was unbroken. He had come too far to falter now. As he pressed on, the weight of his mission bore heavily upon him, but so did the hope of a future where magic was preserved and used wisely.

Tariq's journey through the ancient city of Al-Qamar was far from over, and the fate of the land hung in the balance. With each step, he drew closer to the treasures that could change everything. The entity's sacrifice and the Shadow King's relentless pursuit were reminders of the stakes, driving Tariq forward with a sense of urgency and determination.

CHAPTER 85: WHISPERS OF POWER

As Tariq navigated the ancient, labyrinthine passages of Al-Qamar, he felt a profound sense of urgency. The weight of his mission pressed heavily on his shoulders, and the echoes of battle still lingered in his mind. His thoughts were consumed with the entity he had left behind, holding off the Shadow King and his forces.

Suddenly, the air grew colder, and the passageway before him darkened. Shadows seemed to ripple and move, coalescing into distinct forms. Tariq halted, his senses on high alert. Before him, the shadows took shape, becoming the imprisoned figures he had encountered earlier. One of the shadowy figures, a guardian named Seraphis, stepped forward. His voice was a whisper, filled with an ancient sorrow. "Tariq, you return to us. We have been waiting." Tariq's heart pounded in his chest. "Seraphis, what is this place? Why are you here?"

Seraphis's eyes glowed faintly. "We are the remnants of those who sought power and were consumed by it. Our punishment was imprisonment within these shadows, a fate designed to protect the land from our ambitions. But now, we see a chance for redemption." Another shadow, more spectral than the others, spoke with a voice like the rustling of leaves. "You seek to save your friend, the entity, and to defeat the Shadow King. We can help you." Tariq's eyes widened. "How? What can you do?"

The shadows seemed to pulse with a dark energy. Seraphis continued, "We possess ancient knowledge and power, sealed within us by the guardians. We can bestow this power upon you, but it comes with great risk. To wield it, you must be willing to face your own darkness and embrace the responsibility it brings."

Tariq hesitated, the weight of their offer pressing heavily on him. "If I accept this power, what will become of you?" Seraphis's expression softened. "Our imprisonment was a consequence of our actions. By aiding you, we seek a chance at redemption. If you succeed, our spirits may finally find peace."

The spectral figure added, "But know this, Tariq: power alone will not save you. It must be tempered with wisdom and guided by a pure heart.

The Shadow King fell because he sought power without understanding its true cost. You must not make the same mistake."

Tariq's mind raced. He knew the dangers of accepting such power, but the thought of leaving the entity and the land to the mercy of the Shadow King was unbearable. He steeled himself, his resolve firm. "I will accept your power, but I vow to use it wisely. I will not let it consume me." The shadows began to swirl around Tariq, their energy seeping into him. He felt a surge of strength and knowledge, a connection to the ancient magic of Al-Qamar. The power was overwhelming, but Tariq focused on his purpose, grounding himself in the resolve to protect his friend and the land.

As the ritual concluded, Seraphis's voice echoed in his mind. "Remember, Tariq, true power lies not in domination, but in understanding and balance. Go forth and fulfill your destiny."

Empowered by the ancient magic and the wisdom of the imprisoned guardians, Tariq felt a renewed sense of purpose. He continued through the passageways, now more determined than ever to find the treasures of Al-Qamar and turn the tide against the Shadow King.

The path ahead was still fraught with danger, but Tariq knew he was no longer alone. The spirits of the guardians were with him, their power and wisdom guiding his steps. With each stride, he drew closer to

the heart of Al-Qamar, where the fate of the land
would be decided.

CHAPTER 86: THE VENGEFUL SHADOWS

Empowered by the ancient magic of the imprisoned shadows, Tariq felt a surge of strength and determination. As he continued his journey through the labyrinthine passages of Al-Qamar, the whispers of the shadows filled his mind, revealing their tragic past and their deep-seated desire for vengeance.

The shadows, now a part of him, began to share their stories. Each voice, filled with sorrow and resolve, painted a picture of a time long ago when they were great warriors, protectors of the land and its magic. Seraphis, the spectral guardian who had first spoken to Tariq, began his tale. "We were once the warriors of Al-Qamar, bound by honor and duty to protect the magic of this land. Our strength was unmatched, and our loyalty to the guardians was unwavering. But our greatest enemy was the Shadow King."

Tariq's mind filled with visions of battles long past. He saw the warriors, clad in gleaming armor, wielding weapons imbued with powerful magic. They fought valiantly against the encroaching darkness, their resolve unbroken even in the face of overwhelming odds.

Another shadow, with a voice like the rustling of leaves, spoke. "The Shadow King was once noble, a scholar who sought to harness the magic for knowledge. His ambition consumed him, and he turned against the world, using dark magic to strengthen his power. We fought to stop him, but his strength was too great."

The visions shifted to a cataclysmic battle. The warriors of Al-Qamar clashed with the Shadow King, their magic and might unable to withstand his dark power. One by one, they fell, their spirits bound by his malevolent magic.

A third voice, deeper and more resonant, added, "In his quest for dominance, the Shadow King destroyed us, but the guardians bound our spirits in these halls, imprisoning us within the shadows of Al-Qamar. Our power was sealed away, our voices silenced, until you came." Tariq felt a deep sadness mingled with anger. "You seek vengeance for what he did to you."

Seraphis's voice was resolute. "Yes. Our imprisonment was a fate worse than death, a constant reminder of our failure to protect the land. But now, through you, we have a chance to set things right. We will lend you our strength, but you must use it wisely. The Shadow King must be stopped, not just for our sake, but for the future of Al-Qamar."

The other shadows echoed Seraphis's sentiment, their voices a chorus of determination and hope. Tariq understood the gravity of their request and the responsibility that came with their power. He knew that their desire for vengeance was driven not by hatred, but by a deep love for their land and a duty to protect it.

With each step, Tariq felt the weight of their stories and their sacrifice. The magic that flowed through him was not just a tool for battle, but a testament to the courage and resilience of those who had come before him. He vowed to honor their legacy and to fight for a future where such sacrifices would not be in vain.

As Tariq approached the heart of Al-Qamar, where the treasures and the ultimate confrontation awaited, he carried with him the strength and wisdom of the ancient warriors. Their spirits, once bound in darkness, now burned brightly within him, guiding his path and fortifying his resolve.

The Shadow King would soon face the full might of Al-Qamar's ancient protectors, their power channeled through the one who had vowed to redeem their legacy. The battle ahead would be fierce, but Tariq was ready, his heart and mind united with the spirits of the vengeful shadows.

CHAPTER 87: RETURN TO THE BATTLE

Empowered by the ancient magic and the stories of the imprisoned shadows, Tariq felt a renewed sense of purpose and strength. With the knowledge and power of the ancient artifacts now within his grasp, he made his way back to the heart of the battle, determined to turn the tide against the Shadow King and his forces.

The sounds of clashing magic and battle cries grew louder as Tariq approached the narrow passageway where he had left the entity. His heart pounded with urgency, knowing that every moment counted. As he entered the fray, he saw the entity locked in a fierce struggle, holding off the Shadow King and the mercenaries with remarkable resilience. "Tariq!" the entity called out, a glimmer of relief in its eyes. "You've returned!" Tariq nodded, raising one of the ancient artifacts—a staff imbued with protective magic. "I've brought the power of the guardians with me. Let's end this."

The Shadow King's eyes narrowed, his expression darkening with a mix of anger and apprehension. "You think a few ancient trinkets will save you? You are more foolish than I thought."

With a determined glare, Tariq unleashed the power of the staff. A radiant light burst forth, enveloping the area and creating a protective barrier around him and the entity. The mercenaries recoiled, their dark energy struggling against the newfound light. "Fight with everything you have!" Tariq shouted, his voice carrying over the din of battle. He wielded the staff with precision, directing blasts of magical energy at the mercenaries, forcing them back.

The entity, drawing strength from Tariq's resolve, intensified its own efforts. Together, they formed a formidable defense, their combined powers creating a harmonious blend of light and magic. The mercenaries, though bolstered by the Shadow Sentinels' dark power, found themselves struggling to break through the barrier.

The Shadow King, sensing the shift in the battle, snarled in frustration. "You may have gained some strength, but you are still no match for me!" He summoned a vortex of dark energy, hurling it toward Tariq and the entity.

Tariq reacted swiftly, using another artifact—a shield inscribed with ancient runes. The shield absorbed the impact of the Shadow King's attack, dispersing the dark energy harmlessly into the air. "Your darkness cannot overcome the light of Al-Qamar!" Tariq declared, his voice unwavering.

The Shadow King's frustration grew. He could feel the tide turning, the power of the ancient artifacts and the combined might of Tariq and the entity becoming a significant threat. "You will regret this defiance!" he roared, launching another powerful assault. But Tariq and the entity stood firm. With each artifact they wielded—a sword of pure light, an amulet that amplified their magic, and a staff that called upon the guardians' protective spells—they pushed back against the Shadow King's dark power. The battle intensified, the clash of light and dark creating a dazzling display of magic and determination.

As the fight raged on, the imprisoned shadows within Tariq lent their strength and wisdom. Their voices guided his actions, helping him to harness the full potential of the artifacts and counter the Shadow King's every move. The mercenaries, realizing the futility of their efforts, began to falter, their resolve wavering in the face of such overwhelming power.

The Shadow King, now cornered and desperate, unleashed his most devastating attack. Dark tendrils of energy lashed out, aiming to overwhelm Tariq and the entity once and for all. But Tariq, with the combined strength of the artifacts and the guardians' spirits, met the attack head-on. "Now!" Tariq shouted, channeling all his energy into the staff. A blinding beam of light erupted from the artifact, cutting through the darkness and striking the Shadow King with incredible force.

The Shadow King let out a howl of rage and pain as the light consumed him, breaking through his defenses. The dark energy that had surrounded him dissipated, and he fell to his knees, defeated and weakened.

Tariq and the entity stood over him, their breaths heavy but victorious. "It's over," Tariq said, his voice resolute. "Your reign of darkness ends here."

The Shadow King, his strength fading, looked up at them with a mixture of anger and despair. "You may have won this battle, but the struggle between light and dark will never end." The entity's eyes glowed with a calm, steady light. "True, but today, the light has prevailed. The future of Al-Qamar will be one of balance and wisdom, guided by the lessons of the past."

As the last remnants of the Shadow King's power faded, Tariq and the entity knew that their journey was far from over. The treasures of Al-Qamar had been secured, but the true task lay ahead: ensuring that the magic of the land was used wisely and that the balance between light and dark was maintained. With the guardians' spirits at their side and the power of the ancient artifacts in their hands, they were ready to face whatever challenges the future held.

CHAPTER 88: CORRUPTION OF AL-QAMAR

With the battle won and the Shadow King defeated, Tariq departed the ancient city of Al-Qamar, his heart filled with resolve and the promise of a new beginning. He made his way back to the Sultan's court, eager to report his success and ensure the future of the land. The entity, now freed from the immediate threat, accompanied him, their bond strengthened by the trials they had faced together.

However, not all was well in Al-Qamar. Khalid and his mercenaries, having been left behind, saw an opportunity to seize power for themselves. The dark energies that had once empowered the Shadow King still lingered in the air, tempting them with promises of strength and dominance. As Tariq journeyed back to the Sultan, Khalid gathered his men in the heart of the ancient city. The mercenaries, their eyes glinting with a mixture of ambition and greed, listened as Khalid outlined his plan.

"The Shadow King's power is still here, fragmented but potent," Khalid said, his voice low and conspiratorial. "We can harness it, use it to reshape Al-Qamar in our image. With this power, we can become rulers, not just mercenaries." Farid, ever the skeptic, voiced his concern. "But the Shadow King's power is dangerous. It corrupted him and could do the same to us."

Khalid's eyes burned with determination. "We are not the Shadow King. We will wield this power with discipline and control. The city of Al-Qamar will be our stronghold, and its magic our weapon." The mercenaries, swayed by Khalid's vision, set to work. They began to gather the remnants of the Shadow King's dark energy, channeling it into the ancient structures of Al-Qamar. The city, once a beacon of light and magic, began to change. The dark energies seeped into the walls and streets, corrupting the very essence of the city.

As they worked, the air grew thick with malevolence. The shadows lengthened, and an oppressive aura settled over Al-Qamar. The ancient magic that had once protected and nurtured the city was twisted, its purity tainted by the dark energy.

Khalid, standing at the center of this transformation, felt a surge of power. He believed he could control it, bend it to his will. But even as he reveled in his newfound strength, doubts gnawed at the edges of his mind. The memory of the Shadow King's downfall served as a grim reminder of the dangers of unchecked ambition.

Farid, watching the changes unfold, approached Khalid. "This power is changing us, Khalid. We must be cautious. The same fate that befell the Shadow King could be ours if we lose control." Khalid's gaze hardened. "We will not falter. This is our destiny. Al-Qamar will rise again, not as a city of guardians and scholars, but as a fortress of power."

As the corruption spread, the city's magic responded. The guardians' protective spells weakened, and the once harmonious balance of light and dark was thrown into chaos. The ancient spirits of the city, sensing the shift, stirred with unease.

Meanwhile, Tariq and the entity, unaware of the unfolding corruption, continued their journey to the Sultan's court. They spoke of their plans to rebuild and protect the land, their hopes for a future where magic was used wisely. But the seeds of darkness had been sown. Khalid and his men, driven by ambition and corrupted by the Shadow King's fragmented power, had set in motion a chain of events that threatened to undo everything Tariq and the entity had fought for.

As they neared the Sultan's palace, a sense of foreboding settled over Tariq. He could not shake the feeling that their battle was far from over, and that the true test of their resolve and strength was yet to come.

CHAPTER 89: THE SULTAN'S SCHEMES

In the Sultan's opulent palace, the air was thick with tension and anticipation. The news of Tariq's victory and the defeat of the Shadow King had reached the court, bringing a mix of relief and apprehension. However, as the Sultan stood on his balcony, gazing out at the distant horizon, a dark cloud of foreboding hung over his thoughts.

From his vantage point, the Sultan could see the ancient city of Al-Qamar. What had once been a beacon of magic and wisdom was now shrouded in an unsettling darkness. The city seemed to pulsate with a malevolent energy, its very essence corrupted by the lingering power of the Shadow King.

The Sultan's eyes narrowed as he watched the distant city. "Al-Qamar," he murmured, his voice tinged with both wonder and fear. "What has become of you?"

Beside him, his trusted advisor, Malik, spoke cautiously. "Your Majesty, the changes in Al-Qamar are troubling. The dark energy spreading through the city could threaten your rule and the stability of our kingdom."

The Sultan nodded, his mind racing with possibilities. "Indeed. We must act swiftly to ensure that this corruption does not spread beyond Al-Qamar. But more importantly, we must secure our own power and position." Malik's eyes gleamed with intrigue. "What do you propose, Your Majesty?"

The Sultan turned to face his advisor, his expression resolute. "We will use this opportunity to solidify our control. The people must see us as their protectors, the only force capable of keeping the darkness at bay. We will harness the fear that Al-Qamar's transformation instills and use it to strengthen our rule."

Malik bowed his head. "A wise plan, Your Majesty. But what of Tariq and the entity? They have proven themselves formidable allies and could pose a threat to our ambitions." The Sultan's gaze hardened. "Tariq is a hero to the people, but heroes can be made to serve the throne. We will welcome him back with open arms, shower him with praise and rewards, and ensure his loyalty. As for the entity, we must keep a close watch. Its power is both an asset and a potential danger."

As they spoke, a messenger arrived, bowing deeply before the Sultan. "Your Majesty, Tariq and the entity approach the palace. They are expected to arrive within the hour." The Sultan's expression shifted to one of calculated warmth. "Prepare a grand reception. Let the people see their hero welcomed with all the honor he deserves. We will make him believe that his place is here, by our side." Malik nodded, already issuing orders to the palace staff. "It will be done, Your Majesty."

The Sultan returned his gaze to the distant city of Al-Qamar. He could sense the power shifting, the delicate balance between light and dark hanging in the balance. The corruption spreading through the city was both a threat and an opportunity, one that he intended to exploit to its fullest.

"We will watch Al-Qamar closely," the Sultan said, his voice low and determined. "If the darkness continues to spread, we will intervene. But for now, we must ensure that our own position is unassailable." As the preparations for Tariq's reception were made, the Sultan's mind turned to the future. He knew that the path ahead would be fraught with challenges, but he was determined to emerge victorious. The power of Al-Qamar, both its light and its dark, would be harnessed to secure his rule and protect his kingdom.

As the first signs of Tariq's approach reached the palace, the Sultan donned a mask of benevolent authority. He would play the part of the grateful ruler, all the while scheming and planning to ensure that the true power remained firmly in his hands.

The ancient city of Al-Qamar, once a symbol of hope and wisdom, had become a battleground for control and power. And in this new struggle, the Sultan intended to emerge as the ultimate victor.

CHAPTER 90: REFLECTIONS OF POWER

The Sultan stood on his balcony, watching as the distant city of Al-Qamar writhed with dark energy. The changes in the city were a stark reminder of how volatile the world had become. Power was a fickle and transient thing, shifting hands and allegiances with the tides of magic and ambition.

As he gazed out, the Sultan's thoughts turned inward, reflecting on the state of the world and the many factions vying for dominance.

The world was no longer a place of simple rulers and subjects. Magic had always been a force of change, but its recent upheavals had accelerated the pace of transformation. The Sultan knew that he had to adapt to these changes or risk being swept aside by the tides of power. "Magic has always been a double-edged sword," he mused, his mind racing with thoughts of the recent conflicts. "It can elevate a ruler to greatness or plunge a kingdom into chaos. Those who understand this balance can harness its power to maintain their rule."

The rise and fall of the Shadow King had been a testament to this truth. A once-great guardian, corrupted by his own ambitions, had become a force of destruction. And now, even in his defeat, the Shadow King's influence lingered, threatening to destabilize the delicate balance of power.

The Sultan's thoughts turned to the various factions that sought to control the future. The guardians of Al-Qamar, the ancient protectors of magic, had been instrumental in maintaining order. Yet, their power was waning, and new players were stepping into the void.

"Tariq and the entity have shown great promise," the Sultan thought, his mind calculating the potential benefits and risks of aligning with them. "They are heroes to the people, symbols of hope and resilience. But heroes can be unpredictable, driven by ideals that may not align with the needs of the throne." Then there were the mercenaries, led by Khalid, who had already shown their willingness to seize power through dark means. Their corruption of Al-Qamar was a clear indication of their ambition and ruthlessness. "Khalid and his men are a wild card," the Sultan considered. "They seek power for its own sake, driven by greed and ambition. They could be allies, but only if they can be controlled."

To maintain his place and power in this changing world, the Sultan knew he needed a multifaceted approach. He had to balance alliances, leverage the strengths of those around him, and remain vigilant against threats both external and internal.

"First and foremost, I must secure Tariq's loyalty," the Sultan decided. "He is a hero to the people and a powerful asset. If I can convince him that our goals are aligned, he will be a valuable ally."

The Sultan also knew that he needed to keep a close watch on Khalid and the mercenaries. Their ambition made them dangerous, but their power could be useful if properly harnessed.

"I must find a way to control Khalid," the Sultan thought. "Perhaps by offering him a position of power within my court, I can keep him close and ensure his loyalty." Finally, the Sultan recognized the importance of maintaining the illusion of benevolence and strength. The people needed to see him as their protector, the only force capable of keeping the darkness at bay.

"I will continue to project an image of strength and stability," the Sultan resolved. "Through careful manipulation and strategic alliances, I will ensure that my rule remains unchallenged."

As the Sultan turned away from the balcony, his mind was set on the tasks ahead. The world was indeed changing, but he was determined to adapt and thrive amidst the chaos. With Tariq as a potential ally, Khalid as a controlled asset, and the people's loyalty secured, he believed he could navigate the treacherous waters of power and emerge stronger than ever.

The ancient city of Al-Qamar, now a battleground for control and influence, would be the stage upon which the future of the land was decided. And the Sultan, ever the strategist, was prepared to play his part to perfection.

CHAPTER 91: KHALID'S REFLECTIONS

In the heart of the corrupted city of Al-Qamar, Khalid stood amidst the twisted remnants of what had once been a beacon of light and magic. The dark energies that had seeped into the city had changed everything—its architecture, its atmosphere, and most notably, its inhabitants. Khalid and his mercenaries had not been immune to these changes.

Khalid looked around, taking in the altered cityscape. The once radiant walls of Al-Qamar were now veined with dark, pulsating energy. The air was thick with an oppressive aura, and shadows seemed to move with a life of their own. The city had become a place of unease and foreboding.

Khalid felt the weight of the dark energy within himself. When they had first tapped into the remnants of the Shadow King's power, it had felt exhilarating—a surge of strength and invincibility. But that initial thrill had given way to something more insidious. The power was unpredictable, its influence seeping into his very being.

"We sought power to reshape Al-Qamar," Khalid thought, his mind a tumult of emotions. "But this power is changing us, in ways we could never have anticipated."

His mercenaries, too, were showing signs of this transformation. Once a disciplined and focused group, they were now restless and irritable, their tempers quick to flare. The dark energy had enhanced their abilities, but it had also brought out their worst impulses. Khalid had seen fights break out over trivial matters, and a growing sense of distrust was eroding their camaraderie. Farid, his closest confidant and often his voice of reason, approached him, his expression grim. "Khalid, this power... it's affecting us all. I can feel it changing me, making me more aggressive, less in control."

Khalid nodded, his own experiences mirroring Farid's concerns. "I know. I feel it too. This power is more than we bargained for. But we cannot turn back now. We must learn to control it, harness it, or it will destroy us."

The mercenaries had begun to manifest strange abilities, side effects of the dark magic they had absorbed. Some could manipulate shadows, moving unseen through the city's twisted alleys. Others found they could conjure bursts of dark energy, though these abilities often came with a cost—headaches, nosebleeds, and a pervasive sense of unease.

Zhara, one of Khalid's most trusted fighters, demonstrated her newfound abilities. She raised her hand, and the shadows around her coalesced into a swirling mass. With a flick of her wrist, she sent the shadows hurtling towards a distant wall, where they exploded in a burst of dark light.

"Impressive," Khalid said, though his praise was tinged with caution. "But these powers are unstable. We must be careful."

Zhara nodded, her expression serious. "I can feel it, Khalid. The power is intoxicating, but it's also dangerous. We're playing with forces we barely understand."

Khalid felt the weight of leadership more acutely than ever. The decisions he made now would determine not just his own fate, but the fate of his men and the future of Al-Qamar. He had to navigate the fine line between harnessing the power of the dark magic and falling victim to its corruption.

"We have to stay focused," Khalid said, his voice resolute. "We sought this power to reshape Al-Qamar, to make it our stronghold. We must master it, bend it to our will. The city is changing, but we can use these changes to our advantage." Farid's eyes were filled with concern. "And if we can't control it? What then?" Khalid's gaze hardened. "Then we find a way to mitigate its effects. We cannot afford to fail. We've come too far to let this power consume us."

As night fell over Al-Qamar, the city seemed to come alive with a dark, pulsating energy. Khalid stood on a balcony, looking out over the corrupted landscape. The challenge before him was immense, but he was determined to see it through.

"We will master this power," he vowed, more to himself than to anyone else. "We will control it, harness it, and use it to secure our place in this changing world. Al-Qamar will be our legacy, and we will not let it slip through our fingers."

The path ahead was fraught with danger and uncertainty, but Khalid's resolve was unbroken. He would lead his men through this dark transformation, and together, they would forge a new future for Al-Qamar—one where their power was unchallenged, and their dominion secure.

CHAPTER 92: RETURN TO THE SULTAN'S COURT

Tariq and the entity made their way back to the Sultan's court, their hearts heavy with the knowledge of what had transpired in Al-Qamar. The journey was a somber one, filled with reflections on the battles fought and the sacrifices made. Yet, as they neared the grand palace, a sense of duty and determination settled over them. The future of the land depended on their actions, and they were resolved to see their mission through.

Upon their arrival, the grandeur of the Sultan's palace stood in stark contrast to the corrupted remnants of Al-Qamar. The palace was alive with activity, the air buzzing with anticipation and excitement. News of Tariq's victory had spread quickly, and the court was eager to welcome the hero who had defeated the Shadow King.

The palace gates swung open, and Tariq was met with a chorus of cheers and applause. Courtiers and nobles lined the path, their faces alight with admiration and respect. The Sultan himself stood at the top of the grand staircase, his expression a careful blend of warmth and authority. "Tariq!" the Sultan called out, his voice resonating through the courtyard. "Welcome back, my friend. Your bravery and strength have brought hope to our people. Today, we celebrate your victory and the promise of a brighter future."

Tariq, though humbled by the accolades, felt a pang of unease. The memory of Al-Qamar's corruption and the lingering dark energies weighed heavily on his mind. Yet, he understood the importance of maintaining morale and unity. He bowed deeply to the Sultan, acknowledging the cheers of the crowd. "Thank you, Your Majesty," Tariq replied. "But this victory is not mine alone. The entity and I fought side by side, and the power of the ancient guardians guided us. We have much to discuss, and much work remains to be done to ensure the safety and stability of our land." The Sultan's eyes flickered with interest and a hint of calculation. "Indeed, we must. But first, let us celebrate your return. Tonight, you are our honored guest."

The palace was transformed into a scene of opulence and festivity. Rich tapestries adorned the walls, and tables groaned under the weight of lavish feasts. Music filled the air, and the court danced and celebrated, their spirits lifted by the promise of victory.

Tariq found himself the center of attention, surrounded by well-wishers and admirers. Yet, his mind remained focused on the challenges ahead. He knew that the celebration was but a brief respite, a moment of calm before the next storm.

The entity, ever vigilant, stayed close by Tariq's side. It sensed the underlying tensions and the subtle shifts in power dynamics within the court. They both understood that the battle for Al-Qamar's future was far from over. Later that evening, the Sultan summoned Tariq and the entity to a private audience. The opulent chamber was a stark contrast to the battlefield, its tranquility a reminder of the court's detachment from the harsh realities beyond its walls. "Tariq," the Sultan began, his tone measured and thoughtful. "You have done a great service to this kingdom. But I sense there is more to your story. Tell me, what transpired in Al-Qamar?"

Tariq recounted the events of the battle, the defeat of the Shadow King, and the troubling corruption that had taken hold of the city. He spoke of Khalid and the mercenaries, and the lingering threat of dark magic. The Sultan listened intently, his expression unreadable.

"This is concerning," the Sultan said, his voice grave. "The corruption of Al-Qamar must be addressed. We cannot allow such dark forces to spread. What do you propose?"

Tariq took a deep breath. "We must gather the guardians and the most powerful mages. We need to cleanse Al-Qamar of the dark energies and restore its balance. This will require a united effort, Your Majesty."

The Sultan nodded, his mind already calculating the political implications and the steps needed to maintain his power. "Very well. I will summon the council. Together, we will devise a plan to reclaim Al-Qamar and ensure the safety of our land." As the audience concluded, the Sultan watched Tariq and the entity leave the chamber. His thoughts turned inward, reflecting on the changing world and the many factions vying for power. He knew that his position was precarious, and the balance of power delicate.

"The world is changing," the Sultan mused. "Many seek power, and many will fall in their pursuit. But I will remain. I will adapt, I will scheme, and I will secure my rule. For the good of the kingdom, and for my legacy."

With a final, resolute glance at the door through which Tariq and the entity had departed, the Sultan began to formulate his plans. The future was uncertain, but he was determined to emerge as the guiding force in this new era of magic and power.

CHAPTER 93: THE IMPRISONED PRINCESS

After the grand celebration, Tariq found a moment to speak privately with the Sultan. The recent victories and the ongoing threat of Al-Qamar's corruption weighed heavily on his mind. He knew that there was another critical matter that needed to be addressed—the fate of the imprisoned princess within the relic.

As the Sultan settled into his opulent chamber, Tariq approached him with a respectful bow. The entity stood by his side, its presence a constant reminder of the mystical and complex forces at play. "Your Majesty," Tariq began, his voice steady but filled with urgency. "There is another matter of great importance that I must discuss with you." The

Sultan's gaze sharpened, his curiosity piqued. "Speak, Tariq. What concerns you?"

Tariq took a deep breath, gathering his thoughts. "During our journey and battles, we encountered a powerful relic. This relic, however, contains the essence of a princes. She now remains imprisoned within it, bound by her own magic."

The Sultan's eyes widened slightly, a flicker of surprise and intrigue crossing his features. "The princess, you say? Imprisoned within a relic? Tell me more."

The entity stepped forward, its voice calm and resonant. "The princess, Layla, was a beacon of immense power and wisdom. In a desperate act to protect Tariq and the people of this land she released me and in doing so sealed herself within the relic. This imprisonment, however, has left her in a state of perpetual sacrifice. She cannot be freed without great consequence."

The Sultan leaned back in his chair, his fingers steepled as he considered the information. "And what are these consequences?"

Tariq continued, "If the princess is freed, it could unleash a surge of magic that might destabilize the delicate balance we've been trying to maintain. However, her knowledge and power could be instrumental in cleansing Al-Qamar and protecting our kingdom from future threats."

The Sultan's expression was thoughtful, his mind clearly working through the implications. "This is a complex situation. The release of such power could indeed be both a boon and a danger. We must tread carefully."

The entity nodded in agreement. "We believe that with the right preparations and precautions, we can manage the transition. The princess's wisdom and strength are unparalleled. Her guidance could be invaluable."

The Sultan rose from his chair and began to pace, his robes trailing behind him. "And what of the princess's own desires? Does she wish to be freed?"

Tariq's expression softened. "She has accepted her fate with grace and a heavy heart. Her primary concern is the well-being of the land. However, she has expressed a desire to aid us, to see her sacrifice bear fruit in the form of a lasting peace."

The Sultan paused, his back to Tariq and the entity. "We must consider this carefully. The balance of power in our kingdom is already precarious. Any sudden changes could have far-reaching consequences."

Turning to face them, the Sultan's gaze was firm. "Very well, Tariq. We will proceed with caution. Summon the council of mages and guardians. We will need their combined wisdom and strength to navigate this situation. Prepare the necessary rituals and safeguards. We will attempt to release the princess, but we must be ready for any eventuality."

Tariq bowed deeply, a sense of relief and determination filling him. "Thank you, Your Majesty. We will ensure that every precaution is taken." As Tariq and the entity left the chamber to begin the preparations, the Sultan returned to his thoughts. The world was indeed changing, and the complexities of magic and power required careful handling. He knew that his role as a ruler demanded not just strength, but wisdom and foresight.

The imprisoned princess represented both a hope and a challenge. Her release could tip the balance of power, but it also held the promise of a brighter future. The Sultan was resolved to navigate this delicate path with all the skill and cunning at his disposal, ensuring that his kingdom emerged stronger and more united.

CHAPTER 94: MALIK'S SCHEMES AGAIN

As preparations began for the delicate task of releasing the princess from the relic, the palace buzzed with activity. Tariq, the entity, and the council of mages and guardians worked tirelessly to ensure that every precaution was taken. Meanwhile, the Sultan and his trusted advisor, Malik, watched from the shadows, their minds filled with their own schemes and ambitions.

Malik, ever the opportunist, saw an opening to strengthen the Sultan's power and undermine Tariq's influence. He knew that the entity, with its immense power and ancient wisdom, could be a valuable ally or a formidable foe. Driven by ambition, Malik decided to approach the entity with a proposal, hoping to sway it to serve the Sultan's interests.

One evening, Malik found the entity alone in one of the palace gardens. The entity stood by a tranquil fountain, its form glowing softly in the moonlight. Malik approached with a calculated air of respect and camaraderie. "Good evening," Malik began, his tone friendly yet guarded. "I hope I am not disturbing your reflections."

The entity turned to face Malik, its expression calm and inquisitive. "Not at all, Malik. What brings you here at this hour?" Malik smiled, his eyes glinting with a mixture of genuine curiosity and hidden intent. "I have been thinking about the challenges ahead. The task of freeing the princess is no small feat, and it will require great strength and wisdom. I wanted to speak with you about the future of our kingdom and the role you might play in it." The entity regarded Malik thoughtfully. "What do you have in mind?"

Malik's expression grew earnest, his voice lowering conspiratorially. "You possess incredible power, a power that could be instrumental in shaping the future of our land. The Sultan values your abilities and sees the potential for a strong alliance. With your help, we could ensure stability and prosperity, not just for the kingdom, but for all its people."

The entity's gaze remained steady. "And what would this alliance entail?" Malik stepped closer, his voice taking on a persuasive tone. "Tariq is a brave and noble warrior, but his idealism can blind him to the complexities of rule. The Sultan understands the delicate balance of power and the need for decisive leadership. If you were to ally with the Sultan, together we could guide the kingdom towards a brighter future, free from the shadows of corruption and chaos."

The entity's form flickered slightly, as if considering Malik's words. "You speak of a brighter future, but at what cost? What are the Sultan's true intentions?" Malik's smile grew sharper, though he maintained his friendly demeanor. "The Sultan's intentions are to maintain peace and order. To do this, we must ensure that power is concentrated in capable hands. Your wisdom and strength could be the key to achieving this. Tariq, though noble, may not understand the sacrifices that are sometimes necessary for the greater good."

The entity's thoughts swirled with the implications of Malik's proposal. It understood the complexities of power and the challenges of leadership. Yet, it also sensed the undercurrent of manipulation in Malik's words. The entity had seen the consequences of unchecked ambition and the corruption it could bring.

"Malik," the entity said slowly, "I understand the need for strong leadership. But I must question the motives behind your words. Power for the sake of control can lead to tyranny. What assurances do I have that the Sultan's vision aligns with the true well-being of the people?"

Malik's expression grew more intense, his voice softening to a near whisper. "The Sultan's vision is one of unity and strength. With your support, we can ensure that the kingdom remains stable, that its people are protected, and that the dark forces that threaten us are kept at bay. Think of the potential, the legacy we could create together."

The entity's form shimmered with a mix of emotions—curiosity, caution, and resolve. "I appreciate your candor, Malik. But my loyalty lies with the protection of this land and its people. I will not be swayed by promises of power without clear intentions of justice and righteousness."

Malik's eyes narrowed slightly, sensing the entity's resistance. "Very well," he said, his voice regaining its neutral tone. "Consider my words. The future of our kingdom depends on wise decisions and strong alliances. I hope you will see the value in what I propose."

With a respectful nod, Malik turned and left the garden, leaving the entity to its thoughts. The encounter had planted a seed of doubt and reflection, but the entity's resolve remained strong. It knew that the path ahead was fraught with challenges, and it would need to stay true to its principles to navigate the complexities of power and loyalty.

As the preparations for the release of the princess continued, the entity resolved to remain vigilant. The shadows of ambition and manipulation lurked within the palace walls, but it would stand firm in its commitment to protect the land and its people, guided by wisdom and integrity.

CHAPTER 95: A JOURNEY FOR KNOWLEDGE

As the preparations for freeing the princess from the relic continued, Tariq found himself grappling with uncertainty. The complexity of the magic involved and the potential consequences of their actions weighed heavily on his mind. He knew they needed more than just the council's wisdom— they needed specialized knowledge, techniques that could only be found in distant lands.

One evening, after a long day of consultations and preparations, Tariq sought out the entity. He found it in the same garden where Malik had approached it, the soft glow of the entity's form reflecting in the tranquil waters of the fountain. "Entity," Tariq began, his voice filled with determination and a hint of hesitation. "I've been thinking about the task before us. The magic that binds the princess is ancient and complex. I fear that our current knowledge might not be enough to free her safely." The entity turned to face Tariq, its expression curious and attentive. "What are you suggesting, Tariq?"

Tariq took a deep breath. "There are lands beyond our kingdom, places where magic is studied and practiced in ways we have not yet seen. I believe that to truly understand and safely undo the magic of the relic, I need to seek out these distant lands and learn from their masters. I need to find techniques and wisdom that can aid us in our quest."

The entity's form shimmered with thought. "It is a wise decision, Tariq. Knowledge is power, and the more we understand, the better equipped we will be to face the challenges ahead. But the journey will be long and perilous. Are you prepared for such a task?" Tariq nodded, his resolve firm. "I am. I know the risks, but I also know that without this knowledge, we may fail. I cannot let that happen. The princess's sacrifice, the future of our land—it's all too important."

The entity's gaze softened with understanding. "I will support you in this endeavor, Tariq. Your journey will be difficult, but it is necessary. While you are away, I will continue to aid the council and ensure that preparations here continue. We will be ready for your return."

With the entity's blessing, Tariq began to make preparations for his journey. He gathered what resources he could, consulted maps, and sought guidance from those who had traveled beyond their kingdom. The distant lands he sought were shrouded in mystery, their knowledge and practices guarded by ancient traditions.

On the eve of his departure, the Sultan summoned Tariq to his chambers. The Sultan's expression was a mix of concern and curiosity. "Tariq, I hear you are planning to travel to distant lands in search of knowledge. Is this true?"

Tariq bowed respectfully. "Yes, Your Majesty. I believe that to safely free the princess from the relic, we need to understand the ancient magic that binds her. There are techniques and wisdom beyond our borders that may hold the key."

The Sultan nodded slowly. "It is a bold and commendable decision. I support your quest, and I will ensure that the preparations here continue in your absence. But remember, Tariq, the path you take is fraught with danger. Be vigilant and return to us safely."

The next morning, the palace courtyard was filled with a quiet sense of anticipation. Tariq, clad in traveling gear, stood ready to depart. The entity, the council of mages, and a few close friends gathered to see him off. "Tariq," the entity said, its voice filled with both pride and concern, "you carry our hopes with you. Learn all that you can and return to us safely. The future of our land depends on your success."

Tariq nodded, a determined glint in his eyes. "I will return with the knowledge we need. Together, we will free the princess and ensure the safety of our kingdom."

With final farewells, Tariq mounted his horse and set off towards the horizon, the distant lands and their hidden knowledge awaiting him. The journey would be long and challenging, but Tariq's resolve was unshakable. He knew that the fate of the princess, and the future of his homeland, rested on the success of his quest.

As Tariq rode into the distance, the entity watched with a mixture of hope and trepidation. The journey ahead was uncertain, but they had placed their faith in Tariq. The path to understanding and balance was never easy, but it was a path they were committed to following, no matter where it led.

CHAPTER 96: MALIK'S SCHEME GROWS

As Tariq embarked on his journey to distant lands in search of the knowledge needed to free the imprisoned princess, Malik's mind churned with thoughts of ambition and power. The entity, with its immense strength and ancient wisdom, represented an opportunity that Malik could not ignore. If he could find a way to control or trap the entity, he could use its power to secure his position and influence within the Sultan's court—and perhaps even beyond.

Malik began to devise a plan, one that required careful manipulation and cunning. He knew that the entity was wise and vigilant, and any overt actions would be quickly detected. Instead, Malik decided to approach the situation with subtlety, exploiting the entity's trust and the current focus on the preparations to free the princess.

Malik's first step was to sow seeds of doubt within the entity. He approached it one evening, choosing a moment when the palace was quiet and the moonlight cast long shadows over the garden. "Good evening, entity," Malik began, his tone casual yet deliberate. "I've been reflecting on the recent events and our efforts to free the princess. There is much to consider, don't you think?"

The entity, sensing Malik's approach, turned its glowing eyes towards him. "Indeed, Malik. There is much at stake, and every step must be taken with great care." Malik nodded, his expression thoughtful. "I couldn't agree more. Which is why I've been pondering the nature of power and trust. Tariq's departure leaves us in a precarious position. Without him, the burden of leadership and protection falls heavily on you."

The entity's form shimmered slightly, as if contemplating Malik's words. "I am aware of the responsibilities that lie ahead. Tariq's quest is vital, and I will do everything in my power to ensure our success here." Malik's eyes glinted with a mix of sincerity and deception. "I admire your dedication. But I wonder, do you ever feel the weight of this burden too much to bear alone? The dark forces we face are formidable, and even the strongest among us can falter."

The entity's glow dimmed slightly, a sign of introspection. "I am not immune to doubt, Malik. But I draw strength from the hope and determination of those around me."

Malik seized the moment. "And that is precisely why we must be vigilant. There are those within the court who may seek to exploit our efforts for their gain. Trust is a fragile thing, and we must ensure that our allies are truly aligned with our cause." The entity's gaze sharpened. "What are you suggesting?"

Malik's expression turned grave. "I have reason to believe that there are factions within the court who harbor ambitions of their own. They may see your power as a threat or an opportunity. We must be cautious and ensure that we do not become pawns in their schemes." The entity considered Malik's words carefully. "I will remain vigilant, Malik. Your counsel is appreciated. But I trust in Tariq and the Sultan. Our cause is just, and we will prevail."

Malik's smile was subtle, masking his true intentions. "Of course, entity. Together, we will navigate these treacherous waters. If there is anything I can do to aid you, do not hesitate to ask." With that, Malik left the garden, his mind already plotting the next steps. He needed to create a situation where the entity would be isolated and vulnerable, a moment where he could spring his trap and harness its power.

Over the following days, Malik worked behind the scenes, using his influence to subtly manipulate the court's activities. He arranged for a series of distractions and minor crises that required the entity's attention, gradually wearing down its vigilance and spreading its focus thin.

Malik also began to gather a group of loyal followers, individuals who shared his ambition and were willing to aid in his scheme for promises of power and reward. Together, they crafted a plan to trap the entity, using a combination of ancient magic and deception.

One night, Malik set his plan into motion. He sent a message to the entity, claiming that he had discovered vital information about the relic and the princess's imprisonment. He requested a private meeting in a secluded part of the palace, away from prying eyes and ears.

The entity, ever committed to their cause, agreed to the meeting, unaware of Malik's true intentions. As it arrived at the appointed place, Malik and his conspirators sprung their trap, activating a series of enchanted barriers and spells designed to contain and weaken the entity.

The entity realized the betrayal too late. The enchanted barriers sapped its strength, and the combined magic of Malik's followers overwhelmed it. Malik stepped forward, his eyes gleaming with triumph. "Forgive me, entity," Malik said, his voice cold and calculated. "But power such as yours cannot be left unchecked. With you under my control, we will reshape this kingdom as we see fit."

The entity, weakened but defiant, glared at Malik. "You will not succeed, Malik. This betrayal will not go unanswered." Malik's smile was ruthless. "We shall see. For now, you are mine to command."

As the entity struggled against its bonds, Malik reveled in his newfound power, unaware of the far-reaching consequences of his actions. The balance of power in the kingdom had shifted once again, and the future was more uncertain than ever.

CHAPTER 97: JOURNEY TO THE JUNGLE CITY

Tariq rode through the vast expanse of lands, leaving behind the arid deserts and crossing lush valleys. His journey was long and arduous, but his determination to find the knowledge necessary to free the princess never wavered. Guided by ancient maps and the wisdom shared by the entity, he finally reached the outskirts of a mysterious jungle city known for its magical traditions and unique flora and fauna.

The air grew humid, and the dense canopy of the jungle loomed overhead, casting dappled shadows on the path ahead. Strange calls of unseen creatures echoed through the trees, and vibrant flowers of every hue dotted the landscape. The city, hidden within this verdant maze, was said to be a haven of ancient knowledge and mystical practices.

As Tariq approached the city, he was greeted by the sight of towering trees intertwined with ancient stone structures. The city seemed to grow out of the jungle itself, a seamless blend of nature and human craftsmanship. Vines and flowers adorned the buildings, and the air was thick with the scent of exotic blossoms.

At the entrance, he was met by a group of city guards, their attire reflecting the rich, vibrant culture of the place. They eyed him with curiosity but allowed him passage when he explained his quest.

Tariq was guided through winding streets, bustling with activity. Strange animals, unlike any he had seen before, roamed freely alongside the city's inhabitants. Monkeys with bright plumage swung from the trees, and small, luminescent creatures flitted about, their glow adding to the city's magical ambiance.

He was taken to the heart of the city, where the Council of Elders resided. The elders, a group of wise and venerable figures, sat in a grand hall open to the elements, with the sounds of the jungle providing a constant backdrop.

An elder with a long, white beard and eyes that seemed to hold the wisdom of centuries spoke first. "Welcome, wanderer. We have heard of your journey and the purpose that brings you here. Tell us, what do you seek?"

Tariq bowed respectfully. "Great elders, I seek knowledge to free a princess imprisoned within a magical relic. The magic that binds her is ancient and complex, and I fear that without the proper techniques, we may not succeed in freeing her safely. I have come to learn from your wisdom and to find the means to achieve this goal."

The elders listened intently as Tariq recounted his journey and the challenges he faced. After a moment of contemplation, the lead elder spoke again. "Your quest is noble, and the task before you is indeed daunting. The magic of imprisonment is among the most intricate and perilous. We will share with you what we know, but understand that the path you take will require great skill and understanding."

Over the following days, Tariq immersed himself in the teachings of the jungle city. He learned about the unique properties of the jungle's flora, the mystical creatures that inhabited the region, and the ancient rituals practiced by the city's inhabitants. The elders taught him how to harness the natural magic of the jungle, blending it with the knowledge he had already acquired.

One evening, as the sun set and the jungle came alive with the sounds of nocturnal creatures, the elders gathered with Tariq for a special ceremony. They led him to a sacred grove deep within the jungle, where the energy of the land was at its most potent.

In the center of the grove stood an ancient tree, its bark etched with glowing runes. The elders instructed Tariq to place something of the princess at the base of the tree. They began to chant, their voices harmonizing with the sounds of the jungle, creating a powerful resonance.

As the ritual progressed, Tariq could feel the energy of the jungle flowing through him, connecting with her items. The runes on the tree began to glow brighter, and the air around them shimmered with magical energy.

After what felt like hours, the chanting ceased, and a profound silence fell over the grove. The lead elder approached Tariq, his eyes shining with a mix of exhaustion and hope. "You have learned much, Tariq. The knowledge you now possess will aid you in freeing the princess. But remember, the final act must be performed with great care and precision. The balance of magic is delicate, and any misstep could have dire consequences."

Tariq nodded, gratitude and determination filling his heart. "Thank you, wise elders. I will use this knowledge wisely and with the utmost respect for the balance of magic."

As Tariq prepared to leave the jungle city, the elders presented him with a small vial of glowing liquid, extracted from the heart of the ancient tree. "This essence will aid you in the final ritual," the lead elder explained. "Use it wisely."

With newfound knowledge and a renewed sense of purpose, Tariq set out from the jungle city, the vial of essence safely tucked away. His journey was far from over, but he felt more prepared than ever to face the challenges ahead. The fate of the princess and the future of his land rested on his shoulders, and he was determined to see his quest through to the end.

As he ventured back into the wilds, the echoes of the jungle city's wisdom accompanied him, guiding his path and fortifying his resolve.

CHAPTER 98: LESSONS FROM THE JUNGLE

Tariq remained in the jungle city longer than he had anticipated. The elders' teachings had opened his mind to new possibilities, but he knew there was still much to learn. He decided to venture deeper into the jungle, guided by the belief that the natural world held wisdom beyond what could be taught in books or through rituals.

Tariq ventured into the heart of the jungle, where the dense foliage and the sounds of wildlife enveloped him. The jungle was a vibrant, living entity, each part interconnected with the others. Here, he hoped to learn about the circle of life and the basics of human nature.

His journey took him to a sacred grove, where the trees towered above, their branches forming a protective canopy. In this secluded spot, he encountered an old shaman, a guardian of the jungle's secrets. The shaman, an elderly woman with eyes that seemed to see through time, greeted Tariq warmly.

"Welcome, wanderer," the shaman said, her voice gentle yet powerful. "The jungle has much to teach those who are willing to listen. Come, let us walk and learn."

The shaman led Tariq through the jungle, pointing out the intricate relationships between the plants, animals, and the land itself. She explained the concept of the circle of life, how every creature played a role in maintaining the balance of the ecosystem. "Observe the ants," the shaman said, gesturing to a trail of industrious insects. "They work together, each one contributing to the colony. They teach us about community and cooperation."

Further along, they came upon a majestic tiger resting in the shade. The shaman bowed her head in respect. "The tiger is a powerful predator, yet it hunts only what it needs. It teaches us about strength and restraint." As they walked, Tariq saw the delicate balance between predator and prey, the way plants grew and decayed, returning nutrients to the soil. Each observation reinforced the shaman's teachings about the interconnectedness of all life.

One evening, the shaman brought Tariq to a clearing where animals gathered at dusk. He watched as monkeys played in the trees, their interactions a complex mix of hierarchy and playfulness. Birds sang intricate melodies, communicating warnings, and attracting mates. Even the smallest insects had their role in this vibrant tapestry.

"The animals live by their instincts," the shaman explained. "They do not question their place in the world; they simply exist, each fulfilling its role. Humans, however, have the gift—and the curse—of consciousness. We question, we aspire, we create, and we destroy. This is the essence of human nature."

Tariq pondered these words as he watched a family of deer graze peacefully. "So, our challenge is to balance our instincts with our higher aspirations?"

The shaman nodded. "Exactly. We must learn from the animals, understand our place in the circle of life, and strive to live in harmony with the world. This balance is essential, not just for our survival, but for the fulfillment of our true potential."

Over the next few weeks, Tariq immersed himself in the life of the jungle. He learned to listen to the whispers of the wind, to read the signs left by animals, and to understand the subtle language of the plants. The jungle, with all its beauty and danger, became his teacher.

He realized that the lessons of the jungle were not just about survival, but about understanding the deeper truths of existence. The balance between life and death, strength and vulnerability, independence and community—all these were reflections of the human experience.

As Tariq prepared to leave the jungle city, he felt a profound sense of clarity. The knowledge he had gained from the elders and the wisdom of the jungle had transformed him. He understood now that freeing the princess was not just about breaking a magical bond, but about restoring balance and harmony.

With a heart full of gratitude, Tariq bid farewell to the shaman and the jungle city. He carried with him the essence of the jungle's wisdom, ready to face the challenges ahead. The journey back to his homeland would be long, but he was no longer the same man who had left.

He had become a true guardian of balance, prepared to face whatever trials lay ahead with strength, wisdom, and a deep understanding of the circle of life.

CHAPTER 99: KHALID'S VISION

In the heart of the corrupted city of Al-Qamar, Khalid stood before his group of loyal mercenaries. The dark energy of the Shadow King had seeped into the very fabric of the city, altering its essence and empowering those who had chosen to wield its chaotic force. Khalid's eyes gleamed with ambition as he prepared to address his followers, his mind filled with plans to reshape their world.

Khalid's inner circle gathered around him in the ruins of what had once been a grand hall. The walls, now dark and pulsating with corrupted energy, seemed to echo their leader's fervor. Farid, Zhara, and a few other key members of the group stood at attention, their faces reflecting a mix of anticipation and trepidation.

Khalid began, his voice low but powerful. "We stand on the precipice of a new era. The fall of the Shadow King has left a void, and it is up to us to fill it. The power we have gained from this city is unlike any other. It is a force that can reshape the very foundations of our world."

Farid, ever the skeptic, stepped forward. "Khalid, the power we wield is indeed formidable, but it is also unpredictable. How do you propose we harness it without falling prey to its corruption?"

Khalid nodded, acknowledging the concern. "We must be strategic in our approach. Our first step is gain control over Al-Madina. This city, with its ancient magic and strategic location, will be our stronghold. We will use its power to fortify our position and defend against any who seek to challenge us." Zhara, her eyes glinting with excitement, chimed in. "And what of the people? How will we maintain order and ensure their loyalty?"

Khalid's expression grew stern. "We will rule with a combination of strength and fear. The dark energy we command can be a tool for both destruction and protection. We will show the people that resisting us is futile, but we will also protect them from external threats. In time, they will see that our rule is necessary for their survival."

Khalid raised his hands, as if to encompass the entirety of their vision. "Our rule will not be one of tyranny for its own sake. We will bring order to chaos, structure to anarchy. The magic we possess will be used to rebuild and reshape Al-Madina into a city of unmatched power and influence. From here, we will extend our reach, bringing other lands under our control."

Khalid's eyes darkened slightly. "Balance is a concept for the weak. We will redefine what it means to rule. Light and dark are merely tools to be used. We will wield both, but we will not be bound by their limitations. Our strength lies in our ability to adapt, to control, and to dominate."

As Khalid spoke, the mercenaries felt a surge of energy, a reflection of the dark power that now coursed through their veins. They knew the path ahead would be fraught with challenges, but Khalid's vision filled them with a sense of purpose. "We will be legends," Khalid declared. "Our names will be etched into the annals of history. Al-Qamar will be the beacon of our power, and from here, we will reshape the world."

The group dispersed; each member filled with a renewed sense of determination. Khalid remained in the grand hall, his thoughts already turning to the next steps. He knew that maintaining their power would require constant vigilance and ruthless action. The dark energy was both a gift and a curse, and he intended to wield it to its fullest potential.

As the night deepened, Khalid gazed out over the corrupted city. The transformation of Al-Qamar was just the beginning. His ambitions stretched far beyond its borders, and he was ready to face any obstacle that stood in his way. The world was changing, and Khalid intended to be at the forefront of that change, a ruler of unparalleled power and vision.

CHAPTER 100: MALIK'S AMBITION

In the shadowy corridors of the Sultan's palace, Malik's mind raced with dark ambition. The entity, now captured and weakened by Malik's cunning trap, held a power that could reshape the very essence of the city. Malik envisioned a city alive, bound to him, a living city under his control. This vision was a tantalizing blend of power and immortality.

Malik convened a secret meeting with his most trusted allies, those who had helped him in the capture of the entity. They gathered in a dimly lit chamber, their faces illuminated by the flickering light of torches. "Friends," Malik began, his voice smooth and commanding, "we have achieved what many thought impossible. The entity, with its vast power, is now within our grasp. But this is only the beginning. I have a vision, a plan that will elevate us to the pinnacle of power."

His followers leaned in, their curiosity piqued. One of them, a cunning sorceress named Yasmin, spoke up. "What do you propose, Malik?"

Malik's eyes gleamed with a mix of excitement and determination. "The entity possesses the power to bind life to magic. Imagine a city that is not just a collection of buildings and people, but a living, breathing organism. A city that responds to our will, protects us, and ensures our dominance."

The group murmured in astonishment. Malik continued, "We will use the entity to infuse the city with life. The walls, the streets, the very air will be bound to us. This living city will be indestructible, its power unmatched. And with me at its heart, bound to the city's essence, our rule will be eternal." Yasmin, ever the skeptic, raised an eyebrow. "Binding the city to life through the entity's power is a bold plan, Malik. But how can we ensure that we control it and that it does not turn against us?"

Malik nodded, anticipating the question. "The ritual to bind the city to life is intricate and requires precision. We will perform it in stages, gradually infusing the entity's power into the city's core. By doing so, we can monitor the changes and ensure that everything proceeds according to our plan." Yasmin, her eyes alight with intrigue, added, "And if the entity resists? It is ancient and powerful. It may not submit to our will so easily." Malik's expression hardened. "We will break its will. The entity's power is vast, but it is not invincible. We have the means to control it, to harness its magic. And once the city is bound to us, the entity's power will be fully integrated into our own."

The group dispersed, each member tasked with a specific role in the upcoming ritual. Malik returned to the chamber where the entity was held. The ancient being, now weakened and contained within a magical barrier, looked up as Malik approached. "Malik," the entity's voice was filled with a mix of anger and sadness, "your ambition blinds you. The power you seek to control will only bring destruction."

Malik's smile was cold and unyielding. "You underestimate me, entity. This power will bring a new era, one where I am the master of a living city. You will be the heart of this transformation, and through you, we will achieve greatness."

Over the following days, preparations for the binding ritual began in earnest. Magical sigils were etched into the city's foundations, and ancient chants filled the air. Malik, Yasmin, and the other conspirators worked tirelessly, their determination driving them forward. As the night of the ritual approached, the tension in the city was palpable. The citizens of Al-Madina, unaware of the dark magic at play, continued their lives under the shadow of an impending transformation.

On the appointed night, Malik and his followers gathered in the central square of Al-Madina. The entity, bound by magical chains, was brought forth. Malik began the incantation, his voice rising above the whispers of the wind.

The ground trembled as the ritual progressed. The sigils glowed with an eerie light, and the very air seemed to crackle with energy. The entity's power, reluctantly unleashed, began to merge with the city's core. As the ritual reached its climax, the city of Al-Madina shuddered and then seemed to sigh with newfound life. The walls pulsed with a faint glow, and the streets hummed with a subtle energy. The city was no longer just stone and mortar; it had become a living entity, bound to Malik's will.

Malik stood at the center of it all, his eyes filled with triumph. "Behold, the living city of Al-Madina! Our power is unmatched, our rule unbreakable!" The entity, now an integral part of the city, looked on with a mixture of resignation and despair. The balance of power had shifted once again, but the true consequences of this transformation were yet to be seen.

CHAPTER 101: A DISTURBANCE FELT

Tariq had ventured deep into the jungle city, absorbing the wisdom and knowledge that the ancient and mystical inhabitants had to offer. The teachings on the circle of life, the delicate balance of nature, and the intrinsic connections between all living things had enriched his understanding and fortified his resolve.

Yet, as he prepared to delve even further into the depths of the jungle, seeking more hidden knowledge, he felt an inexplicable unease. It started as a faint whisper in the back of his mind, a subtle disturbance that gradually grew into a gnawing anxiety.

One evening, as the sun dipped below the horizon and the jungle began to hum with nocturnal life, Tariq sat in quiet contemplation. He closed his eyes, reaching out with his senses, trying to understand the source of his disquiet.

Suddenly, a vision flashed before his eyes—a vision of the entity, his loyal and powerful friend, bound and suffering. He saw dark magic swirling around Al-Madina, the once-great city now corrupted and twisted. Malik's face loomed in the vision, filled with ambition and malevolence.

Tariq's eyes snapped open, his heart pounding. "Something is terribly wrong," he murmured to himself. "The entity is in danger. Malik has betrayed us, and Al-Madina is becoming a living nightmare." As Tariq packed his belongings, preparing for a hasty return, his mind raced with thoughts of how everything had spiraled into chaos. He remembered the beginnings of his quest—the hope and determination that had driven him to seek the knowledge necessary to free the princess. But now, it seemed, the forces of darkness and ambition had outpaced his efforts. "How did it come to this?" Tariq thought, his brow furrowed. "So much chaos, so much treachery. We sought to bring balance and peace, yet the shadows have grown deeper and more insidious."

He thought of the Sultan's court, the machinations of Malik, and the corruption spreading through Al-Qamar. The delicate balance they had tried to maintain was on the verge of collapse, and the stakes had never been higher. Determined to save his friend and restore order, Tariq set off on his journey back to Al-Madina. The path through the jungle was fraught with dangers, but his resolve was unshakable. Every step he took was fueled by a deep sense of duty and a burning desire to right the wrongs that had befallen his homeland.

As he journeyed, he reflected on the lessons he had learned in the jungle city. The circle of life, the balance of nature—these were not just abstract concepts but vital truths that must be upheld. He understood now that true power lay not in domination but in harmony.

CHAPTER 102: KHALID'S AMBITION UNLEASHED

In the heart of the corrupted city of Al-Qamar, Khalid stood atop a high tower, his eyes fixed on the distant horizon. The dark energies that now suffused the city had transformed it into a formidable stronghold, and Khalid felt a surge of pride and power. His mind, however, was already turning towards his next move.

Khalid watched as the Al-Madina responded to Malik's dark rituals. The buildings seemed to breathe, the streets pulsed with energy, and shadows danced in every corner. The transformation was both awe-inspiring and terrifying. "This is just the beginning," Khalid thought, a grim smile spreading across his face. "If Malik can infuse a city with life, then so can I. But I will take it further. I will lead my city to conquer, to dominate. Al-Madina will be just the first in a series of conquests." He turned to Farid, his loyal second-in-command, who stood nearby. "Farid, we've seen what Malik has done. It's time for us to act. Prepare the men. We're taking the battle to them."

Farid's eyes widened in surprise but quickly shifted to determination. "As you command, Khalid. We will be ready." Khalid descended from the tower, his steps purposeful and resolute. He summoned his key officers and outlined his plan. "We will use the power of this city to descend upon Al-Madina. Our forces, combined with the dark energies we've harnessed, will be unstoppable. We will crush Malik and his followers, and the power of the living city will be ours." Zhara, one of his fiercest warriors, stepped forward. "What about the people of Al-Madina? They will resist."

Khalid's expression hardened. "We will show them the futility of resistance. The city itself will aid us. Those who submit will be spared; those who resist will be destroyed."

The preparations were swift and efficient. Khalid's mercenaries, now augmented by the dark magic they had absorbed, readied themselves for the impending battle. Al-Qamar responded to their intent, its energies amplifying their strength and resolve. As night fell, Khalid stood at the forefront of his army, his eyes gleaming with anticipation. "Tonight, we make history," he declared. "We will descend upon Al-Madina and take what is rightfully ours. This city will be the heart of our new empire."

With a roar, Khalid's forces began their descent. Al-Qamar now a colossal war machine, moved with them, its structures shifting and changing to support their advance. The ground trembled as they approached Al-Madina, the air thick with the promise of conflict. As they reached the outskirts of the city, they were met with resistance. Malik's forces, alerted to the impending assault, had fortified their positions. The battle began in earnest, dark energies clashing and exploding in a symphony of chaos.

Khalid led the charge, his presence a beacon of dark power. His men fought with relentless ferocity, their abilities enhanced by the city's corrupted magic. The streets of Al-Madina became a battleground, with buildings and structures coming to life, attacking and defending with a will of their own. Amidst the chaos, Khalid sought out Malik, knowing that a decisive confrontation would determine the outcome of the battle. As he fought his way through the city, he could feel the pulse of the living city's power, urging him onward.

As the battle raged, Khalid could see the potential of a city bound to his will. The power to reshape, to dominate, to control—it was within his grasp. The chaos of the battlefield only fueled his ambition, driving him to push harder, fight fiercer. "This is what it means to wield true power," Khalid thought, a fierce determination in his eyes. "Not just to possess it, but to command it, to reshape the world in your image. Al-Madina will be mine, and from here, we will conquer all." The battle for Al-Madina had begun, and with it, the fight for the future of the land. Khalid's ambition and Malik's dark rituals clashed in a contest of wills, each seeking to bend the city—and its power—to their own ends. The outcome would determine the fate of all who lived in the shadow of these formidable forces.

CHAPTER 103: THE BATTLE OF THE LIVING CITIES

The night was illuminated by an otherworldly glow as the two living cities, Al-Madina and Khalid's corrupted stronghold, Al-Qamar prepared for battle. The air crackled with magical energy, and the ground trembled as ancient powers clashed. The once serene landscape now bore witness to a confrontation that would determine the fate of the land. Khalid, standing at the forefront of his army, raised his hand, and Al-Qamar responded. The streets shifted, walls extended, and structures reformed into defensive and offensive positions. His mercenaries, empowered by the dark energies coursing through the city, charged forward with a ferocity that seemed almost unnatural.

Across the battlefield, Malik stood resolute, his eyes glowing with the dark magic he had harnessed. He commanded his forces with precision, the living city of Al-Madina responding to his every command. Buildings transformed into towering golems, streets became rivers of molten lava, and trees sprouted limbs to entangle the invaders.

The clash of magical energies was both breathtaking and terrifying. Khalid's forces wielded their newfound powers with deadly efficiency. Zhara, with her shadow manipulation, became a whirlwind of darkness, striking down enemies with lightning speed. Farid, now able to summon spectral warriors, led his phantom army into the fray, their ethereal blades slicing through Malik's defenses.

Malik countered with equal ferocity. He summoned elemental spirits, their fiery and icy forms wreaking havoc on Khalid's ranks. The ground beneath Khalid's forces erupted with jagged crystals, impaling those who were too slow to react. Malik's command of the city turned every corner of Al-Madina into a potential trap.

The battle raged on, each side pushing the other to their limits. The living cities themselves seemed to come alive, their structures groaning and shifting as they absorbed and redirected magical energy. Al-Madina's buildings glowed with an eerie light, while Khalid's city pulsed with dark, ominous shadows.

Khalid, seeing an opportunity, called upon the full might of his city's power. The ground beneath Al-Qamar began to crack and split, dark tendrils of energy reaching up to entangle the city's defenses. "We will break them!" Khalid roared, his voice amplified by the magic around him.

Malik, undeterred, unleashed a torrent of elemental fury. Firestorms swept through Khalid's ranks, and torrents of water washed away the dark tendrils. The air was filled with the deafening sounds of battle, the clash of steel, the roar of flames, and the crackle of lightning.

As the battle reached its climax, Khalid and Malik faced off amidst the chaos. Their magical energies collided in a dazzling display of light and darkness. Khalid's eyes burned with ambition, while Malik's glowed with the cold, calculating intensity of a seasoned strategist.

Khalid summoned the full power of Al-Qamar, his body surrounded by a swirling vortex of shadows. "You cannot stop us, Malik! We will reshape this world in our image!" Malik responded with a wave of his hand, summoning a barrier of pure energy. "Your ambition blinds you, Khalid. This power is not meant for tyranny!"

The two leaders clashed, their powers creating shockwaves that rippled through the battlefield. Buildings crumbled, the ground shook, and the sky seemed to split with the intensity of their confrontation. Khalid's dark energy sought to consume and corrupt, while Malik's magic seemed to spread death and decay.

As the battle reached its zenith, a blinding explosion of light and shadow erupted from the center of Al-Qamar. Both cities groaned in response, their energies reacting violently to the clash of such immense power.

When the dust settled, the battlefield was a scene of devastation. Both Khalid's and Malik's forces lay scattered, exhausted and wounded. The living cities, drained of much of their magical energy, stood in eerie silence, their once vibrant structures now dimmed.

Khalid, wounded but defiant, struggled to his feet. "This is not over, Malik. We will rise again." Malik, equally battered, met Khalid's gaze with steely resolve. "The battle may be over, but the war for the future of our land has just begun."

As both leaders retreated to regroup, the citizens of Al-Madina emerged from the shadows, their eyes filled with a mixture of fear and despair. The battle had shown them the true power of their city, but also the devastating consequences of its misuse.

Days turned into weeks as Tariq traveled with relentless determination. Finally, the outskirts of Al-Madina came into view. The city, once a beacon of life and wisdom, now loomed like a dark monolith, pulsating with a sinister energy. Tariq's heart ached at the sight. "Hold on, my friend," he whispered, thinking of the entity. "I am coming for you. Together, we will set things right."

Tariq, having felt the disturbance, quickened his pace towards Al-Madina. He knew that his presence would be crucial in the battles to come. The lessons he had learned in the jungle and the wisdom he had gained were now more important than ever.

As Tariq approached the city, he knew that a confrontation with Malik was inevitable. Malik's ambition and treachery had brought about a new darkness, one that threatened to engulf everything Tariq held dear. Tariq's resolve hardened. He had learned much on his journey, and now it was time to put that knowledge to use. The fate of the entity, the princess, and the entire kingdom rested on his shoulders.

With a deep breath, Tariq stepped into the living city of Al-Madina, ready to face the challenges ahead and determined to restore balance and justice to his land. The battle of the living cities was but a prelude to the greater conflicts ahead. As the forces of light and darkness continued to clash, the future of the land hung in the balance, waiting for those with the strength and wisdom to guide it to a better tomorrow.

CHAPTER 104:
REFLECTIONS OF THE
ENTITY

Amidst the chaos of the battle between Khalid's and Malik's forces, the entity found itself bound and weakened, forced to witness the clash of powers from within its magical prison. Its once vibrant glow had dimmed, and its thoughts were a tangled web of pain and reflection.

The entity's thoughts drifted to the nature of subjugation. It had always known power as a means of protection and balance, but now it was being used as a tool of control and domination. Bound by Malik's dark magic, the entity felt the weight of its imprisonment keenly. "How did it come to this?" it wondered. "To be subjugated by those who seek only to exploit and corrupt? Power should be wielded with wisdom, not tyranny. Yet here I am, a prisoner to the very forces I once sought to guide."

The entity's mind wandered to the countless civilizations it had observed over the centuries, each grappling with the delicate balance of power and freedom. It had seen rulers who governed with benevolence and others who ruled with an iron fist. The latter always led to corruption, suffering, and ultimately, downfall.

As the battle raged outside, the entity reflected on the insidious nature of corruption. Malik's ambition had twisted the noble goals they once shared, turning them into a dark quest for domination. Khalid, too, had succumbed to the allure of unchecked power, his city becoming a weapon of conquest rather than a beacon of hope. "Corruption begins in the heart," the entity mused. "It starts with a desire for more—more power, more control, more influence. But as that desire grows, it consumes the very essence of what makes one human. Ambition without restraint becomes a poison, seeping into the soul and turning noble intentions into dark obsessions."

The entity's own power, once a source of guidance and protection, was now being used to fuel Malik's schemes. It felt a profound sorrow for the path Malik had chosen and the suffering it had wrought upon the land.

The entity's thoughts turned inward, to the personal struggle it faced. Bound by Malik's magic, it was now forced to fight against its own father, the Shadow King. The memories of their time together, before the darkness had consumed them, came rushing back.

"We were once protectors of this land," the entity remembered. "My father and I, wandering the desert, seeking knowledge and wisdom. But the very magic we cherished became our downfall. My father's quest for vengeance led him down a path of darkness, and I too became a prisoner to the very powers we sought to understand."

The entity's heart ached with the realization that it was now pitted against the one it had once loved and revered. "Why am I forced to fight against my own blood? How do I reconcile the duty to protect with the pain of betrayal?"

Despite its despair, the entity clung to a glimmer of hope. It knew that Tariq was on his way, driven by a determination to set things right. The bond they shared, forged in the fires of battle and tempered by mutual respect, was a source of strength. "Tariq will come," the entity thought with resolve. "He understands the true nature of power and the importance of balance. Together, we will find a way to break these chains and restore harmony to the land."

The entity's reflections gave it a renewed sense of purpose. Though imprisoned and weakened, it would not succumb to despair. It would endure, waiting for the moment when it could once again stand beside Tariq and fight for the future, they both believed in.

As the battle outside raged on, the entity's thoughts remained focused on the lessons it had learned. The nature of subjugation and corruption, the pain of

fighting against its own kin, and the hope for a brighter future—all these reflections strengthened its resolve.

The struggle for Al-Madina was far from over, but the entity knew that with Tariq's return, there was still a chance to reclaim what had been lost. The path ahead would be fraught with challenges, but the entity was ready to face them, armed with the wisdom of its reflections and the strength of its resolve.

CHAPTER 105:
REFLECTIONS OF A
BATTLE-SCARRED LAND

Tariq rode into the city of Al-Madina, his heart heavy with the weight of the destruction that lay before him. The once magnificent city, now a battleground of twisted magic and broken dreams, stood as a testament to the chaos that ambition and power could unleash. The air was thick with the residue of dark energies, and the ground was littered with the remnants of a fierce conflict.

As he dismounted his horse, Tariq took in the scene around him. The streets, once bustling with life, were now eerily silent, save for the occasional groan of a collapsing structure or the distant cries of those still caught in the fray. Buildings that had once stood as proud symbols of the city's heritage now lay in ruins; their beauty marred by the scars of battle.

Walking through the desolate city, Tariq couldn't help but reflect on the nature of the suffering that had befallen everyone involved. Each individual, driven by their desires and ambitions, had become a prisoner of their own making. He thought of the entity, his loyal friend, now bound by Malik's dark magic. "The entity, with all its power and wisdom, is a prisoner to its own sense of duty and devotion," Tariq mused. "Its desire to protect and guide has been twisted into a chain that binds it to suffering."

The Sultan's Power

The Sultan, too, was not free. "The Sultan is trapped by his own need to maintain power and control," Tariq reflected. "His decisions, driven by fear of losing his throne, have led to a series of betrayals and dark alliances. He is a prisoner to his own crown."

Malik and Khalid's Ambitions

Malik and Khalid, the two men whose ambitions had sparked the current conflict, were perhaps the most tragic prisoners of all. "Malik, with his insatiable thirst for power, and Khalid, with his relentless drive for conquest—they are both consumed by their ambitions. Their desires have led them down a path of destruction, and now they are bound to the chaos they have created."

The Shadow King's Vengeance

The Shadow King, whose presence had cast a long shadow over the land, was driven by vengeance. "The Shadow King is condemned by his own hatred and desire for revenge," Tariq thought. "His actions, born from a place of deep pain, have only perpetuated the cycle of suffering."

The Princess's Love

And then there was the princess, the heart of Tariq's quest. "The princess, imprisoned within the relic, is a prisoner to her own love and sacrifice. Her desire to protect her people has led her to a fate of endless confinement. She suffers because of her selfless love."

The Nature of Desire and Suffering

Tariq's heart ached with the realization that all these individuals, each driven by their desires, were condemned to suffer. "Desire, in its many forms, can be a powerful motivator," he reflected. "But when unchecked, it becomes a chain that binds us to our own undoing. Power, love, vengeance, ambition—they all lead to suffering if not tempered by wisdom and balance."

Despite the devastation, Tariq knew that hope still remained. The lessons he had learned in the jungle city, the wisdom he had gained from the elders and the shaman, had taught him that balance was the key to breaking these chains. "We must find a way to restore harmony," he resolved. "To free ourselves from the prisons of our own making and create a future where wisdom guides our desires."

With renewed determination, Tariq set off towards the heart of the city, where he knew Malik and Khalid would be locked in their final confrontation. He knew that to end the cycle of suffering, he would need to confront them both and find a way to release the entity and the princess. As he walked, the city seemed to whisper its own reflections, the echoes of its history mingling with the hopes for its future. The path ahead was fraught with challenges, but Tariq was ready to face them, armed with the knowledge that true power lay not in domination, but in understanding and balance.

CHAPTER 106: TARIQ'S DECISION

As Tariq made his way through the desolate streets of Al-Madina, his mind raced with thoughts of how to end the suffering and chaos that had enveloped the city and its people. He knew that to restore balance and free those imprisoned by their desires, a great sacrifice would be needed. It was then that a daring plan began to form in his mind—a plan to use the relic to bind himself and free everyone else.

Tariq knew that the relic, which held the princess, was a powerful artifact capable of both binding and liberating the essence of individuals. It had been used to imprison the princess in an act of selfless love and sacrifice. Now, Tariq hoped to harness its power once more, but this time, for a different purpose.

His plan was simple yet fraught with danger. Tariq would use the relic to bind himself, channeling the energies required to free the princess, the entity, and even the Shadow King from their respective imprisonments. By becoming the focal point of the relic's power, he would absorb the dark energies that had corrupted the city and its inhabitants, sacrificing himself to restore balance and harmony.

Tariq took a deep breath, his resolve unwavering. He knew the risks, but he also understood that this was the only way to save everyone. He would confront Malik and Khalid, using the relic to draw their powers into himself, thus breaking the chains that bound them all.

Tariq approached the central square where Malik and Khalid were locked in a fierce battle. Dark energies swirled around them, their powers clashing in a display of raw, destructive force. With the relic clutched in his hand, Tariq stepped into the fray, his presence commanding their attention.

"Malik! Khalid!" Tariq's voice rang out, cutting through the din of battle. "This must end now. Your ambitions have brought only suffering and chaos. It's time to restore balance and free those imprisoned by your desires." Malik sneered, his eyes glinting with malice. "And how do you propose to do that, Tariq? You are but one man."

Tariq raised the relic, its glow intensifying. "I will use this relic the heart of Al-tahnia to bind myself and absorb the darkness that has corrupted this city.

In doing so, I will free the princess, the entity, and even the Shadow King. You will be freed from your ambitions, and the land will be restored."

As Tariq began to chant the incantation taught to him by the elders of the jungle city, the relic's power surged. The ground trembled, and a bright light enveloped him. Malik and Khalid watched in awe and fear as the relic's magic took hold. The energies of the dark magic that had permeated Al-Qamar and Al-Madina began to flow into the relic, drawn towards Tariq. He could feel the weight of the darkness pressing upon him, but he remained steadfast, his thoughts focused on the goal of freeing everyone.

One by one, the chains of magic that bound the princess, the entity, and the Shadow King began to dissolve. The princess, her form shimmering with newfound freedom, emerged from the relic, her eyes filled with gratitude and sorrow. The entity, no longer bound by Malik's dark magic, stood tall, its glow restored. Even the Shadow King, his vengeful spirit tempered by the relic's power, felt the weight of his imprisonment lift.

As the last of the dark energies were absorbed into the relic, Tariq felt his strength waning. He knew that his sacrifice was complete. With one final effort, he directed the relic's power to cleanse the city of its corruption, restoring it to its former glory.

The citizens of Al-Madina, freed from the dark influence, began to emerge from their homes, their eyes filled with wonder and hope. The city, once a battleground, now stood as a beacon of renewal and harmony.

As the light from the relic faded, Tariq fell to his knees, exhausted but content. The princess knelt beside him, her eyes filled with tears. "Thank you, Tariq. Your sacrifice has saved us all." Tariq smiled weakly, his vision fading. "It was worth it, to see the land restored and the people free. Remember, true power lies in balance and wisdom, not in domination." With those final words, Tariq closed his eyes, his essence merging with the relic, becoming a guardian of balance for all time.

The entity, now free, looked to the horizon, its purpose renewed. "We must honor Tariq's sacrifice and ensure that such darkness never takes hold again." Malik and Khalid, their ambitions shattered, stood in silent reflection. They had been freed from their desires, given a chance to rebuild and seek redemption. The princess, her heart heavy with sorrow and gratitude, vowed to carry on Tariq's legacy, guiding her people with wisdom and compassion.

The land of Al-Madina, now a symbol of hope and renewal, thrived under the guidance of those who had been freed from their chains. Tariq's sacrifice had taught them the true nature of power and the importance of balance. His legacy lived on, a testament to the enduring strength of selfless love and the unbreakable spirit of those who seek to protect and restore harmony.

The End

Amanbir Dhade has always been fascinated by the mysteries of antiquities and the grandeur of ancient civilizations. With a deep appreciation for history and culture, Amanbir finds inspiration in the stories and artifacts of bygone eras.

When not immersed in the past, Amanbir enjoys bringing these influences to life through the vibrant strokes of oil painting, creating works that echo the timeless beauty of ancient art. This passion for the old and the mystical weaves seamlessly into his writing, where history and imagination intertwine.

In this novel, Amanbir invites readers to embark on a thoughtful journey of reflection and imagination, hoping to spark a sense of wonder and contemplation. Through the pages of this book, may you find a window to the past, a mirror to the present, and a doorway to endless possibilities.

www.ingramcontent.com/pod-product-compliance
Lightning Source LLC
Chambersburg PA
CBHW061508020726
47502CB00006B/1987